WHITE

MINK

Ivey and
Belle Chase

WHITE MINK

A Southern Tale

WHITE MINK, A Southern Tale
Copyright © 2016 by Ivey & Belle Chase Second Edition

BELLE CHASE BOOKS
Printed in United States

belle.chase@mail.com
iveysayshello@yahoo.com

ISBN -13 978-0-692-92575-1

DEDICATION

This book is for all who lost their mother when they were a child. This book is for women born beautiful. This book is for those born poor. This book is for those who love loving so much that they forget to love themselves. This book is for those who struggle to survive the best way they know. This book is for those who feel they should live each day as if it were their last.

"Not even a sparrow falls to the ground without God's notice . . .

And that the glory of God expresses itself in the lilies of the field"

Matthew 10:29 & Luke   12:27–28

Table of Contents

1

Velvet Gardens 1954

Two White Tobacco Growers
A Slave Girl Belonged to One
One Gun Shot
One Man Dead
Her Name Was Velvet

Amber streetlights faintly overhang the tree-lined street as the taxicab crawled, searching for the entrance of the Velvet Gardens, a large plantation house that had been converted into a bed-and-breakfast. Twenty-year-old Josephine Walker, sleepy and tired, peered from the back windows, looking for a sign along the sloping fields of braided grapevine stalks.

"There it is. Look to the right." The young woman pointed to a light in the distance. The driver turned the yellow cab onto a graveled stretch shouldered by rows and rows of orchard trees, now winter bare. The headlights pierced the dark lane leading to the long, rectangular, two-story redbrick colonial with grand white columns supporting the triangular arch over a porch entrance. A long iron chained chandelier hung in front of the white double doors.

The black cabby cautiously stopped where the road met a circular drive that surrounded a garden of evergreens, pines, holly, and magnolia trees decorated with winter holiday ornaments. Concerned, he said, "I don't think they take coloreds here. Are you sure this the right place?"

"Yesss, it is," she replied, exaggerating her response. "How much do I owe? And why did you stop here? Please, take me to the door."

"It may cause more trouble than necessary," he responded dryly, as he sat low in his seat. "This here is Robert E. Lee's town, not Ben Franklin's." Dogs in the back kennels barked. "It'll be ten dollars."

"Don't worry. They are expecting me. Here's your money." Josephine passed a bill to him, then hurriedly hopped out the back with her small overnight bag in hand, "I'll walk the rest of the way." She'd heard enough tales from her grandmother before leaving Philadelphia.

"You might have to go around back of the house. Coloreds don't generally go in the front," he said staring at the great white front doors of the house.

"Got it. Thanks again," she said shutting the car door before he could begin his repeated warnings about the Jim Crow South. She was tired of being told to watch where you go, watch what you say, look for the colored signs. Don't look directly at white folks.

It was 1954.

Sticking his head out the car window, he spoke with concern, "I'll sit for a while."

It was midnight, windless and foggy. Josephine's small heels crunched the fine gravel around the circle of decorated trees standing in a colorful stately manner as she looked up at a light on the top floor of the house. After what seemed like an entire city block, Josephine finally climbed the steps of the portico. A barely readable epithet was etched in a black marble plaque next to the doors.

Two White Tobacco Growers
A Slave Girl Belonged to One
One Gun Shot
One Man Dead
Her Name Was Velvet

She sensed jealousy was the cause. She heard stories of men and women killing each other. Especially in bars. She lifted one of the imposing iron circular knockers that had two small rifles crisscrossing each other, wondering if it would fire. *Clack. Clack.* She stepped back and turned around to find the cab. Suddenly it appeared to be a wagon pulled by horses with soldiers riding shotgun. Some were walking across the damp fields or marching up the road, lugging packs, wounded, fatigued.

The driver flashed the headlights on and off.

Relieved, Josephine turned to knock again when one door opened with a gust of wind. Penelope LeNoire stood in a pink fluffy night robe with matching slippers. She was fiftyish, with long wavy hair and a long Southern drawl, "Hello, missy?"

"I'm Josephine Walker. Are you Miss Porter?" she asked, holding her hand out. Penelope stepped away to look toward the driveway, avoiding the girl.

"No, no. Is that your cab?"

"Yes, ma'am."

"Is he able to take you to the back?" Penelope waved to the cab to come to the house, but he believed it meant the girl was safe, so he turned and left.

"No, ma'am. He's afraid. I'm here to see Rita Jane."

Perplexed as to what to do with Josephine framed in the doorway, Penelope continued, "I guess it is frightful to ask you to walk around to the back by yourself, now. Let me call Rita Jane for you. Wait here, dear. Don't move now."

Penelope stepped backward into the foyer where a grand oak staircase ascended to the second floor. A long hallway ran alongside of it to the kitchen's swinging doors at the back section of the house. To the left and right of the foyer were hallways leading to the east and west wings of the house.

"It's so late, I guess it'll be all right for you to come in for a minute."

"Thank you, ma'am," Josephine said, gripping tightly the handles of her purse and bag to channel nervousness.

"I'm Penelope LeNoire," slyly masking her displeasure at seeing this girl standing in her home. "You are lucky I peeked out the window and noticed the car. Otherwise, you may have had to return home. Come into the parlor."

Penelope led the way down the west hall and through the first door into a large room decorated in the federalist period. Adjoining the room was a library which could be seen through French double doors.

"I have no idea what Rita Jane's plans are. I am off tomorrow to New York. Let me ring her in the carriage house. Have a seat."

Josephine sat quietly on the edge of the high-backed sofa, intimidated by the scale of the room, the high ceilings and draperies. There was matching sky-blue details throughout the room. Penelope watched the girl, noticing a resemblance to her mother, as she dialed the table telephone near a sitting chair.

"Rita Jane is a wonderful woman. We've known each other since we were toddlers," she said. After a few rings she hung up. "There is no answer. Come with me to the kitchen. She may still be preparing the carriage house out back for you."

The little woman moved quickly as if carried by a wind of her own, rolling down the hall with walls papered with tiny apricots on a beige background. Oak floor boards gently scuffed from traffic echoed the sound of their steps toward the kitchen. Josephine followed, keeping pace as she passed open doors to a dining room with a long mahogany table and at least twenty chairs. Two crystal chandeliers, each with four tiers, hung over the ends of the table. Heavy drapes covered the floor-to-ceiling windows. Then through the swinging door at the end of the hallway, they entered a spacious yellow kitchen with yellow cabinets and speckled black Formica counters. "Did I say who I am?" Penelope asked.

"Yes, ma'am. Penelope."

"Miss Penelope LeNoire, owner of the Velvet Gardens." She opened the back door to look for a light in the upper floor of the carriage house, that had ornate Victorian trim and a gable framing its pitched roof and windows. Trestles full of climbing rose branches graced the sides of the wooden building. The lower floor housed a cigar-rolling operation.

"Rita, Rita Jane," Penelope called in a voice barely above a whisper. Hardly enough sound to travel the distance of three feet. She shut the door. "Well, I guess I'll have to figure something out. It's eons past midnight and no one will interrupt their sleep to take you to a hotel room. Rita expected you around six to pick up the suitcase and leave." This was untrue. They had argued over the girl staying the night.

"I am sorry to be late. My train from Philadelphia was delayed in Washington, D.C., where the colored people had to change trains to the southern service line."

"Oh my, my." Penelope patted her cheek, pretending disbelief, well aware that the trains segregated after Washington.

Josephine sensed the woman disliked her. Her sleepy eyes closed for a moment, recalling the long wait in the colored section. She tried her best to speak in a friendly voice. "Seemed like a long time before the porters counted the seats for the new riders to board."

Not mentioning that the new riders were white. Or that the train had oversold tickets to the colored-seating section and even to the baggage car where blacks often stood. Nor the argument between a woman from New York and the porters over leaving her Negro maid to take the next train to Florida. She'd had a medical condition that might flare up. The black porter had insisted that if the maid was not in a separate car, it could cause trouble passing through states that didn't allow mixing of the races.

"Because of this situation, the next southern train could not enter the station," Josephine continued. "I'm sorry. I had no choice but to wait for the next train."

She left out that another woman had insisted that she had the right to ride the train free of coloreds. She'd argued that the New York woman and her colored maid should not board the train but wait for the next one, further delaying the departure.

Lowering her wispy voice, Penelope explained, "Then you understand the policy here in the South. It's the same at the Gardens. This house does not let rooms to Negroes." She pretended embarrassment but was actually happy to confront the girl about the racial policy which Rita Jane had forced her to ignore.

Angry, Josephine said, "I will leave if you want. But first, where are my momma's things? I can go find a room elsewhere!" The woman who had first appeared glamorous was nothing more than a mean liar, she thought.

"No. No. Please, don't raise your voice. I have guests sleeping. I am a decent person and seeing as your cab left you on my doorstep, you can stay one night. Just one night. Rita will hang me if I let you leave now. We can discuss it tomorrow. Reputations are important here. What people say or think can influence a business." Penelope explained, giving her a stern look. "And, our prices exclude many."

"I have money. I'm not here to beg." Josephine had two hundred dollars for emergencies, believing she had more than enough for a taxi from Virginia to Philadelphia if necessary.

"As I was speaking, it's about money. No need allowing people to stay who can't pay the full price because of a pitiful situation. You understand." The older woman moved past Josephine, to lead her back through the hallway to the front. "Come, let me show you the room," Penelope whispered in her slower drawl, remembering how she had argued heatedly with Rita over a colored girl staying in the house, knowing it was against the rules. And how only servants slept in the basement when necessary.

Rita Jane expected Josephine to arrive the day after Penelope left for New York, but the train was sold out for that day. Penelope accused Rita of going behind her back. How could she trust her anymore?

Josephine asked, "Did you meet my mother, Miriam Walker?"

"Not sure I have. So many guests. We've been in business since 1926. Let see, it's 1954. Shush, folks are sleeping."

Strained silence fell between them until they reached a front bedroom door off the west wing. Opening it, Penelope said, "This is Rita Jane's private bedroom. I don't think she will mind if you sleep here." She flipped on the overhead lights. "Lovely, it has a private bath. It is a special room; it once was the master bedroom for a tobacco planter. Actually, my grandpoppa. It rents at a higher rate."

Josephine began to dismiss everything Penelope said as a lie. "May I see my mother's suitcase?" she asked. Standing still in the hallway, ignoring Penelope's obvious pride in the lavish pink brocade wallpaper, the swirling motif in the rug, and the large antique white bed and canopy frame.

"I believe Rita Jane has it. She will be in the kitchen at six to prepare breakfast. Please let's go to bed now."

Disappointed and suspicious, after having traveled so far, Josephine didn't want to wait until the morning. "Ma'am, I really would like to see my mother's suitcase tonight."

"It's late. Do not disturb the house roaming around now." Penelope was annoyed that she had to contain her distaste of this sleepover. "You can lock yourself in." Then she shut the door to end the conversation.

After locking the door, Josephine sat on the bed, fighting the feeling that maybe her grandmother had been right about the hateful South, the lynch mobs, the dirty separate public places. The idea that Josephine wanted to go to Richmond where her mother was killed had set Grandma Philly into a torrent of bad words. She was not sparse with words as to her dislike of Miriam, even insinuating that she was not worth a free train ride to recover her belongings.

It made Josephine more determined to meet people who had known her. Rita Jane's letter opened a window of fresh air. It brought life to her imaginations of her mother. No one was going to stop her from getting the last things her mother once touched, even if it was only one garment.

Penelope retreated to the kitchen to climb the back, narrow servants' steps to a third-floor attic loft. Each step reminded her of the need for money to keep the place going. Yes, she'd wanted to sell the house a thousand times over. But if she did, who would she be? Where would she go? She'd wasted precious sleep talking to the young black girl. Who was she, coming down here, questioning her?

If only one of her many workers hadn't been afraid to help clear out the basement, that was filled with trunks of curtains, clothing, boxes, books from the days of her great-grandparents, stacked on top of personal articles left by guests over the years. She hated to throw out happy reminders of when the business had flourished. But the workers were afraid of Polly's hanging cards that she called her keys to miracles. Rita Jane was not.

Together with Rita, she began the task of sorting out the storage area. Suddenly Rita became excited, "This suitcase belongs to that woman, Miriam, Jules's friend. How did it get here?"

"Who, what are you talking about?" Penelope knew it was Miriam's. She thought it had been thrown away that fateful night. She was angry with herself that she had not seen it before Rita.

"Oh, and here's the coat Jules gave her." Rita took a white mink in a plastic cold-storage sack off a clothing rack. "This was in the carriage house wasn't it. How did it get down here?" turning to Penelope.

"Nonsense." Penelope quickly took it. "It's Mother's."

"It's not Mary Margaret's," replied Rita Jane. "Jules bought the coat. I remember him showing it to me."

"If Jules gave it to someone, he had no business. Mother bought it. Hugh told me."

"Hugh?!" That's crazy. I don't believe it." Rita was confused, knowing Hugh was not one to lie about anything.

Penelope ignored Rita's puzzled face and surveyed the coat for damage, or blood stains from Miriam. Seeing none, she decided to wear it Christmas in New York. She'd impress her cousin and lover, Pierre. Before she could put the mink aside to take the suitcase, Rita had picked it up again, opening it to find a little girl's photograph.

"How sweet. This must be Miriam's girl. Jules told me she had a child. I must find her address. She will love to have these things."

Now, tonight, Miriam's daughter was here. Reminding Penelope of Jules and Miriam's affair, the scandal he caused leaving that woman to die. As Penelope neared the top floor, she softened, remembering her love for her grandpoppa. He'd spent his last days in the room, remembering that black girl from long ago. An afternoon didn't go by without him talking about her.

His wife, Ann, had passed many years before. As a child, Penelope had followed him everywhere, sitting quietly on the steps, waiting for him to come out. Sometimes she peeked through the keyhole. What could he be doing in there alone, she wondered?

One day she thought she believed she saw Velvet. Penelope imagined her lying on the big bed, alluring, striking. Once she thought the woman had stolen her eyes from her head, because her little eyes followed every move she made. The little girl saw her turn the covers back, then pat the bed, inviting a lover to join.

Penelope had heard Velvet was a runaway from another tobacco planter fields. She'd matured, becoming open and satisfied with herself. She didn't have to work with her hands. She'd elicited lust and desire in

Grandpoppa's eyes. Warm and sultry eyes, open and pleased when he dressed her in his wife Ann's clothes.

Penelope remembered sitting in the narrow stairway, waiting and waiting for Grandpoppa to come out. Mary Margaret would start calling, "Penelope! Penelope!" Momma pretended she didn't know where Grandpoppa had gone or where her little girl was. But she knew. She knew he was in there with Velvet. "Penelope! Penelope!" Mother kept calling until she had to scurry down the wooden steps, making as much noise as possible. She'd wanted Grandpoppa to hear her, hear her jealousy. She'd wanted him to know she was there. She'd wanted her mother, Mary Margaret, to know too.

All she'd wanted to do was sit in the staircase and look into the keyhole. Every afternoon, one big bed. Not much up in that room but old Grandpoppa remembering that black woman. Then there was only Grandpoppa, alone. Now it was her haven. She understood why Grandpoppa came up here. The only place where she could find warmth. The only place where sleep came easily.

It would be all right soon. Calls for rooms started coming after she voiced her opposition to the federal government's tampering with state rights on segregation. Supporters were reaching out to her, enticing her to join the cause. But her mind continued to drift back to the white mink. Her breath was sucked out of her mouth when she saw the fur and suitcase. She'd been certain all traces of Miriam at the Velvet Gardens were gone. Now her child sleeps below.

2

Folding Regrets

Rita Jane refused to answer the telephone call from the big house, knowing it was Penelope. Their argument earlier that day still lingered in her mind. It was outrageous to think the young girl's stay would taint the reputation of Velvet Gardens because of her skin color. Rita was black too.

"We can't have that girl in here. I regret we found that damn suitcase. Now we are arguing over a stranger. Rita Jane, I am sorry you feel the need to change the way we've always done things here. We—we never catered to blacks. Our independence depends on certain kinds of people with money. It's about money. Not race. You've become attached to some notion about this girl. I can't figure it out, but I don't want to fight." Penelope retreated to her room before Rita could say another word.

The white suitcase sat on a stuffed chair in the carriage house. It was quiet and still, waiting to be owned again. But it kept Rita restless. She had watched over it from the day it was discovered, afraid Penelope would try to destroy it. She'd opened it several times to empty the contents, only to repack them neatly once again. She dared not wipe the dark dried stains of blood off the handle. It was Miriam's blood.

Guilt kept her awake many nights, wondering what she could have done to prevent the woman from dying. After finding the photograph, she began to imagine the emptiness that saddled Josephine growing up. Thinking the young girl's mind probably wandered off as she watched other children with mothers. Feeling the loss of an imaginary person who would give comfort in sad times, and laughter at happier moments.

Inside the suitcase, Rita kept a copy of the *Richmond News,* reporting the death. The papers lied, saying she was a guest of Velvet Gardens. Rita had read it often, trying to understand why they lied. The article created chaos. A flurry of crime hounds posing as casual guests invaded the Gardens to question staff. Some told different accounts of what they'd seen at the river the morning Miriam was found.

* * *

Police boats were already in water when the blood-orange sun rose, overtaking the streetlights that lingered longer than usual. In the cold rapid river was Miriam Walker in a royal-blue dress ballooned around her waist. The muddy water slapped her nude breasts as her head lay backward on a restless pillow, bobbing up and down, revealing a neck as blue as her dress from strangulation marks. She was discovered by a fishing boat.

Police pushed back the gathering crowd while forensic police photographers snapped pictures from all angles. News reporters tried to get answers from the police or from the crowd. There was no identification on the girl.

Benjamin Blackstone, a young officer, arrived when the body was pulled from the water. He looked closely at her face which was swollen from the trauma. Then the face of the girl at the raid flashed in his mind.

He bulldozed the crowd, trying to recognize other streetwalkers, hoping to shake them down for answers.

"Anyone have a name for the girl?" Blackstone yelled at the mute faces that stared out over the water. As frightful as his demeanor was, no one wanted to leave, soaking in the stillness of a cold body where life past into another world. He approached the captain.

"Owen, I know this girl. She was a waitress at the Brown Derby, not far from here. I'd like to work the case."

"You're not a detective."

"I won't interfere with the detectives, but I have some leads." He'd remember a glimpse of Jules LeNoire reaching out to her during the raid.

"Sure, sure, not my type of case. Probably another poor girl selling. Just give what you find to me first."

Blackstone left and drove to the Brown Derby club to find anyone cleaning up from the night before or preparing to open for the day's business. It was locked. Next, he called Gene, the owner, at home.

"Her name's Miriam. She didn't work much after the raid. I fired her a few weeks back. Why?"

"She was found dead in the James, this morning."

"I had nothing to do with it. Why are you calling me? Are you trying to shut me down? Why do you guys do me like this? I pay my coverage. The lunch bag is delivered on time to the police desk on Marshall and you still run in here. No warning. A big night and there's a raid. Why you guys do that? Scared the hell out of my good customers."

"We have to make some heat now and then. We need our jobs too. When the machines press us about a joint operating a sideshow that tourists and everyone in the city knows about but no one ever gets busted, what do you think we should do?"

"Keep me out of the news. My business doesn't need it."

"Any relatives you know of?"

"Said she had a daughter and aunt here. She was from Philadelphia. A good person. Shame. Think she got involved with the wrong people here. Thinking they really cared about her."

After the evening paper ran her picture, waves of calls jammed the police board. Most were anonymous tips. Some sleuths went to the precinct to talk to detectives privately only to give suggestions on how to find the killer. Others were angry there were not enough police on the streets.

The next morning the Velvet Gardens was under siege by police, blaring sirens. Whipping around the grounds on false statements that Miriam Walker had been killed by Jules. But Jules was at a ski resort in Switzerland. The police stayed all morning, frightening guests and the workers with questions. Only after a dozen calls to friends by Penelope did the police retreat. She was disappointed that the police commissioner and his wife, Estelle, gave no warning before their arrival.

Harassing calls came by the dozen to the Velvet Gardens. People just wanted to trash talk the place. A big house was still standing. Penelope believed Blackstone had started the rumor that Miriam Walker lived secretly in a room. Worse words came from Vera Gold, her aunt, who took out several ads promising one thousand dollars for information. The desire for the money drew out evil intent in everyone.

The reward was a year's salary for most working people. It encouraged bookings by annoying guests who looked for truth in the whisperings and lies they'd heard. No one faulted Mrs. Gold for pressing for an investigation. But she was too controversial for white folks. Uppity for most with her money and land. So her push to solve the case was dismissed as a Negro woman seeking to show off her clout.

* * *

Rita Jane finally was able to turn off the bedside lamp, knowing the girl had arrived, hoping sleep would overcome the day gone by. She noticed lights in the attic room and wondered why Penelope was not asleep. Earlier, she had watched the little woman walk up and down the halls, stopping from time to time before a family portrait, seeking approval from the image as to whether she should reject a run for public office.

Penelope spent the most time in front of her mother, Mary Margaret, a quiet, dignified woman who had constantly fought off strangers invading her privacy. Now Penelope welcomed freeloaders who supported politicians who opposed the Supreme Court ending segregation in the public schools. They sat around all day, talking about how Penelope was perfect for the next election, without paying a cent for their tea.

The names they called other people disturbed Rita. They tried to use codes when she entered the room. "Miss Rita, how is the day treating you so far? More joyous than yesterday, I pray."

"Don't mind the talk, Rita," Penelope would say. "They aren't talking about you. It's the others."

The burden of handling the stream of visitors, calls, boxes of paper, signs, and buttons became oppressive. Answering calls from supporters or staffers for the Action for Our Private Rights disturbed her. When Rita Jane refused to answer the telephones yesterday, Penelope called her beauty salon for Esther Mae, the shampooer, to help with the administrative chores. She needed help with the paperwork piling up in stacks around the dining room. She needed Esther, who could type and answer calls pleasingly, do errands and other sorts of things. More importantly, she could pick up the mail from the post office that often contained threats. The woman would be a shield. A good one against black opposition.

Esther Mae was vocal at the white salon about her belief that blacks were better off with their own kind, no matter what the circumstances. It served no purpose for their little brown children to sit next to white children to learn about white people and their history from Europe. Keep our children to ourselves, just make their situation and circumstances better. Penelope enjoyed discussing the campaign with her.

It was better for both that Esther Mae was hired. It was not awkward for Rita Jane as much as for Esther Mae, who was ashamed that money had her doing an injustice. Rita Jane was never really recruited or suited for the task of campaign canvassing. Nor did Esther Mae understand that Rita Jane was not a servant. Most assumed because she was black and was the ward of Polly, she had inherited the role of housemaid. Esther Mae and Rita Jane had met when they both attended Miss Della's beauty school shortly after high school.

Finally, Rita turned away from the light in Penelope's room, sleepily thinking of the holiday things she would do tomorrow, getting the pig's head and feet for pickling, shelling peas, making baskets for the laborers.

3

Restless Night

As the night went on, the steam radiator beneath the window whistled and rattled, overheating the room. Josephine's throat was already dry and scratchy from the cigarette and cigar smoke that had filled the railroad car during the six-hour train ride. She got up to pull back the heavy drapery and crack open the window next to the queen-sized bed. The holiday lights in the shrubbery circle were off but the front porch chandelier cast a misty light out front.

Groggy, she realized she'd fallen asleep in the new dress that had cost so much. She didn't care. She was tired. It was her first trip alone. Her grandmother had complained that she'd spent too much money on a worthless trip. Josephine knew her grandmother loved her but there were times when it was overwhelming. Her seventy-year-old Grandma Philly kept hinting that she should marry and start a family. She feared Josephine would be alone once she passed. But the young woman was not going to be forced into marriage based on what Grandma Philly thought was right or wrong.

She climbed back onto the high bed fully clothed, prepared to run for her life if necessary. Closing her eyes to thank the heavenly angels for the last pieces belonging to her mom, she drifted off to sleep. A voice softly whispered, "Josephine. Josephine." Then a man's voice begged a woman to get into the car. Too tired to awaken, she turned over again, wanting to remain asleep, but the talking outside continued.

She opened her eyes slightly. A car door slammed. A woman wearing white left a black sedan and called to the girl. "Josephine. Josephine." A man pleaded for her to get into the car. Josephine sat up, afraid to breathe. Her heart was pumping quickly. She wondered if she was dreaming.

Crouching toward the window, she hid behind the heavy drapes. But there was no car. Puzzled, she pushed the window open farther to allow the cool night air to wash over her face. After a few minutes, she returned to bed but couldn't fall asleep, wanting the dream to repeat, to hear the soothing voice call her.

Lying on top of the covers, prepared to run to the window, she closed her eyes. Someone whispered, "It's me, Mommy." A warm feeling filled the room. It filled with love, and a golden light. The voice called again, "Josephine, my little cupcake." Josephine sat up, searching the room for the woman. There was no one. She rushed to the window.

With joy, Josephine saw a woman in white far along the road. The airy figure walked toward the edge of the circle of trees. A car followed the sleek, tender, and youthful woman, whose hair was pulled up in a ballerina bun. She stopped and stood like a statute. Josephine scrambled out of the room barefoot, running down the hallway to the large front doors.

Upstairs, Penelope was awakened too by an approaching car. She heard Jules's voice, laughing, as he had the first night he came home with Miriam. The sound of his voice talking with that woman unnerved her. She opened the attic window to see if Jules had arrived for the holidays. To her surprise Miriam stood at the circle looking up at her. Shocked, she stepped back and held her chest to quiet her pounding heart. *Dear Mother, what is this? It can't be Miriam. It must be another tramp. Why was this woman standing there in the dead of night?* She turned from the window. Images of Miriam wearing the white mink flashed through her mind, creating an eerie feeling. Already groggy from two previous pills, she took another sleeping pill, afraid to look again, and returned to bed.

Josephine stood barefoot on the stone steps and waved to the image of the woman. "It's me, Josephine." The woman gently smiled. The black car pulled next to the woman in white. There were two men and a driver.

"Don't! Don't get in!" Josephine ran down the brick steps toward the woman. "Wait! Wait! Come here!"

She ran faster, almost around the whole circle before the door of the black sedan opened and a hand reached for the woman.

"No, no, don't get in the car. Please!" Josephine cried.

But the woman disappeared into the darkness of the car. It slowly approached Josephine, who could see that the woman was truly her mother, sending tremendous warmth of love to her. Josephine trotted alongside the slow moving car, grabbing at the door handle as it went around the circle.

"Stop! Stop! Stop!" But the car sped down the desolate road. Josephine drenched with joy and sorrow chased after it, yelling for it to come back. As quickly as it appeared, it was gone. Cold and shivering, she walked back to the house, constantly turning to see if the car returned. She stood on the steps waiting, hoping it had not been a dream. When daylight came, she was forced to accept it all passed into the night before.

Reluctantly she shut the doors with hesitation, hurting to think it was a dream. In the bedroom she cried into a pillow with joy. "I saw her. I saw her." Repeating it until she fell asleep.

4

Smoked Bacon

At six a.m., Rita Jane moved around the kitchen, pulling dishes and occasionally stirring grits on the stove. Bacon and a dozen eggs sat on the counter waiting to be cooked. The smell of coffee drifted throughout the house. The radio played softly on the counter near the sink. She loved food. Her Southern cuisine was well known, as were her baked goods that garnered the highest bids at charity fund-raisers.

Looking up from beating a bowl of pancake mix, she watched two blue birds peck each other on a Magnolia branch in the small circular garden at the back of the house. She couldn't wait for the tree to blossom with large white flowers, or for the pink azaleas and red roses to regrow. The small shrubbery was decorated in Christmas ornaments with a winged angel on top of her favorite pine.

The kitchen door swung open and Josephine rushed across the room, wearing the now bed wrinkled dress. She was barefooted and ready to exit out the back door to cross the grounds to the carriage house.

Rita turned to her, surprised. "Mornin'." She'd checked on the girl earlier, but the door was locked.

Josephine looked back to find an attractive, slim woman wearing an apron at the sink.

"I'm looking for Miss Rita Jane."

"That's me."

"Oh! It's me, Miriam's daughter."

"Yes, yes. Where are your shoes?"

"I was in a hurry."

"Was the room comfortable?"

"Oh, I saw my mother. I saw her. She came to me."

Puzzled, Rita turned away to tend to the bacon slab she was slicing.

"Do you believe me?" Josephine asked, excited about the vision.

"It's not what I believe, but what you want to believe. Have a seat, breakfast is almost ready."

Trying to appease the strange woman, Josephine continued. "Do you understand what it means? I mean, I am so grateful you wrote me."

Rita moved to the stove to turn on the burner, then placed a skillet on top. "Have a seat at the table. I'll get the suitcase in a minute."

"Yes, ma'am." Not wanting to upset the woman, she sat down but couldn't keep still, twisting in the chair at the table.

"When Hugh returns with Jules, he'll take you down to the station. It won't be long. You can eat breakfast first."

"I want to stay longer."

Rita inhaled heavily as she leaned over to change the radio to jazz. Then went back to placing thick slices of bacon in the hot skillet, trying hard to ignore the girl's confused excitement. After watching Rita Jane for a few minutes, not understanding the woman's silence, Josephine sensed she needed to leave quickly.

"Where is the suitcase, Miss Rita? Can I see it now? Then I'll be on my way."

"Oh, yes, yes. It's in Polly's room. You wait here."

Rita walked down a hallway off the kitchen that led to two bedrooms and a bath. She returned with a white suitcase that caused squeals to erupt from the yawning, sleepy girl.

"Mighty fine, isn't it? The white has not yellowed over the years."

"Did you meet her?"

Silent, Rita Jane returned to picking at the frying bacon, stopping now and then to nervously push back curls falling into her face. Josephine resembled Miriam so much it made her uncomfortable

"Not really, but honey, there is so much more in the suitcase about your mother than I can tell. It was about fifteen years ago. I don't want to say stuff that may be nothing more than guessing." She couldn't share she believed her mother was meaning to blackmail Jules. Or that she still stayed up nights asking herself how or why did Miriam die.

Josephine snapped open the suitcase, to find a satin lining of baby pink roses with little green leaves. The scent of jasmine and rose tickled her nose. A French perfume bottle, half empty, sat on top of the newspaper article. Everything was neatly packed. She sneezed again and again.

"Bless you and me," said the older woman, continuing to prepare food platters for the morning buffet in the dining room.

Josephine opened a card. *With all my love, J.* Who was J? Then the voice of her mother spoke as she picked up a pink silk slip with lace trim: "Do not hate him. He is kind." The girl stared at the slip then looked at Rita, who was holding a coffeepot, ready to leave the kitchen again.

"Did you hear her?"

"Who?"

"My mother. Who is J?"

Rita Jane was silent.

"Tell me. Something happened between them. You're afraid to tell me. Who is J?"

Uncomfortable, she quietly spoke. "I am not afraid. J is Jules and I can't speak for him or your mother. I don't know the answers you're looking for."

"My mother is speaking to me. I can't leave. I can't go." She sneezed and sneezed.

"If people hear talk like this, it can cause trouble for you. People will place all their bad luck on you. They'll say that you're the cause of their problems. It all happened 'cause you're speaking with the devil."

"Are you trying to scare me?"

"I hope so."

Jo sneezed. "It's all right if she speaks to me. She's always in my dreams" Ignoring any further advice, she read a telegram from Paris.

Urgent. Stop. Dear Miriam. No, cannot return. Stop. See P. Discussed. February 21, 1939.

Rita left to take food trays into the dining room while Josephine sniffed and shuffled through the suitcase. There were stockings, two dresses, one black with roses, another orange with red and white trim. A gold compact of powder makeup, lipstick, a gold ruby ring. There was a silver whisky flask, initialed J. Finding black-and-white photos of her as a baby brought a smile. She read an unfinished letter on pink stationery, handwritten by her mother.

Dear love of all loves, I miss your touch. Your face is always before me. There is nothing else to see in the world. I can't sleep in a cold bed knowing you are near a war. Our love is greater than our color. The heart always wants to love.

She stopped reading, wondering if the letter had been written to a white man. She'd never imagined her mother being in love with a white man.

Rita returned, alarmed to see Josephine holding several envelopes with French postmarks and Jules's return address, upon which Miriam had placed kiss marks. She had meant to take them out of the case this morning. It was too late now.

"Who is Jules?" Feverish and sweaty, she sneezed. "When can I meet Jules?"

Josephine's curiosity caused Rita to change plans for Hugh to drive her to the station. "I think it best if I drive you down to the train station, sweetie. I have to pick up some small things for the holiday baskets."

"You mentioned in your letter that Mr. Jules was coming to meet me. I'm not leaving until I meet Mr. Jules."

Rita Jane stood over her and quickly spoke. "No, you cannot stay here any longer. The rooms are for whites only. I made a big fuss for you to stay in my room last night. No more nights here."

Rita's change in mood shocked Jo. "Okay, don't worry. I have an aunt downtown. Aunt Vera. She lives on Church Hill, I think." Sensing Rita Jane was lying to make her leave, she tried to think of a way to stay longer, or to come back that night.

Rita was relieved the girl had relatives nearby, knowing Penelope would not suffer another night of her in this house.

The girl continued. "Yes, Aunt Vera. I visited every Easter and a month in the summer. I can't wait to see her."

"Does she know you're coming? We can call her now."

Out back, Hugh honked the horn to let everyone know that Jules had arrived. Josephine recognized the black sedan as the one she'd seen last night. She ran to the door but was unable to undue the lock. She yanked hard in a frenzy. *Maybe her mother was in the car. Who was she with?* Crazed with joy, she watched as Hugh, an elderly black man, suited and wearing a heavy overcoat, labored his frame out of the front seat, leaving the motor running. He'd wondered why Mr. Jules wanted to come to the back when the protocol had always been the front.

Rita Jane, surprised by Josephine's aggressive behavior, opened the door, allowing the girl to race out. She tried to speak to her as to what she was doing but Josephine was frantic. All she could do was follow to see what the girl would do next. Jules was startled by the barefoot girl running toward him. He remained seated, suffering from a slight hangover from last night. His mouth opened. His face paled, thinking she was Miriam. Hugh was speaking but he couldn't hear.

"Mr. Jules, do you want me to take your trunk up to the carriage house or the big house?" Hugh asked again, peering into the back window. "Mr. Jules?" He hardly recognized the tensed face that was jovial a moment ago, suave, smooth, happy to be home.

"Hello, Mr. Jules? Where is she? Where is my mother?"

Hugh was surprised. "What is it, girl?"

Josephine was standing next to the car, knocking on the window which agitated Jules further.

"Hugh, please get in. Get in and take me away!"

The old man re-entered the car causing Josephine to rush in front of the car to keep it from leaving.

"No, no, stop it girl! Leave him be!" Rita screamed.

Hugh swerved around Josephine and sped toward the back road.

"Who is that child?" Jules asked, pulling out a handkerchief to wipe his nose.

"I'm not sure, sir." Hugh had recognized Miriam's features in Josephine and was certain Jules did too. The old man enjoyed the privilege of being a confidant, which required ignorance without a second thought about truth.

"Stop, stop, stop, stop! It's me!" Josephine raced after the car with all her might, yelling as it sped past the kennels, passing the early morning workers outside tending the plots, and onto the public road.

"Where to, Mr. Jules?"

Jules was sad, looking at his passport, wondering if he should leave for Paris. "The Aladdin Club," he answered. "I need to say hello to some old friends."

Ella, a land tenant, waved as the car passed. Josephine, out of breath, stumbled in the roadway exhausted. Ella eyed her with strangeness. "You lost girl?

5

Another Teardrop

Inside the dining room, two guests, married teachers, were eating breakfast. They whispered disagreements about last night. "I don't know why you refuse to believe I heard a ghost," the wife said.

The husband laughed. "It could have been anyone running around outside. This place has a number of workers on-site."

"And what about the gunfire?"

"I do admit to seeing a black car going down that lovely road. It must have backfired."

"She looked like a bride."

"Why, because ghosts look white? Eat up. The food is delicious Southern cooking."

Another guest entered, a young man working on a thesis regarding the failures of the Reconstruction. "Howdy. Anyone else hear the spirits?" he asked.

The couple laughed.

"This charming house has a lot of history," the young man commented.

"My wife insists there was a ghost roaming the grounds last night."

"Strange, I had a dream about a woman. I think she was soliciting, or being abducted. By the way, I am Rob Wilson, working on my doctorate."

"We're high school teachers from Connecticut, math and science. Beth and Joel Rockland. Pleased to meet you."

"Was this a red-light district?" Beth Rockland asked when Penelope entered the room, wanting to thank the guests and inquire about their stay.

"Honey, every district has a red light." Giggling at her pun, Penelope passed around newspapers, one to each guest.

"I mean, the girl I saw walking up and down the road early this morning."

Nervous the guest had seen the same woman she'd seen last night, Penelope explained, "Girls are girls. I have allowed a woman or two who seemed to have been battered at home in for coffee from time to time to talk. Then there are clients who sneak women in and out while I am asleep. Sometimes they show up lost and confused."

Rob Wilson continued, "Like ghosts. I heard that spirits haunt the house." He chomped down on a crispy slice of bacon.

"Now, now, that's a good one." Penelope smiled. "From time to time we have visitors of that sort. It is an old house on very solemn ground in Virginia. Anyone from the 1600s may show up."

Rob added, "The few calls I made to check on the Velvet Gardens, said folks reported sightings of a black woman named Velvet who walks the halls here."

"Then you have to believe the Civil War still rages on out there over those fields." Her smile froze. She wanted to leave the room, but not with an unpleasant picture of Velvet Gardens at the table. She stood still, like an attentive servant, listening.

"Well, we are in the South. People tend to have great imaginations. It could have been someone from the Underground Railroad," Joel Rockland quipped as he sipped his coffee.

"Or soldiers lost in battle," suggested Beth, enjoying the line of conversation.

"What are you suggesting?" Penelope pretended polite interest. "Ma'am, the entire South is historically full of displaced people. Isn't that our American history?"

"She's right, dear. The South is full of people not properly buried from the wars."

"Many wars." Penelope sighed, longing to get out of the room.

Rob Wilson continued. "Let's see, the Revolution, the War of 1812, the Civil War, the American Indian wars, slave revolts."

Penelope deflected their disrepute of the South. "There you are, thousands of souls. None will be found at Velvet Gardens. My grandfather thrived on goodwill. He provided work, food, and very good cigars and wines from these thousands of acres." Not mentioning the slow sale of twenty-five hundred acres over time, mostly during the Depression at boll weevil rates. She continued. "We grow lots of vegetables and have a vineyard. We make the fine wine we serve during lunch and dinner. Cigars and wine can be purchased. Let me know if you're interested," she said, hoping the banter was over. "Enjoy your breakfast." She attempted to retreat.

"One question. How many slaves were held here?" Joel asked as he stood to fill his plate with more food from the buffet.

"Not to boast, but we had more than a hundred slaves at one time. The house was built around 1830. Grandpoppa told me Union troops quartered here for a while, ransacking it before our loyal Confederates pushed back." This was one of her righteous lies.

"My research suggests that once the importation of slaves was abolished, slave owners began the practice of inbreeding, and often fathering several children to increase their holdings. Is that true of your bloodline?" asked Rob, stirring butter into his grits.

"I find that ridiculous, sir. Can you excuse me for a moment?" She smiled as best she could against the insult.

Beth spoke up. "The Velvet girl. Do you know the story?"

"I think we need more smoked bacon. Please excuse me," Penelope said. As she left, she overheard Rob's explanation.

". . . she was a concubine slave of about fifteen or so and then she disappeared . . ."

"What the hell do they know about our way of living?" Thought Penelope as she walked down the hall, shamed by guests who were eating at the very table that held fond memories of family, who dressed in suits and gowns for each other's pleasure, enjoying their heritage. Now strangers were fascinated by the glasses, place settings, and silver candelabras, hoping to see blacks running away from slave catchers, or some poor young soldier lying bleeding out on those wonderful fields. She worried that Josephine and Rita Jane might come up the hallway and incite more disgusting conversations.

She entered the kitchen to find the back door open. Furious, she saw the two walking back toward the house with Ella not far behind.

"Mr. Jules does not tolerate foolishness like ghosts. It was better he didn't stop. Maybe he had other business." Rita consoled the tired girl.

"When is he coming back? I have to talk to him. I saw my mother get into that car last night. Why didn't he stop so I could talk to him? Why, Miss Rita?"

Once inside the kitchen, Penelope glared at the girl who had tears running down her cheeks, while Rita cuddled her.

"Were you outside on the drive last night?" Penelope demanded.

Josephine stiffened.

"Were you outside last night? The guests say they saw someone. Neighbors have called the police because they saw a woman walking up and down the driveway." She continued.

"It was her," Josephine replied. Excited, she turned to Rita. "I told you. She came. Believe me. I saw it last night. It wasn't a ghost. It wasn't a dream." She sneezed. "I saw my mother get into that black car. Why didn't he stop so I could talk to him?"

Penelope was looking at the girl nervously. "Who is she talking about?"

"She saw Jules and Hugh this morning."

"And Miriam Walker, my mother," Josephine said with pride.

Penelope's anger rose. "Your-your mother is dead. Hear me, now. You didn't see your mother, or anybody else! Rita, it's best if you take this girl to the train station before the police arrive." Quickly she turned to ascend the back staircase, wanting to avoid any further encounters with the last guests before it shuttered for the holidays.

The kitchen was still warm and comforting with scents of bacon and coffee helping Josephine's anxiousness to ease as the radio played soft music. Rita Jane prodded her to sit and eat but she would not, too preoccupied with why Jules would not speak to her. Josephine began to sneeze uncontrollably.

"You need some medicine for that cold. Still no shoes. Sit still here. I have something that will stop that sneezing right away. My momma Polly was very good at herbs. She healed many workers. Helped women with labor." Rita didn't mention miscarriages and abortions.

"I'm fine." Weary from being awake most of the night, she lay her head on folded arms. She wanted to see the river where her mother had been found. She sneezed again. "Oh, my head. It aches."

"I'll be right back." Rita disappeared behind a kitchen door to descend steps to the basement, never fearing the hand-drawn cards of clowns and animal heads, angels and devils dangling on a string tied to the doorknob of Polly's private room. The old raccoon tacked on the door was only meant to frighten off unbelievers. She jingled the cards first, as Polly had instructed for permission to enter and obtaining guidance from a higher source once inside.

Upstairs, the music from the radio was interrupted.

"Good morning, listeners. Your news on the hour from WTTP. The body of a young woman was discovered in the James River this morning. Authorities suspect foul play. The homicide unit is investigating. Anyone with information is asked to call..."

Josephine raised her head to listen intently. "Was the radio repeating her mother's death?"

"The last death of a strangled woman in the river was fifteen years ago, a Miriam Walker. The police are asking your help to identify the woman. All calls will be kept confidential."

Her caramel face turned gray with fear. The announcement confused her. "Who, who is he talking about?" The radio continued.

"Anyone with information, please contact the Richmond police."

Her mind raced from one thought to another. Overlapping each other, pushing each new one away in a split second. She held her head between her hands, wondering if the woman she had seen last night was the same one now found dead. Or was it her mother. Was her mother killed again? She questioned whether she'd really seen or heard anything last night. She sneezed. Her chest was congested.

Josephine charged through the kitchen doors, up the hall with the suitcase in hand, only to bump into the departing guests in the front foyer with Alice. Sight of the black girl horrified the short and stout woman with red pixie hair. She tried hard to keep a calm voice as the bedraggled girl rushed past the guests into the bedroom. The married couple looked at each other in surprise. Alice smiled and lied.

"She's a domestic."

Alice managed the reservations and accommodations on a small salary. Neat and serious, she enjoyed sending the guests off with a blessing for safe travel with courtesy maps of the city's historic sites. Included in the goodwill was a pitch to buy a bottle of wine or a cigar. And, in an unobtrusive way, she also inspected what they carried out, to minimize the loss of linen and artifacts from the house.

She'd grown up on the land, inheriting a small parcel given to her grandfather, an overseer for Penelope's Grandpoppa Franklin. She lived with her husband, Roy, the son of a former sharecropper, and her son, Talbot. He and his father oversaw the tobacco crops and cigar making.

Alice twitched from trying to control her outrage over Josephine's appearance before the guest at the front door. She couldn't wait to report the incident to Penelope. The Rocklands walked down the brick path through a wooded area toward their car, while Rob Wilson still curious, continued to chat with her at the front door, holding a small transistor radio, from which he heard the river tours were cancelled. Investigation of a woman's body found in the river was under way.

Although speaking with compassion, she was indifferent to his disappointment over his inability to stare into the murky water, inhale the swampy smell, conjure up slave cries and money changing hands, or imagine Indians fishing along the river. She'd heard it all, the city with big dreams, the promise of a rebel country right here on the

James River. She offered him a complimentary cigar and hastened him out to the taxi waiting for his departure. Alice slammed the doors shut and raced to Josephine's bedroom door.

Josephine ignored Alice's repeated knocking. She wanted to get to the crime scene at the river quickly to identify herself. The police might talk to her, give her clues about her mother. But the knocking at the door caused her lungs to feel hot. Her feet were cold as she slipped on her short heels. Now she understood about the black car, the white coat, and the telegrams. "These people must have done something to my mother," she thought. "They will kill me too if they think I know."

Rita was still inside Polly's room. She pulled the long string to the hanging lightbulb above the high wooden workbench where Polly mixed her seasonings and potions. The shelves were lined with jars filled with spices for cooking or herbs for healing. The room had the wonderful smell of an apothecary. Bags of leaves, roots, and branches, collected from the nearby woods, or grown in her private garden were still hanging on the walls. Polly often prepared poultices and teas for ailing workers and house members.

Rita Jane remembered the formula Polly made her drink to slow down the hunger for food or the strange wanting she had as a little girl that she could not express. It tasted like the wine served at the big fancy meals with guests. Polly's last words before passing away were, "Don't let it eat you away, Rita Jane. You're still a good child, but I have to go. Don't let it bother you. You take your medicine."

She'd believed something in Rita Jane's mind was causing her to eat too much, eating to keep it fed. Polly believed the drink would keep it from eating up the body of her child. Rita became a round bundle by then. It was hard not to eat Polly's good cooking. That's all. Polly was always in the kitchen, or in the gardens cultivating her special vegetables and herbs. She'd made sure the hogs were killed properly and the animal cut right for curing in the smokehouse.

The whole idea of drinking that stuff was foolishness. Still a teen when Polly passed, no one forced her to drink the special juice anymore. Then again, no one's cooking was as good. It was foolishness to everyone, even Rita Jane, but Polly insisted. It was to keep evil doings away. Polly was a serious woman that could give a look that stayed a long time on a person, long after they stepped back.

Rita reminisced as she moved the jars of herbs, oils, incense, powders, feathers, beads, mixing bowls, and utensils on the shelves, looking for the herbal tea for colds. On the workbench table were clay jugs filled with wine, candles, and wooden spoons. It was not there. She had to make some. But she couldn't find Polly's book of practices with all her scribbled notes of secret formulas learned from her mother and other slaves. Her recipes would bring luck, money, ward off the evil eye, and restore health to the mind and body.

Resigned she wouldn't find it quickly, she reached to turn off the light when her eyes fell upon the small black stones Polly often shook when she was worried. "Perhaps one of these will help Josephine," Rita thought. She knew how worrisome dreams and nightmares could be. She'd had her share.

Polly repeatedly said, "Don't let anything press on your mind that keeps you from sleeping. Rid yourself of the trouble. When the mind goes, you're nothing but a living ghost. Lost in the world and the life God gave you."

6

Arrested

What a morning it was for Penelope, waiting for that girl to leave. There was no need to wait any longer. Standing on the front portico wearing the white mink, she looked for the arrival of the police to arrest Josephine. Audacity of that girl to refuse to answer Alice. Disrespectful people needed to be set straight complained Alice. Penelope in turn called her admirer at the police station, Lieutenant Martin, asking him to make a house call.

The sleepless girl scurried to the front doors juggling her mother's suitcase and purse, only to find Penelope. Stunned to see Josephine open the doors behind her, she lashed out.

"How dare you disgrace my front door? Go back!"

With uncombed hair and tired eyes, Josephine ignored the woman's pointed finger and clamored past down the steps. Suddenly a vision of her mother in the white mink appeared. Blood was running down her legs. Her neck was blue. *"Leave, baby girl. Leave."* The voice was alarming.

Josephine's mind blurred again. "You killed her, didn't you? I know you did. Look at the blood on the coat."

A police car traveled up the driveway toward the two.

"There is no blood on this coat. You crazy child!" She raised her arms to flag the officer's attention. As the sleeves reached eye level, the sight of red spots along the cuffs and sleeves caused her to scream.

Alice rushed from her office to the doorway.

"Miss Penelope, are you all right?"

"She did it. Look at the blood," Josephine yelled back at the two women as she ran to the circle of tall evergreens.

Penelope felt faint. The blood was dripping near her feet.

"She left blood here. There is blood on the steps. Why didn't you clean it, Alice?"

Alice frowned, wondering if the young girl had bewitched the woman.

"Miss Penelope, there's no blood."

"There is, there is. Clean it up. Get someone to clean it up now, before the officer comes. I'm not crazy. Just clean it up!"

Penelope took off the coat and entered the house shaken.

Josephine continued to run past the officer, down the gritty road, fearing for her life. Visions of her mother so near, yet so far blinded her way. Alice's son, Talbot, in his Chevy station wagon nearly hit her as he headed toward the big house. He had finished delivering goods to wholesalers downtown. Noticing that she was cute and about his age, he stopped the vehicle to get a good look at the girl with wild hair and half dressed in wrinkled clothes.

She was dizzy and couldn't see her surroundings, trying to reconcile visions of her mother last night. She ignored Talbot and continued to rush toward the main street. Angry her mother died, leaving her. She was tired of the hushed talk she was a child of rape. Or that her father had not accepted her.

She was tired of the nightmare, the screams she imagined her mother cried when she was being assaulted by him.

"Wake up, Mommy, wake up. Who's bothering you?" Josephine had known as a child that her mother met men in dance halls, but she made it home every night. She wasn't a whore, just young and pretty. It was fun to meet guys and drink, laugh. Sometimes her breath smelled of alcohol when she kissed her good night. It was okay.

Talbot called out his car window again, "Miss, are you okay? There's no bus around here."

She dropped her bag.

"I'm Talbot. Where are you going? Can I give you a ride?" He stepped out his car to call t her.

She questioned the tall, lanky young man's sincerity. His eyes were calm and friendly. It confused her. Was he trying to pick her up? Was he peering, looking for something within, signaling she could be had?

"Wait. Where are you going?"

Maybe he could be trusted. Maybe he could take her to Church Hill where Aunt Vera Gold lived. She remembered the little park on the hill. On the way she would buy flowers to toss in the river. Watch them float without tears. There was a chance she could find her mother's grave before she left. It had to be with Aunt Vera's. She stopped and looked at him hopelessly. Then ran again to the main road.

He got back inside his car and watched her in his rearview mirror run like crazy. Then he saw the same unmarked police car he'd seen on his way home. Driving up and down in front of the Garden. When it stopped the end of the gritty drive, he turned around to catch up with the girl, sensing trouble.

Josephine reached the main road unsure, which way to go. There were no sidewalks on this country road, so she stood in the street trying to figure out a direction. The unmarked car past her. Josephine did not recognize it at first, even though the scratchy noise of the two-way radio penetrated the air. It sparked a memory of police with radios and guns strapped to their waists the day they found her mother's body, whispering to Aunt Vera as she cried loudly how she couldn't save her Mimi.

Josephine grew suspicious of the black car. It brought to mind Aunt Vera's superstition. Never wear anything black including shoes or handbags. Only witches wore black because the black hand was always working in all ways through all people and places through black. But Miriam loved black dresses. Vera repeatedly told her not to wear the color in her house.

The black car stopped and sat across the street for a minute. Then it made a U-turn in front of her. She pulled her coat collar tighter around her neck.

The man inside rolled down a window. "You want a ride?" the man asked. "Taxi? I don't mind giving you a lift. What's your price?" he said in a slow, confident drawl.

She looked away from the unshaven white man, rough looking with dark circled eyes. He'd been up since 6 a.m. when homicide called, having just jumped in bed at 3 a.m. after playing poker with friends. The morning river scene of another girl dead made him anguish over another one dying. How did he let that happen?

He had a right to a night off from watching the tramps, night after night. Fellow officers began to wonder if he jumped into the game and became a pimp. He talked like he was their daddy. But he hated their musty perfume, sweaty from walking up and down the sidewalks. Cigarette breath coated with alcohol. When another died, their family blamed the police. Where were they when the girl ran away? He guessed he was getting too personal with these women.

The officer leered hard at Josephine. He saw that face somewhere. Not sure why. He yelled, "What's your name?"

She turned her back to him. "Please leave me alone."

The radio began to squeak and squeal for a pickup of a young black woman. He listened and figured she was the one. Blackstone got out.

"I see you aren't from this area. Your accent ain't right. It's 'yes, sir,' or 'no, sir,'" strolling around the car to confront her.

Talbot stopped abruptly in front of the patrol car. Josephine picked up her bag and started to walk quickly toward him. But the officer grabbed her arm.

"Don't run, baby, don't run." The rough-looking white man, who hadn't shaved in three days, then yanked her closer to handcuff her wrists.

"What's up, Blackstone?" Talbot asked as he approached, recognizing the officer as a member of his father's hunting club.

"She's under arrest."

Josephine screamed. "Please, no!"

"Why? She was a guest at the Gardens."

"No, she wasn't. She was soliciting you. I saw the two of you."

"That's a lie."

"Miss Rita," she yelled. "Miss Rita! Tell Miss Rita, please!"

"Back off, kid. I'll call your folks on you."

"We didn't do anything. You're wrong." Talbot followed the officer.

"Go on. Get away." The officer took Jo's bags and threw them in the front passenger seat.

"No, no, give them back to me. Please!" Josephine cried.

Talbot stood there helplessly, watching as the officer forced Josephine into the police car. Hugh pulled up to the scene. Talbot tried to flag him down, but the old man only waved an acknowledgment, knowing Jules in the backseat did not want to stop and interfere with Officer Blackstone. They continued toward the house. Upon seeing another police car parked at the front of the house, Jules directed Hugh to the carriage house in back.

Rita rushed out to the front portico looking for Josephine, after hearing the row she had with Penelope, she shook the little black stones harder. Talbot pulled up to the front evergreen circle.

"Come on, Miss Rita," he said, excited and upset. "The police arrested the girl. Said she was soliciting me. It was not true. I offered her a ride. That's all."

The police car was no longer visible. "Stop, Talbot."

"No, Miss Rita."

"Stop! There's no use."

He banged the steering wheel with both hands. "Why? We have to help. I know that bastard. He hates black people. Now he's got my name mixed up in it." The young man was upset. He was determined to get Blackstone.

"I'm going to talk with my mother. She'll have Miss Penelope get her out of jail."

"Don't put yourself in it. I'll handle it."

He looked at her with doubt, then drove off, set on finding out why the girl had been arrested.

* * *

The police car raced down the two-lane street, skipping lights, with the siren blaring.

"Officer, please, let me go," Josephine pleaded.

"Uh-uh, you were loitering, resisting arrest, assaulting a police officer, and obstructing justice." He radioed in that he had the suspect. "Yeah, I think she's the one you want. Roger."

Josephine cried, looking left and right as the blocks went by, trying to remember the way.

"May I have my bag?"

"What's in it? Drugs? Or your getup for night walking?"

"Please, I've done nothing wrong."

"Yeah, in the wrong place. This is the Velvet district."

They passed through one red light after another.

Velvet again. Her mind whirled with confusion.

"The slave girl that lived in that house?" he said.

"I am not Velvet."

"You look just like her. Who gave you that fur coat? That hat? Someone buy it for you?"

She thought he must be crazy. She didn't have any hat or fur coat.

He sneered. "The slave girl caused a man to lose his mind. You must have heard the story. Well, in these parts everyone is related. He was my people. This was tobacco land. Owned by my family until that happened. You see, I cruise this neighborhood a lot. Looking for the girls, looking for the Velvets who are out to ruin a man. That killing caused an upheaval in my family. Yeah, I know it was generations ago, but it is my history. Girls getting in a man's mind. He thinks he owns her, but she owns him. Can't get enough of that young black girl. Every day until he lost his mind when she walked off."

She cried over his prattling. Her wrists ached from the cuffs. She couldn't sit up straight. Glancing in the rearview mirror, he no longer saw her, causing him to fear she was trying to unlock the back door. He pulled to the curb at Broad.

Josephine rose when he stopped, and began rocking back and forth, crying hysterically. Tales of the unjust South rose in her mind. At the curb waiting for the traffic light to change was a group of men and women, white and black. They stood, unable to proceed even though the red signal changed to green, to red, to green, and back to red several times. The group could not lift a foot, mesmerized by the big man who jumped out of the squad car to unlock the back door and grab the crying girl's coat to make her sit still.

He shook her. "Shut up! Shut up!" He slapped her face hard.

"Help me! Help!" she cried at the people on the sidewalk. They became wooden puppets, stiff from fright, propped on the curbside. The assault did not raise a hair of courage to intervene. Only Odessa broke free from the group awakened by the slapping of the young girl's face. Outraged to see a man beat a woman, a white man too.

"Officer. Stop. Stop. I'll report you!"

Blackstone yelled, "Get back!"

Josephine screamed. "Please, miss. Help me. Please!" She tried to wriggle out of the car. He shoved her back down into the seat. There was a struggle, so Blackstone pulled out his gun and hit her across the cheek with the handle. A loud moan filled the car. Once out of the backseat, he slammed the door and waved his gun at Odessa. The older black woman stepped back. The officer returned to the driver's seat, then tossed the white suitcase and purse onto the street. He snorted.

"Hookers don't need clothes."

When the bags hit the street, Josephine blacked out and slumped sideways as the patrol car sped off. Two homeless, unkempt men in worn coats and shoes rushed to grab the bags, knocking, and falling over each other.

One dove for the suitcase, thinking no one would object. But Odessa quickly grabbed the white bag. "Get your hands off. Get, get, before I call the police," she said.

The other bystanders staring straight ahead, walked around the scuffle for the bags, pretending they had not seen the altercation in the police car. Traffic had backed up and a siren was heard approaching. The feisty panhandlers, fearful of dealing with the police, let go of the white one and ran off with the purse.

Odessa stood in the street, unable to move, feeling how precious the white suitcase must be to the girl. Cars moved slowly around her. One driver, upset over the backup, stopped inches from her hip, and blasted his horn hoping to intimidate her to move. Boiling from what she had just witnessed, she stood defiantly, soaked with pity for the girl. The car, finding her invincible, backed up and jetted away.

7

Jules Arrives

Ella mumbled as she dipped a mop into a pail of hot water mixed with peroxide. With long sweeps, she swung the wet mop across the portico, questioning whether Miss Penelope was losing her mind. Alice didn't tell her whose blood was supposedly on the steps. She bent lower to inspect the brick surface in search of just one blood spot. Just one spot.

Not seeing anything infuriated her. She believed Miss Penelope was trying to keep guilt from choking her mind. She'd heard talk that Mary Margaret and Polly had been into meddling with babies. And Polly had prospered with those herbs. Everyone knew those well-to-do women of the Fortune 500 club had been here, having Polly work on them. Even old Dr. Davis knew. She'd seen him come by now and then to check up on women. "Lot of blood on their hands, now on their minds. It was finally catching up to her children," she thought.

After firmly instructing Talbot to go back to his work, Rita Jane stood and looked down the roadway, worried about Josephine. Feeling responsible for her fate. Walking toward the house she wondered what Ella was doing.

"Why are you moping in this cold weather? You're making the steps icy. And what is it that you are using?"

"It's bleach. Some peroxide. Cleaning up blood."

"Where?"

"Alice said Miss Penelope saw blood. Maybe her conscience is rotting. This is the spot where that girl's mother died."

"How do you know?"

"Heard it," as she continued to swab the bricks with the cleaning solution.

"Rumors run like rivers, Ella." Rita Jane stepped past the woman.

"And so do blood. I've seen it."

Rita wrinkled her brow in disbelief. "If it does, you've seen nothing of the kind here. And stop that talk about Penelope. You hear?"

"Why you speaking to me like that? I've worked here long enough to know what is right around here. It ain't right anymore."

"If you want to keep working here you should stop talking about what you see or hear in this house."

"Why are you takin' up for her? She ain't got a liking for you. But you're just like her though."

"Ella, if you don't like your job or me, or Penelope, you can leave."

"Can't leave. Owe too much for the house and farm goods we get. If Scotty could get one of those factory or railroad jobs, we would be soon gone. But then we figure you folks would track us down to pay our back loans and debts."

"Do you want me to tell Penelope you're unhappy and you're leaving?"

"Tell her whatever you want. I was expressing myself. I've known you since you were a teenager and I watched Miss Polly hover over you. Now if you are better than me and like them and you want to protect her, go ahead. I've done no harm. I do my job. Just expressing myself. Just like if I tell you that she's ready to kick you out of this place. Watch and see, like I do. I see a lot." She dipped her mop into the bucket and turned away from Rita to splash the steps.

Ella's words challenged Rita Jane's heart. She stared at the woman's back with contempt, condemning the confidence the woman displayed in an attempt to put her in her place, on the assumption that because of their race they were equal, they were from the same fabric of society, wealth and education did not separate them, and her hardworking loyalty meant she could speak rudely.

It set Rita's mind back to childhood. Although she'd attended the same black schools as the children of the workers, she was driven to and from school by Hugh. Her classmates watched her climb in and out the big black car, whispering she didn't know where she belonged. But living in the big house did not make her feel welcome either. She noticed the delight guests expressed when the darker hand served the white porcelain teacups. Rita knew Ella received more respect from whites because of her darkness.

Polly would shoo her away, saying she was too light for these folks. But she watched from the next room the treatment the white guests and friends of the family gave the darker hands serving dinner. The talk was heartier, friendlier once they saw the contrast. It boosted their pride in their white skin.

Rita stood at the front door, wondering if this made Ella feel superior. In spite, with her hands on the front door knobs, she turned to the cleaning woman to ask a question, wanting the woman to acknowledge the privilege she had to enter the front doors. In a very composed voice to prevent Ella from detecting she had unhinged any insecurity about her identity at the Velvet Gardens, she asked "Where is Jules?"

"They went on to the back." The older woman continued to dip her mop to splash water across the steps, never looking up, in order to avoid Rita Jane's display of arrogance by walking through those doors.

"Ella, have a blessed day."

Rita Jane entered to find Penelope and Lieutenant Martin, a broad-shouldered man, early forties, in a dark police uniform, standing intimately close in the foyer. He held a box of cigars in one hand and Penelope's hand in the other.

"Thank you, for arresting her. It means a lot to me."

Rita coughed as she leaned back against the door, breaking their amorous trance.

Pulling his hand away, "My duty, Penelope. You needn't worry about anyone questioning you about the river death today, even though they appear similar to the last one, years ago. But we did get a call from Mrs. Ross about a woman in a white coat roaming down your street last night. So I had to ask a few questions."

"Mrs. Ross is pure trouble. Constantly complaining about my guests, or traffic tying up the roads. It's her daily bread," Penelope replied. "I don't think she saw any such person last night."

"She did describe a black car similar to the tips we received from people who came out the bars. Said it cruised up and down Canal and Main a few times."

"Oh, a black car? Well, she may have seen the taxi. We did have one late arrival." Penelope pointed her eyes at Rita, annoyed. Rita was quietly listening. Then Penelope blinked her eyes flirtatiously at the officer to distract him.

"Have another box of cigars, Officer Martin."

He stacked the second box on top of the first. "Thank you, ma'am. I know I'll enjoy them." Then they just stood there, affectionately smiling at each other. Rita decided it was time to break their false intimacy.

"Officer, a young lady, my guest, was arrested. I don't know why? Can you find out why? Can you stop the car?"

"Don't bother the officer," Penelope chided. "He's leaving." Penelope escorted officer toward the doors.

Martin took out one of the cigars. "I was told she came late, refusing to leave, only to break in without anyone knowing. Is that right, Penelope?" He sniffed the tobacco.

"Of course, and stealing," added Penelope.

"Stealing what!?" Rita yelled. "Why, Penelope? She did nothing to you." Rita moved toward the policeman. "Please, officer, I invited her. She was my guest. Where is she!?"

"She's okay. One of my officers saw her loitering." He hurried to leave, worried about the flack he'd get for the false arrest. He opened the doors. "Very grateful for the cigars. Happy holidays to you."

"What precinct?" demanded Rita Jane.

"I'm not sure, call Second Street. They handle most Negroes." Sly y, he turned to Penelope. "You will be at the toy giveaway today, won't you? The commissioner's wife is expecting you. She told me to remind you when she heard you called for a car. She's very happy about your work with the school board drive."

"Yes, sir." She smiled real hard to cover up her surprise regarding an appearance at an event she'd already told Estelle she was not going to make. She had reservations on the noon sleeper to New York. How could she say no after having Josephine arrested?

"Not a word is written about this call in my reports," he said, entering his patrol car. "Thanks again. These are the best cigars in town. You always have a good crop."

"Thank the graces of the good Lord for over one hundred years," Penelope replied, standing on the portico and waving the officer off.

"Officer, please, check on the girl, her name is Josephine, Josephine Walker. Have her released." Rita Jane pleaded.

"Don't worry, miss. She'll be released in twenty-four hours. I'm sure it was just a misunderstanding." He rolled up the window and started the engine to drown out the two women arguing as they reentered the house.

"If you go down to the station they may implicate you in all kinds of nonsense that girl conjures up. We can't get involved," Penelope begged.

"It was my fault she came. She could be in danger with those white men. What if her grandmother calls? I can't leave her be."

"You should not have invited her."

"I have a right to guests."

"Not without my approval."

"I own part of this house."

"Why Grandpoppa left you part of his estate is strange to me. And your share is smaller than what was given to the descendants of Mary Margaret, which you are not." Throwing her hands up in the air for dramatic emphasis, she continued, "Maybe Polly had something to do with it. But I rule the house and its goings-on." She whisked out of the foyer and into the east wing. A door slammed as she entered her father Zachary's library.

Rita Jane was weary of Penelope's denouncements. She'd wanted to leave Velvet Gardens for good, but Hugh insisted she stay. A growing distrust was growing between the two women. A growing battle to keep Penelope from subordinating her. She was not a servant.

She walked to the back of the house, hoping to enlist Jules to help with the police. He sometimes preferred the carriage house, where the second floor was an open loft providing privacy from Penelope and her workers. Out back, Hugh and Jules were unloading a set of brown designer steamer trunks, three luggage cases, and fancy gift boxes with the aid of Ella and her husband.

"Rita Jane Porter, *ma cheri*," he called, opening his arms for a hug. Jules was exotic with an ever-present tan, suggesting a mixed-race heritage with white features. His dark wavy hair had streaks of gray now. But he was still slender and sophisticated in a suit and tie as usual under a full-length black cashmere coat and expensive Italian leather shoes. At twenty-five he went to Paris to meet a high school friend studying perfumery. He stayed.

His letters home spoke of living in a villa and befriending café society. But he actually lived in a fifth-floor walk-up in a transient hotel with a false balcony overlooking wrought-iron spires atop the narrow buildings in the Latin Quarter. The small room had a lumpy bed, face basin, and a filthy toilet down the hallway shared by other residents. The continental breakfast of coffee, croissant, jelly, and butter every morning made up for the discomfort. It was all he could afford on his monthly allowance then.

The escalating war in Europe made living difficult. Expats were energized by his stories of the Confederate South where his grandfather had fought in the Civil War. Soon he became a choice delicacy at dinner parties. He survived, living a life as imaginative as he wished without fear of truth smacking him down. Soft, sweet with words, he charmed everyone in France as the heir to a tobacco plantation.

In Virginia, he was the accomplished editor of a notorious newspaper that was fire bombed by the Nazis for its clandestine support of the French Resistance during World War II. Not far from the truth, fortune placed him at a dinner party attended by the newspaper publisher, Monsieur Marche. Marche was enchanted by the Southern aristocracy as depicted in *Gone with the Wind.* He was fascinated by Jules's stories of his grandfather and the slave plantations, and the mysterious Velvet. He hired Jules by dinner's end.

His embellished lifestyle meant nothing unless he visited home each year shamelessly telling fanciful stories of his achievements even when it was brought to his attention they'd heard a different version the last time. He kept their attention each Christmas because he returned with a trunk filled with bottles of wine, candies, ties, cologne, and perfume. The scents were so exquisite.

Then he met Miriam one holiday trip. Night after night she came to the carriage house. He could not rid his feelings for her. She stayed on him longer than expected. Eventually his employer in Europe threatened to fire him. Unable to say goodbye face-to-face, he left, leaving money and instructions for Hugh to meet Miriam.

His returns to the states were sporadic and short after Miriam's death. He had not been home in five years. But it was best that he came this year to reestablish his American roots, he told his friends in France. There was rampant fear of roundups of persons suspected to be Nazi sympizers during the war years. He was not, but some acquaintances at parties were. Also, the suitcase was found, which worried him, because it contained his love letters.

If he is associated with any murder, or death in the U.S., it would be an excuse to detain him in Paris for questioning about his friends, about Miriam. It could mean a lengthy time in jail until money was secured for him to a post bond and obtain a lawyer.

Rita hugged Jules. Her large brown eyes were full of tears.

"Darling, live the good life. Stop the tears." Speaking in French, he kissed her forehead. "My, not one wrinkle."

She tried to smile. "Why did you drive off earlier?"

"I forgot to go to Lulu's Bakery to pick up your favorite coconut rum cake with cherries."

Hugh interrupted them. "Up the stairs, sir, or to the big house?" He knew Jules was lying to Rita. They'd gone to his lawyer, not a pastry shop. There were more patrol cars than usual for a slow holiday in the capital on Marshall Street. The newsstands at the John Marshall Hotel carried headlines about the death of a woman in the James River.

When Jules had arrived earlier, the sight of Josephine caused his throat to swell, his mind swirled with guilt and remorse. The young girl's face made the years separating Mimi and he vanish.

"Upstairs for now. I am not sure if I want to stay in the big house yet. Here, these are for you. I'll take this bag, and you take these packages." Jules filled her arms with fancy boxes wrapped with ribbons, smelling like perfume and candies. "I have a very special wine for you."

She tensed. "I haven't had a drink in years."

"Good, you'll enjoy it even more. I know you're trying to stay clean but a nip or two for me will not take you over the edge."

The two walked toward the big house, his arm around her shoulder. Penelope stepped out onto the back porch wearing the white mink. Then imitated a shiver to cover the bristling thoughts of dealing with Jules.

"Oooh, it's cold. Hugh," she called to the bowed shoulder man. "Can you warm my car and bring it to the side of the house?"

"Yes, ma'am. As soon as I finish with Mr. Jules's bags."

Jules gripped Rita's upper arm at the sight of Penelope.

"Welcome, brother."

He charged toward his sister who began to grin, pleased that she had cracked his nonchalant attitude. "How did you get that coat?"

"I purchased it for Mother. You have no claim to it." She pushed her shoulders up and tugged at the collar to cover her neck. Her eyes became vengeful thinking how Mary Margaret willed clothes and jewelry left by that Velvet woman to Rita Jane. Grandpoppa should never have given them to that woman in the first place. Mary Margaret had insisted that Rita have those clothes because she was a descendant of that woman. But they really were Grandmother Ann's. *Now they want to take my mink? No,* she thought.

"I bought that coat." Jules was livid because it was the mink in which Miriam laid nude upon his bed many nights. It held desire he longed to have again.

"No—no. This mink is mine. You have no claim to it."

"I will see that you will not either." He spat.

Approaching the circle was Esther Mae. She was hesitant to exit her car after seeing Jules and Rita but Penelope waved her on. Penelope wanted her to accompany her at the toy drive to gather names of black parents for a future campaign mailer.

"Mornin', Esther." Rita Jane broke the tension, sensing the woman was ashamed to be seen by her. She understood people needed money. Rita wondered if it was better than washing dirty hair.

"Mornin', Rita Jane." Esther smiled with relief that she wasn't hated for working in a beautiful house like the Velvet Gardens. She felt it raised her stature as an aspiring business woman. Hugh drove Penelope's Buick from the lot behind the carriage house to the bottom of the back steps and waited.

"We'll talk about the coat later, Penelope."

"Of, course we will." She replied as she entered the waiting vehicle with Esther.

"Let's carry on with better things," Jules said to Rita. The two walked to the carriage house. Agitated, he said, "Why does she insist on going after black people? I keep telling her it's wrong. Wrong. I hate to have my name associated with it. Honestly, I am ashamed. And where is that girl with the suitcase?"

"Penelope had her arrested."

Jules stopped in disbelief, then hurried up the carriage steps. "Incredible. Wicked."

"We need to go downtown and bail her out, Jules. She needs a lawyer. Should I call Art?"

"Art? Aristotle Strickland? Are you still talking to him? A glass of wine is better than that old lover." Relieved and comforted by the clean and airy loft as he remembered, he went into the bathroom to wash his face, hoping the conversation about the girl was over. Rita Jane paced, frustrated that he was ignoring the seriousness of it. He returned to the room and lit a cigar from the humidor.

Watching him with sadness, she remembered the weeks Miriam had stayed at the carriage house. No one could stop them. He was fascinated by the girlishness in a woman full of lust.

"That woman's daughter is in jail because I invited her here. I am to blame," Rita was sorrowful.

"How I miss these cigars. Have you set aside the boxes as I asked? I need more this year. They bring superb people to my attention. I am afraid to have them shipped. You know tobacco is not grown—"

"Shut up! Listen to me!" she interrupted.

He ignored her anger, then from a bag, opened a bottle of wine and poured a glassful. Then began unpacking his bags.

"Jules, that girl can be killed."

"You know there's nothing I can do about that. Just as I was unable to prevent Mimi from dying. Sometimes I wish I had taken her to France. But she had a child and was too restless, too young to be happy just in my bed."

His mind drifted to the week after the raid at the Derby when he called to see if she'd returned to work. He'd wanted her to visit him again in the carriage house. She was hesitant, wanting to leave Richmond, away from her aunt. She hadn't been making much money since the raid. Folks with big money were afraid to return. So, he promised her a nightly salary if she came to the Velvet Gardens. He arranged for Hugh to pick her up one block from the club. She came. Night after night. He knew it was foolish to continue the affair. One week after Jules's departure, Hugh was instructed to take an envelope of cash along with his address to her at the regular spot where she was picked up. And explain why he had left suddenly with a promise they would meet again.

"Stop lying to yourself and me. You left her pregnant and hid behind Hugh. You let her die." Rita couldn't stop the rush of words, feeling relieved of the pent-up emotional turmoil. "She screamed and screamed on those front steps thinking you were going to come back and take care of her. Saying you were going to keep her. How many black women do you prey on in France? How many black babies do you have in France?!"

Drawing on his cigar, he turned to her. "None." He exhaled a cloud of smoke. "Does it matter now?"

"Does it matter? Yes! You helped kill her."

"And they are after me!" He tossed a newspaper at her. "Read it. Seems her sordid life is fashionable now.

Headlines in all the papers. Her love affairs with the high social register of Richmond makes me guilty by association, doesn't it?"

"There's no mention of your name," she consoled him.

"Has the sleeping killer awakened? Another nightmare for a family." He reddened and continued to unpack, then repacked, uncertain if he would stay.

"I tried to help. I sent Penelope a dozen telegrams to help her. I was not coming back to deal with the girl. I was not marrying her. I sent her letters telling her to get an abortion. What happened?"

"Penelope made a mistake," said Rita. "Hugh knows—"

"Hugh knows nothing! You cut her up. You and Penelope, two jealous bitches cut her up!"

"Jules, you're crazy, out of your mind."

"Hugh told me you or Penelope tried some of Polly's tricks on the girl. Cheap voodoo formulas from some crazy book. Instead of sending her to the person like I asked.

Rita was offended. "What do you know? There is nothing voodoo about what Polly did to help women. Nothing is voodoo if it helps."

"If so, then why is Miriam dead?"

"How should I know. No one knows what was wrong with her. They say she just showed up at midnight, screaming to be let in at the front door, complaining about pain and bleeding. Ella told me Penelope started shooting a rifle at her, yelling, calling her Velvet. Telling her to run or she was going to kill her on the doorstep. Miriam started screaming for help, for the police. Hugh took her away. That's all I know. I never saw her that night."

He picked up the slowly burning cigar from the ashtray. He drew on it, then exhaled another cloud of smoke.

"You're lying," he said.

Rita Jane glared at him in disbelief. "I don't need to lie to you."

"Hugh did not take her away. It was another car. He thinks Penelope arranged for her to be taken away to some hack woman. Ella said it all happened after you and Penelope took her to the basement to work on her."

"Ella's a liar."

"How did she get in the river?"

"I don't know." Rita tired of arguing about Miriam's death walked to the top of the steps to leave. "Why did you come back? You lied about coming home to meet the little girl left behind. Didn't you? Wouldn't even stop to say hello when she ran after your car."

Calmly, deflecting her criticism, he asked, "And where is the precious suitcase?"

"She took it. Probably with the police by now."

This sent a chill through his chest. The police may discover letters establishing their affair.

"Rita, get ahold of Art, and let me know if he finds the girl." He should have stopped the automobile when she tried to talk to him. *But could he trust Art to retrieve the bag in confidence,* he worried.

"He's not returning my calls. Josephine did say she had an aunt in Richmond. Vera."

"Vera?"

"Yes."

"Vera Gold is dead."

"Dead?" Rita became upset the girl lied to her.

"I met the woman once before leaving. Very influential with the black community, particularly on Church Hill. She didn't like me." He poured another glass of wine. "One for you, *cheri*?" he asked. "I was white trash. No. She called me rich white trash. Out to gutter her niece. There was a rumor she considered a contract on my life."

8

Loving Right, Lovin' Wrong

Vera Gold did all she could to find her niece's killer. Deep inside she believed Jules LeNoire was responsible. Miriam was in a bad way after he left. Miriam's mother, Mae, hadn't done well with men either. Picking the wrong man to love was an invitation to living hell. Vera hated to think her niece's destiny was to die young like the rest of her family.

Vera faced sending Miriam's child off to unknown relatives after her health began to fail. She'd wanted to keep Josephine, but her days were filled with completing her last wishes, preoccupied with each day being the last. It was hard to keep a child happy in that state of mind. Even more difficult was filling the void in a child missing her mother.

The most worrisome question was whether Josephine would suffer the same fate as Miriam or her grandmother, Mae, dying young. It was decided that Josephine should go and live with her paternal grandmother.

A year after Miriam's death, Vera waited in the train station for Gloria Tate's arrival from Philadelphia.

Little Josephine in her yellow-and-white dress clapped at each speaker announcement. Excitedly she'd ask, "Is that it?"

"In a few more minutes. You'll hear the whistle," Vera answered patiently. People stopped to say how pretty she was. It was a chore to keep her in the colored seating section. The elderly woman looked upon the child with fondness, then a wave of sadness washed it away. The little girl's face was Miriam's face. She hated sending the girl to Philadelphia, the city her dear sister thought was a reprieve from the oppressive South.

Vera had distant relatives on farmland in Powhatan, a few cities away, her birthplace and Mae's. Their father, Rufus, bought nineteen acres from his former slave owner in 1874, earning the money as a paid laborer rebuilding the city of Richmond after the great fire set by the retreating Confederates.

Rufus was free to leave the state but stayed, believing the North would not treat him any better than the people whom he'd known all his life. His roots were deep in Virginia. Farming was profitable after the war because food was scarce. He did so well with his crops that he was able to buy rental property in Richmond. He knew there was a large population of blacks looking to reside on their own terms. The lack of good housing often forced ex-slaves to return to their masters as sharecroppers.

Vera was already working in Richmond as a domestic to get away from farm work. One Saturday while helping her father clean one of his rooming houses, she met Will Gold carrying a heavy duffel bag. He was moving into a single room with two older brothers after serving in World War I. He impressed her when he put down his heavy bag to help her mop the halls. She knew he was a good man.

They married and bought a house on Grace Street. At one Thanksgiving dinner, Will's older brother Sam met Mae there. He was a widower with two small children and he was looking for a new wife. Mae was thirty and anxious to be married. Everyone discouraged her from marrying Sam, but he was tall, cinnamon, and freckled, with sandy red hair. A woman could not refuse him a smile when he spoke. But behind the good looks was a cold streak that surfaced after Mae and he moved to Philadelphia, leaving his first set of children in Virginia with in-laws. Mae wanted a bigger life and no warnings could prevent her fate. Sam was hers and he insisted they were in love and others were jealous, trying to keep them apart.

She swooned when she saw Philadelphia, an old city full of jazz joints, beauty parlors, theaters, and blocks of black-owned stores. A black renaissance was in full swing. Demand for factory workers and railroads attracted Sam along with other migrant blacks and whites from the Southern states. Railroads offered free passage for those willing to work in their yards. The noble city on the Delaware was a beacon of prosperity to free men and runaway slaves where the sidewalks didn't wash away with rain.

The dance halls, fancy and big as the white ones in Richmond, excited Mae. At night they filled with men and women polished in fine suits, dresses, hats, furs, shoes, and jewelry, arriving in Model Ts. Hair so pressed and shiny, one could see the reflection of the ballroom lights. From one club to another Sam and Mae danced every Saturday night. Then the Great Depression set in like a heavy cold. The sidewalks became hard and bitter concrete to the less fortunate. With four daughters they struggled to stay off the street. Miriam was the eldest. Then Babs, who died at age eight. Then came Marie and Maddie. They lived poorly even though Sam had two jobs during the Depression era. He hid money and began to see other women. Mae fell sick but told no one. It lingered for a year before the farm girl with lovely cream skin and wavy raven hair passed at the age of forty-two without Sam saying a word about her death to Vera or Will.

A train whistling as it entered the station brought Vera's thoughts back to Josephine who jumped and clapped her hands again. Josephine knew this was the train. Vera wondered if she would recognize the woman whom she met years ago at the funeral of Miriam's younger sister, Marie.

Josephine and Vera stood near the doorway peering at each passenger as they entered the station, looking down for bowed legs.

"Hello, there." The woman pushed through the crowd, carrying a shopping bag of toys. The bowed legs of the well-groomed woman in a spring suit with gray hair in a French roll smiled brightly.

"How do you do, Gloria. Was your travel comfortable?" Vera asked.

"It was fine. Come here, sugar, and give Grandma a hug." She held out her arms. "Now we don't need to talk on the telephone, do we?" The little girl smiled, finding the attention warm. She reached up to the woman who smelled of gardenias.

"I always meant to get to Philadelphia, but after my sister Mae passed, then Marie, and Miriam here, I never got too far past Washington, D.C."

Little Josephine held up her bag, "See, Grandma, I have a suitcase. Like it?"

"I truly do, sugar."

"Can I take you to lunch? Across the street is a good rib place," Vera offered.

"We won't have time. The next train north arrives in thirty minutes. We can sit and talk, though, can we?"

"Yes, in this section." They walked through the doors to the designated area for coloreds.

"Haven't been south in a while, it's still the same."

"I didn't think it was right to pass Jo onto a cousin."

"I appreciate that," Gloria said.

"After her mother died, I wanted to keep her. She was the last of my sisters. And... well, you would have had to come soon." Vera was choking with tears.

A woman recognized Vera. "Hello Miss Gold."

"Hello." Cordial but not recognizing the woman.

"Just want to thank you for your help with that school donation. The one for the after-school books."

"It was God's gift."

"Don't let me interrupt. But I saw the ad in the paper about the reward. Your niece. I think I know—"

Grandma Philly listened and watched Vera flush. "Dear, I can't discuss it right now. It has a number to call. My lawyer is handling it."

"Sure, sure. I'll be in touch with him."

"Please do. We appreciate any information. Thank you."

"Thank you. I'll let you be, now." The woman moved on.

Vera lapsed into silence, staring at her hands. She recalled her distress over the police's refusal to investigate Miriam's death. Their refusal to provide information or pursue the little evidence and leads they had, infuriated her. She believed the LeNoires paid to have it covered up to protect Jules. It pushed her to use her own money to get answers. The reward notice had been posted and circulated in all the churches, barbershops and beauty parlors, liquor stores too. No one seemed to care. Some said it wasn't Jules but one of his friends. Some said Miriam was too whorish to merit concern. Vera knew she'd come from a good family but suffered a lifetime of despair from an early age.

Inhaling heavily, she said, "That brings to mind something. I would prefer Josephine not experience the separate schools. I could send money for private ones."

"Don't you worry, ma'am. She will do fine. The schools are bound by their neighborhoods, but I will see that she is raised with pride."

"Good, good. I know you will care for her with all your heart."

Vera thought back, searching for a handkerchief in her small purse. She'd arranged for Miriam to move to Richmond, hoping to give her a better life. Miriam had written Vera a little card, telling her of the misery of living with Sam after her mother's death.

* * *

Vera and Will did not have children. Once in a while they took in a child until the mother or father could do better. After Mae passed, she wrote Sam insisting the three girls, then twelve, eleven, and four, live with her. They'd spent their summers with her growing up. But Sam would not have it. Summers in Richmond were enough. He was afraid she would spoil his girls. They had to live within their means. Vera's flair for the big and fancy made him look like a loser and it made Mae sad.

She believed Sam was angry and envious of Will because they prospered. They worked hard, despising the servitude they saw in other blacks working for a living. They maintained the family farm for a while, raising chickens and hogs, selling the eggs and curing and selling the hams to church members or local stores. He bought two taxicabs after selling some rental properties. They sponsored fund-raisers for different charity causes. They gave annually to students who needed books or tuition.

It was upsetting to hear rumors that Sam had the three girls on the sidewalk while he worked in a car lot cleaning vehicles, watching them beg for change from passersby who thought they were too cute to be wearing soiled dresses. They were very attractive girls. He refused help from Will. Even so, Vera continued to send money to Mae, after her inheritance share was spent.

Sam hired babysitters, but it was becoming too much for him alone. Miriam was grief stricken and incorrigible. She refused to go to school, often sitting in her mother's empty bedroom, the room she hadn't been allowed in while Mae was alive. He'd scold her that Mae was too sick for children, not to bother her. He did have a favorite, Marie, who could do no wrong, and was allowed to visit with Mae in her sickbed as much as she wished.

Miriam began to argue with her father. He expected her to watch her younger sisters after school. Instead she walked the streets, suddenly grown. She missed her mother and began to steal or beg for cigarettes. Then she acquired a taste for liquor. It made her feel alive. She became an alcoholic at thirteen.

Overwhelmed, he took Miriam to the Bureau for Colored Children for placement in a foster home, first of many she ran away from. Miriam believed her younger sister Marie was the blame, wanting all of Sam's affection to herself. Alone, he could not care for Maddie, the toddler, either, so he placed her in a foster home too. He kept only Marie, for whom he bought gifts every payday to keep her sadness away. Marie was not happy, not without her sisters or her mom.

The Great Depression lingered. The next year he decided to marry a woman of means, whom he thought was worth his time. She was Gloria Tate, a widow with two sons, and the nickname Philly. She'd heard that he was a womanizer. He'd heard she was a lesbian. But she owned a row house on Oxford Street and took in boarders. With hope of material comfort, Sam married Gloria and moved in with Marie.

Shortly before Easter, Marie became feverish. A doctor was called but it was too late; she died at the age of thirteen from rheumatic fever. Miriam did not meet Philly until Marie's funeral. She liked Philly's warmth, and she grieved Marie's death.

Philly did not. She grew jealous of Sam's over affection for this one daughter. After Marie's death, Sam was unreachable, stone. No one could console him, so Philly allowed Miriam to stay to help his grief.

A year after Marie's passing, Miriam was unhappy living with her father and Philly. He began to call her Marie, her dead sister. He'd visited Maddie now and then in foster care, and called her Marie too. Miriam refused the name, but Maddie identified with the name in order to gain her father's attention and love; and began telling everyone she was Marie.

In a letter to Vera, Miriam said Philly's son, Percy had raped her. He was twenty-two. She was fourteen and pregnant. No one believed her. Sam wanted the son to confess but he denied it. Philly was about to kill all of them. She had worked hard to be an upstanding person, calling Miriam a liar and a whore. Philly was a strong woman, having left the hills of Staunton with two boys after her husband died, determined to live without shame.

Rape would mean the death penalty. Maybe life in prison. Oh, why ruin his name? She pleaded with Miriam to tell the truth. Back and forth it went for weeks. Philly resolved that they marry. Sam was not too happy about having his fourteen-year-old daughter marry.

Sam finally agreed to sign the marriage papers, telling Miriam she could leave the marriage if she wanted to, but that he wanted her to stay. Miriam hated her father and her new husband. It was Sam who had caused her mother to suffer, and now causing the black hand to strangle her youth.

Miriam refused to be near Percy. She hated his guts for ruining her life. They argued constantly until Philly encouraged him to leave the house, fearing he would turn up dead, poisoned. He joined the army before Josephine was born. Still, Miriam was unhappy in the house. She was Sam's little Marie, quelling the grief for his other truly beloved daughter.

Then Philly began watching Miriam, gauging her infidelity toward an absent husband, calling her friends to find out what she was doing. She was often out playing cards or drinking in bars. Sam was getting tired of it too.

* * *

Another incoming train whistled coordinated with the loudspeaker, calling out the northbound stops which caused Josephine to clap happily. Vera and Josephine rose but Philly stayed seated, struggling to bring her mind to the present from the guilt of Miriam's death. The sound of the train whistle brought back the memory of the day Miriam left Philadelphia.

Philly had agreed to drive Miriam and the baby to the 30th Street station for the trip to Richmond, hopeful that at the last minute, Miriam would leave the little girl with her. Overcome with anger that this teenager was leaving with her son's child, the child she'd first despised, Philly's hand kept shaking in her pocket.

Miriam had always considered her evil, with devilish ways. "What's in your pocket? Why do you keep shaking your hand?"

"Just cold hands. Trying to keep 'em warm."

Then Miriam saw a handsome man with a cigarette. They smiled. She wanted to speak to him. So, she asked for a cigarette.

"Is that necessary with the child?" said Philly.

"Why not? We're out in the air."

The young man held her hand as he lit her cigarette. Philly rattled her pockets harder. Miriam felt a strange sensation in her heart. The older woman had killed a chicken when she heard Miriam was leaving. She put blood on the matter. Her eyes were on fire with a Bible in one hand and chicken bones rattling in the other.

Quietly, Philly spoke. "Don't take the child away from me. She's the only thing I have. Go on with the fella if you want."

"This is my child. She stays with me." Miriam stepped back from Philly's dark eyes possessed with hatred. Her mind was concentrated on how Miriam had entered her house and cursed it. All the old woman wanted was Miriam to leave without Josephine.

The man asked, "Is there a problem? Can I help?" Miriam stood behind him. Hoping to block the deadly eyes.

"It's my child. Go, Philly. Go on home."

Philly knew she had made a scene. "You'll see. You'll come to no good." Shaking her hands hard in her coat pockets as she walked through the crowd, never hearing from Miriam again.

Now she plans to raise the little girl with lots of love and protection against evil. She prays God will give her that redemption.

The train from Florida bound to Philadelphia was loading passengers and making its final announcements. Even though Josephine knew Philly only by telephone calls, she was not afraid to leave with her because she had a pretty shopping bag full of gifts, lots of sweets too. She hugged her Aunt Vera for the last time, not understanding the sadness in her eyes.

"I'll ship the rest of her things. I didn't want to load you down with bags knowing you have to change trains," Vera said.

"Don't worry, I have plenty."

"She has some favorites. Maybe I'll get up there to see you before Christmas."

The trio walked to the train platform. Josephine pulled her Grandma Philly's hand, anxious to board.

"Give Auntie Vera another hug," Philly said, attempting to slow the child down and allow the white passengers to pass and board. Then Philly picked up the child and tickled her, causing giggles. The little girl stopped for a moment to wave to Vera before she disappeared into the crowd.

Vera never made it for Christmas. She was suffering from breast cancer. In the end, a trust was established in the Virginia Commonwealth Bank for the little girl. Philly received a letter from the trustee lawyer but ignored it. Once a year, an interest check arrived in Philly's name to buy Christmas gifts but she never cashed them. They would manage without it. She never told Josephine about the money, fearful the child would want to learn about her mother. Philly didn't want Josephine to love anyone but her.

9

Odessa

Driving in the midst of heavy traffic and holiday shoppers, Odessa wondered what she was going to do with the white suitcase. She felt bad she wasn't able to get the other bag from the bum. Another unexpected chore in a day full of plans, seemed to be the way of life for her.

Odessa was on Broad Street to buy a festive tablecloth for the dining room and to drop off toys that her office had collected for the Greater Richmond Christmas Toy Drive. Next, she was to pick up Hattie, a sorority sister, by noon. It was her year to host her college sorority sisters for the Christmas weekend. They'd eat, drink, play cards, and see a show. Now she was a witness to police brutality.

She decided to leave the suitcase with the police and let them locate the girl even though she did not like dealing with them. They kept tabs on her unnecessarily. She was a respectable social worker dealing with juvenile offenders. In a telephone booth outside the Second Street police station she called her husband, Minton.

"Hello, Mint. It's me. I'm running late."

"Are you okay?" he asked.

"Yes, yes." He always worried when she was alone downtown. "I'm going to the police to report an incident."

"Odessa, do you want me to come? What happened? Are you hurt?" he asked fearfully.

"No, no. I'm fine. Can you please pick up Hattie when she calls? At the Greyhound station. The bus from Raleigh."

She had no idea whether Art was at this office or would pick up the telephone. Being the head of a tennis academy kept him on the go. Usually to a wealthy widow's villa in Florida during December.

"I don't feel good about you going in there alone. You know how they are."

"I know exactly how they are. That's why I am going in there."

"If trouble starts—"

"I will call you."

Her activism with the NAACP, gathering signatures and holding rallies to help the plaintiffs in the school desegregation cases, or raising money to challenge Richmond's overcrowded schools and segregated districts, kept her under surveillance. After the Supreme Court ruled against separate but equal education earlier that year, she periodically received hate mail or bomb threats. Sometimes white people sat in their cars in front of her house for hours.

None of it deterred her.

"In whose problem are you meddling?"

"Mint, I need to keep going. I'll be home shortly." She took a deep breath, straightened her jacket, gripped the suitcase, and then walked not too slow or fast to the station doors. Making sure her steps were evenly paced, not out of step with her hips and not too far in front of the shoulders. A walk that suggested her thoughts were not rushed or random.

She looked at her appearance in a store's plate window, pleased with the reflection of a professional woman in her better overcoat and dress. Her makeup was as fresh as when she left her bedroom this morning. Always putting on her Garbo eyebrows and scarlet lipstick, pancake makeup with her hair pinned off her neck.

Behind the tall reception desk facing the entrance was a dashboard with wires and telephone receivers on hooks. A large blackboard that listed patrol cars and officers' names hung behind the officer who manned the desk. She stood eye level with the top of the high counter. The officer did not raise his head from his note writing to acknowledge her.

"Officer, do you see me?" she asked.

Instead, he answered a telephone call, peering over her head toward the entrance doors. After the call he immediately radioed a patrol car to go to an apartment building regarding an attempted break-in.

After he hung up, she exploded. "I want to speak to the captain," she yelled.

He said nothing, ignoring her. He wrote more notes and turned to put papers in a metal bin behind him for pickup and distribution. The radio crackled in the background from patrol cars radioing their locations.

"Captain Hall," she yelled. "Captain Hall! I want to speak to the captain, right now!"

"If you yell one more time, I will arrest you for assaulting an officer!"

"Arrest me now. Captain Hall!" she yelled again.

"Okay, okay." He dialed, waited, then said, "The line is busy."

"Then call the commissioner. You must be relief."

"I am the sergeant on duty." Another officer entered from a back door who recognized Odessa. He'd handled the investigation of a suspicious package sent to her home a few months ago.

"Good morning, Miss Odessa. More hate mail?"

"No. I have a suitcase that belongs to a young woman. She was beaten by a man. Not sure if it was an officer or not. He was not in uniform. But he threw her belongings cut of the car. Did you bring a young Negro woman into custody this morning?"

"No, ma'am. Why do you think it was a police officer?"

Odessa was perplexed. "The man put her in handcuffs, and when I approached to stop him from hitting her, he pulled a gun on me. Either way, it is a crime to hit a woman. It needs to be investigated."

"There was no incident reported this morning. What are you talking about?" the seated officer asked with a cold stare.

"I saw it." Punctuating each word through tight lips, "The-young-lady-was-beaten. Then he threw this suitcase out of the car."

The seated police officer held his hand up to quiet her, in order to listen to a radio report.

"Roger. Will send cars out for assistance. AP-five. Ten-four. Roger.

"You must be talking about a domestic incident. We do not handle husband-and-wife affairs," the standing officer continued.

"No, this was a police officer!" She was adamant. "He had a gun."

"Did you see a badge?"

"No."

"Was the car marked POLICE?"

"No. I saw it. I saw it. It was shameful." She was pained that the officer was trying to raise doubts about what she saw.

"*If* you saw an officer, and I say *if*. And *if* the officer hit a person in his squad car, it was because they had to be subdued."

"Let me speak to the commissioner," she insisted.

"You can catch the commissioner at the toy giveaway. I think he and Miss LeNoire will be appearing together," replied the seated officer.

The LeNoire name infuriated Odessa. She stamped her foot to rid her mind of the sound. A woman who does not have a child of her own but speaks out for the safety of others with bigotry. Odessa can hear her lies. *'The old South must not be fragmented, torn apart. We can mend our ways together.'* Distressed that she was not able to get the officer to admit he was protecting another officer who had violated the girl's civil rights, she walked away. The standing officer called out, "You might want to try the hospital."

Odessa did not look back, horrified to think the girl was injured that badly. She ignored the terrible feeling in her stomach. Hurriedly she drove to the outdoor toy giveaway where workers were decorating tables with red cloth. She waved at a few familiar parents who stood in the Santa line with their children. A truck with mounted speakers filled the air with holiday music as workers walked around ringing bells.

As she crossed the street carrying two shopping bags of toys, she saw Esther Mae jotting down notes on a pad while talking with Penelope and the police commissioner's wife, Estelle. This stung Odessa, knowing the church had paid Esther Mae's poll tax so she could vote for the first time in November's presidential election. The state's annual voters' registration tax equaled the average monthly salary of a white man.

Esther Mae was thirty-five and never could afford the tax. She had never voted. Pastor Poindexter promised to take up a collection if she volunteered several hours for the church. Odessa knew the woman was ambitious, wanting more in life than living on tips as a beautician. Esther smiled upon seeing Odessa and broke away from the two women.

"Good morning, Miss Odessa." Esther seem pleased with herself.

"Good morning to you. You look right professional today."

"I got a job working with Miss Penelope."

Odessa held back her disappointment. "Well, I hope she's paying you well." She handed the toys off to a worker who asked if she needed a receipt. She shook her head no while listening to Esther, not wanting to make eye contact.

"Yes, I'm her assistant. She's preparing a campaign to run for school board. She liked my manners."

"Esther, if you needed a better job than a beautician, why go to her? She's against our kind."

"We'll see." Esther sensed Odessa's displeasure. "Everyone deserves a chance. No one is all bad. She says she has great plans to improve our schools. She will raise money to build a new high school." Penelope waved at Esther to return. "I have to go. But if you be needing anything or help call me."

"Certainly."

Estelle, a seasoned woman in cat eyeglasses recognized Odessa. "Miss Odessa, how are you?" Walking quickly to shake hands.

"Good to see you, Miss Estelle."

"The same. The commissioner was supposed to give a speech with Penelope but cancelled. So, here I am."

"Oh, I was hoping to speak with him. I witnessed a young lady being assaulted by a police officer today. I am trying to locate the girl and the name of the officer."

Estelle felt pinched. "I don't really interfere with that sort of stuff. I am sure they will hold the officer accountable. But what I wanted to hear is how you feel about Miss Penelope running for the school board."

"I have no opinion," Odessa said dryly.

"Well, I can say I've listened to her go on and on about the need to preserve and protect our youth. I am not sure if her heart is really there. But I think she'll grow into doing the best for all. What I mean is I don't want you to think my friendship with her is against your race. I want to be assured you get that message to your fellow workers."

"Miss Estelle, you're welcomed to address them at our meetings at the church on Thursday evenings. You need no special invitation."

"Oh, that might be too political. Anyway, I want you to know I agree with what you're trying to do, but my open support can cause the commissioner to lose his clout, maybe his job. Some might try to ambush us and run us out of town," she said, hoping to elicit sympathy from Odessa, who smiled. "You understand?"

"Partly. I've seen many leave Richmond after risking their jobs and reputations for pushing back on prejudice. Having everyone turn against them, showing them their backs, and saying it was none of their business and they shouldn't have spoken out."

"Odessa, I speak as best I can. I am only one person."

"In a social position to makes others listen."

The conversation was getting too testy for Estelle. "Well, keep up the good work. We need you. I hear some politicians are meeting to write new legislation. They've raised a quarter of a million already and they call and call to recruit people like me and Penelope, afraid the colored signs will come down soon. Hope I can be of help to you too, Odessa." She walked away with a plastered smile in order to speak with the Santa who just arrived.

The conversation saddened Odessa. *Why can't she get the support to run for public office and win? Was she too bossy, too smart?* She was only forty-five. A social worker for twenty years working with families, babies, the homeless, and single mothers. Her husband, Mint, was a track coach and teacher at Armstrong High. They owned a house.

"But they won't vote for you," Art had counseled. He'd worked on her campaign to sit on the city council, and the previous school board election. His belief was people were afraid they'd lose their jobs if they showed too much support for a black person over a white one. Then again, public office is not for everyone.

How do you explain Penelope? worried her. *The socialite never had a child, did not attend public schools. How can she represent anyone on a school board?*

"Having some sort of competition with Penelope LeNoire is a waste of your precious energy. Leave it alone. Bottom line, where are we going to get the votes? People still have a hard time registering. The poll tax is too high for many." Minton tried his best to sober her ambition.

Finally, she arrived home. Minton stood at the front door relieved to see his wife. She smiled but her mind was still churning as he kissed her cheek. *Why are we cowards? Where is our courage? Those kids at Moton had it. They went on strike. They refused to sit in classrooms with rain pouring on their heads. Now we are supposed to let state officials stop the Brown case from taking affect?*

Her old college friend Hattie joined them at the door with a glass of brandy. It was a long wait. Minton and Hattie had chatted quietly trying to keep the holiday spirit while listening to Nat King Cole. Now and then each took a turn to look out the window for her car, worried.

Mint asked, "What happened? Why did you go to the police?"

"A young girl was beaten by a cop. I was trying to return the suitcase that he threw in the street." She entered the living room with Josephine's bag, taking off her overcoat and gloves, avoiding Minton's glare that condemned her easily given compassion. Hattie handed her a glass of brandy.

Her friend held her glass up. "Cheers to O, for every broken arm, to every broken heart, with the strongest shoulders, willing to hold up the entire world of trouble."

Drink in hand, she sat on the sofa, thinking how to groom herself to recruit votes. "Maybe I should try again."

"No, Odessa. No." Mint shook his head. "You have tried three times. People are too afraid of women in public office. Aren't you tired of the hate mail?"

"No. Besides, that was before the Supreme Court ruled. We have to make sure it's enforced. We have to fight. We can't let them continue with the schools this way. Boys and girls are truant. Dropping out, getting into trouble. Always begging and borrowing to raise bail for them. Or they sit home or stand on corners dreaming, instead of learning. Why?"

"How are you going to do it?" asked Hattie.

"Smearing that Penelope woman won't get you elected," Minton added. Realizing he was making his wife more despondent, "I'll leave you ladies after my sweet rolls are done." He walked to the kitchen, speaking over his shoulder. "Paul called while you were out. He was worried."

"What did he say? How is he?"

"Fine. Called to say he got tickets for us to see the Platters at the Apollo tomorrow." In the kitchen he finished packing a bag of food and drinks for the trip to see their son who attended college in New York. Mint visited often to keep his son from Virginia and learning of Odessa's knack for agitation. His son needn't worry about their safety.

"That is a pretty suitcase." Hattie noticed it by the front door.

"It's the girl's. The police told me she may be in the hospital."

Mint came back to kiss his wife.

"Keep her locked down," he said to Hattie. "Please. I don't want to come and—"

"And what?" Odessa interrupted, looking at her husband fearlessly.

"Come home and have to kill a few crazy people," he replied, irritated. "It's one thing to be in the struggle and another to trash folks." He'd warned her to keep the issues clear about what she wanted. "Jealousy over that white woman running for office is no need to create a scandal."

"Bye." She waved her glass at him.

The music on the radio was interrupted by a newsbreak just after he'd driven away.

"A strangled woman was found in the James River this morning. The police are requesting any information as to her identification or suspects..." Odessa turned up the radio.

"Is that your girl?"

"I don't think so, but maybe. Let's call the hospital. I need to call Art too."

"Odessa, you have the calm and peace to stop a hurricane. Why are you having a fit over this strange girl."

"Only heaven knows." She answered

10

The Toy Drive

Penelope was relieved when Odessa drove away. She'd feared another public confrontation. They often argued at board hearings, accusing each other of using the school platform to self-promote which was not far from true.

Her leisure class was losing clout with fellow Southerners whose social status was also being challenged by the surge for equal rights. Politics was turning genteel tea parties into bulldog fights. A new breed wanted power by showing they could stop the federal government. But they were not her kind or on anyone's social register. She had to stop them too, by stepping up and proving her historical importance was still relevant.

She often complained to Estelle that Odessa was the mastermind of trouble in Richmond, by using race to propel herself into city affairs. "Change can't be based on race. It has to be about competency and righteousness."

"According to whom?" Estelle asked, poking Penelope's arm for emphasis as they walked along the lines of children waiting for Santa. "What about the politics of the white color?"

Penelope looked at Estelle strangely. "Are you testing me? I am not understanding."

"Are you color blind?"

82

"What? Who is? Certainly not Odessa. A committee member told me she sent the senator a flyer with a picture of a little black girl called Jenny Brown closing the lid of a coffin on a black bird named Jim Crow. What an awful thing to do. The flyer said, 'There was no use trying to dress him in new laws, 'cause he is about to be buried for good.' Well, they sent the FBI straight to her door for threatening the good senator. She doesn't know her place."

"My dear, she does. It's what motivates her."

"She's black and will stay black."

"Certainly. Look at these youngsters. Innocent. But you have two lines. One for whites and one for blacks. The whites go first. Why? Why do they get to go first to get toys? In a few years it will be one line, Penelope. That's what she's working at. Come on, let's shake some of those little hands." Estelle walked away, passing a choral group as it strolled through the crowd singing carols. One member handed out candy canes from a large stocking. The lines wrapped around the corner, everyone waiting for a turn to speak to Santa and receive a toy. Cheerily Estelle bent down to speak to a few children in line.

Penelope soured at the prospect of talking to the little squealing know-nothings. *Oh, why,* she lamented, *am I not on the train to see Pierre?* She loved her cousin, but her father had threatened to kill both in their wedding bed if they married. They were soul mates, complicated by being in the same family. Pierre had been upset when he'd learned that she would not arrive until nearly midnight. She should have called Lieutenant Martin to say she fell sick. Even if he was kind to have that crazy girl arrested.

Penelope looked for a way out. Her feet were cold. Uncomfortable in high heels and sheer stockings, she wondered if she was too made up and whether wearing the white mink was a good idea. The constant commands from Estelle irritated her. Then she saw a photographer snapping away. The prospect of having her picture taken for the papers prompted her to join Estelle to shake hands with a few colored parents, in hopes of good press.

* * *

Two blocks over, Blackstone, still on duty, patrolled for suspicious activity around Broad Street where shoppers darted back and forth across the street decorated with holiday lights and ornaments. Suddenly a group of teenage girls with shopping bags, laughing and talking, inattentive to cars, stepped off the curb in front of him. He hit the brakes hard. Josephine's bruised face appeared in his windshield. Jolted by the image, he turned on the wipers to erase the sight.

He froze. Horns from backed up traffic began honking but the sound did not shake the memory of his rage against Josephine. He'd meant no harm. It was his uncontrollable temper. It was a mistake. He had no hatred for coloreds.

People gathering on the sidewalk gawked at him, wondering if he was okay. Horns continued to honk bringing him back to his whereabouts. He sped away, around the corner to find his childhood friend Joe Rogers in the middle of the street directing traffic around the toy drive.

He yelled over the squeaking kids and carol singers. "Joe! Joe! What's happening?"

Joe leaned into his window. "Nothing much. Except the chief's wife and Queen Penny called for coverage. Are we still on for bowling tonight?"

"Wouldn't miss it." Blackstone stared at Penelope, who was posing for photographs.

A kid ran across the street. "Hey, hey, you. Get back in line. Got to go." Joe tapped the car's hood and returned to directing the flow of cars and people.

Blackstone was happy that Joe was still his friend. They often joked about their third grade fight over Queen Penny. She'd sat two desks ahead with painted red nails, a real belle in her pressed little dresses, a constant chatterbox about her plantation, the servants, the tobacco fields. And how she drank whiskey with her poppa at bedtime. He couldn't sleep at night, waiting for the next day to hear more of her lies.

Unable to hold his secret, he shared his dream of kissing her pretty face with Joe, who insulted his feelings by laughing and saying she was nothing but a nigger. Then Joe told Penelope that Benjamin Blackstone had said it. She burst into tears. Mrs. Fisher, their teacher, had asked, "Why are you crying, Penelope?" Before she could speak, Blackstone jumped Joe, punching his face hard. "Stop! Stop, Benjamin!" She scurried down the aisle of desks to pull the boys apart.

The teacher sent Penelope to the girls' room to wash her face, then scolded the class that bad language would not be tolerated. Such things were not said to white girls. To call Mr. LeNoire's daughter a nigger was a sin. It was nonsense to Blackstone's father, who wished he'd been in the classroom that day. He would have told them the truth. Penelope was the daughter of a slave woman's child. From that day on Penelope looked down her nose at Blackstone. Her father, Zak, put her in a private school the next day.

Blackstone sat across from the toy giveaway. Trying hard to figure out if she was white or black. She looked as white as any other white person, no blunt nose, no kinky hair. Her hair had darkened but she kept it bleached blond to be a boss bitch. Her freckles were always covered with makeup.

He drove closer to where Penelope stood to observe her further because she didn't appear in public too often, preferring to be driven around by Hugh or sending servants to handle her business. When she noticed his stare, she sniffed at him, then kissed Estelle good-bye. Then instructed Esther Mae about the mail, reminding her to return anything out of the ordinary back to the postal clerk.

Blackstone wondered what they were up to with this campaign. Maybe they think that light colored hair coming out of her brain makes her the glorious right. She isn't right. Thinking back to his father.

Blackstone could see his father's face, red with anger after hearing what had happened. "No reason to be fighting over a nigger gal." he said. His granddad had owed a tobacco plantation and was as well-off as any other respectable landowner. They'd had twenty slaves or more. It all went bad when a slave girl ran off to the LeNoire farm and they refused to return her. That family got away with the girl and killing Granddad, then they took the plantation. Care of the land became too much. Those bastards took it. They stole our heritage."

"She didn't belong in the school anyway. Coloreds had their own school. She ain't worth the heartache. Nothing but the offspring of a thief and a slave. Remember that," he said.

Blackstone drove past Penelope as she hurried to Hugh, who was sitting in the black sedan waiting to take her to the train station. He thought about all the rumors he'd heard. They said she'd had herself fixed so she could not have kids. She was afraid of the truth, and no white man here would marry her. That's why she ran a whorehouse.

Nonsense to him, because he'd watched her every chance he could get when she was outside the Velvet Gardens. Even had his buddies radio her whereabouts to him. So far nothing unusual except lots of out-of-town folks and well-to-do women stayed there, sometimes a doctor or two came by. No one talked.

He followed the Buick for a few blocks, wondering if he could break her—bankrupt her. Why had she wanted that girl arrested? Why? And then that mink. Why was she wearing it around these poor kids? When she saw him following her in the rearview mirror, she told Hugh to slam on the brakes, hoping he would rear-end her. Quickly, the officer swerved and sped off.

11

The Reward

Rita Jane was awakened irritated by screams. *Who is screaming? Who is it?* Next to her bed sat an empty bottle of bourbon and a tall glass. She feared she was hallucinating and promised not to drink today. Wobbly, she walked into the kitchen to finish the baskets for the five families who worked the fields and sometimes helped with the small winery. Polly started the tradition so long ago. It was only right to keep it going with a good chunk of homemade hog's head cheese, two pounds of black-eyed peas, five pounds of corn meal, a dozen cigars, and a small bottle of Virginia gin.

This morning, it seemed like each step she took, a telephone rang. Rita wasn't sure if it was her mind or if the house phones were really ringing. Was it the business line in the office that rang every half hour for a party reservation on New Year's Eve? Or was it the family line in the kitchen and library? Penelope's private line in her bedroom and parlor rang more often with committee people, which was no one's responsibility except Esther Mae's now. Many of the day workers were off until the new year.

Rita stopped answering the calls. She could not keep arguing with Josephine's grandmother, who had left six messages and cursed out all the staff. She was angry, crying, accusing Rita of lying and threatening to call the police if her precious granddaughter didn't call home by tomorrow.

She stared dizzily at the encircled garden where the racehorses in her mind went around and around until they fell. Why had the girl lied about her aunt? She was worried more than ever that the girl would not get out of jail. It was her fault for encouraging the girl. Maybe it was her own deep want. To find a mother she never knew.

Polly had told her that her mama was a ghost. A ghost that would worry her to death trying to find her. "No need to go looking for her. I'm your mother. I'm the one who's raising you and loves you. The other person is just a stranger out there in the world. A ghost." Rita wanted another drink to calm her nerves.

One drink today. That's it. Just one more drink. A little one.

The cabinet in the dining room where all the fine bourbon and sherry were kept was locked. Penelope had taken the key, knowing Jules would empty the contents. Penelope was good at counting the bottles and levels. But Rita had her own stash in case of an emergency hidden in the pantry behind the rice, beans, and grits. She stood before the cabinet, holding back the urge as long as possible.

Hugh was walking with a slight limp toward the carriage house. The limp was never noticeable unless he had a problem. He kept saying he was going to retire to Florida. But he couldn't give up his concern about the place, he still carried on as an all-around handyman and overseer, treating the sharecroppers with respect. He often said that he was born here free, raised here free, and intend to die here free. He was the youngest of Polly's three sons. Hugh treated Rita like a little sister even though she'd been raised in the big house with her own bedroom, often sleeping with Polly in a room next to Mary Margaret.

Since Jules's arrival, he was constantly in attendance. Just his way. Hugh walked around the garden of seasonal plants he was forever tending to keep pretty. He'd made the garden to remind Rita Jane that this was home. There was no need to run away from the Velvet Gardens. 'Be still, listen to the land. Hear it speak. When you do, you'll know you belong.'

At nineteen, Rita Jane ran away with Art who left Richmond in defiance of his father to play the tennis circuits. She wrote Hugh to say she was safe. He was the only one to write back, begging her to return; he was tired of answering everyone's rolling eyes, insinuating she'd gone bad. Pieces of the sky fell when Art ended their affair. He met her at the train station to bring her home and promised to make her a garden.

He'd made sure the garden had lots of roses, saying love is as sweet and pretty as a rose, with thorns to prick pain when one is careless.

Now she wondered how long Hugh would be around to hold up the sky. He knocked at the carriage house door, fiddling with a newspaper in his hand. Jules looked out the window, smiled and waved. Hugh waved back with the newspaper. Jules indicated that he was coming down. When he emerged in his bathrobe and pajamas, Hugh handed the paper to him. A sheet of worry covered his face. The two men looked solemnly at each other before going upstairs into the carriage house.

She twisted her curls, trying to hold off that one drink. She rehearsed lie after lie that she'd planned to tell Miss Philly. She dialed, then hung up after one ring. Thinking it might be better to wait to speak to Art first. But to call Art would invite pieces of the sky to fall. They had not spoken in one year. *Yes, staying sober and recovering from Art,* she thought. But today, he was the only person who could help.

Odessa, Rita, and Art knew each other from high school. He was the boy every girl wanted. He stood out at six foot three, slim and chiseled, resigned to be a bachelor to the end. He was his father's pride. His father, Arthur Strickland, was a longstanding criminal lawyer in the city, who'd raised him as a prince. His family were patron members of various black society groups, independent big shots. His father was a tennis enthusiast who'd organized a small tennis club in Richmond to play other black tennis associations in Hampton, Norfolk, and Newport News.

Rita and Art began seriously dating after high school. She was in love with his dream of playing Wimbledon. He loved her elusive quality; that she lived like a black Southern belle. Art won a college scholarship but tried to postpone entering school in order to play pro. His father would not give him a penny, forcing him to try his luck alone.

Rita Jane tried to forget their love affair. Never challenging his interpretation of their relationship or discussing the rumors of his getting strung out on heroin after he hurt his knee in a tennis tournament. His father pulled him through a few arrests for possession. He told everyone it was her fault because she wouldn't marry him the first go-around. She'd wanted to marry white, but he'd convinced her to run away with him. Then he began dating white.

She came home. He married someone from Georgia. It was the first of a series of marriages and divorces. Each time they fell apart, he grew more certain he loved her the most. But she would not have him back.

Remembering her affair was the best excuse that she needed a drink. She filled a large water glass with liquor from her stash and turned on the radio. The drink convinced Rita that calling Art was an emergency after all.

A few swallows of the hot liquid let her sway to the band music as she calmly dialed his home. No answer. She tried his office. After five rings he answered. "Art, I need your help. There's a girl who was arrested. Can you locate her?"

"Rita?"

"Yes. Art, please help. I'm scared to death. Penelope had a girl arrested. Josephine Walker."

"Yeah, Odessa called earlier about a girl who was beat up by the cops. She didn't know her name. What happened?"

"Beat up? Oh no, Art. I'm so sorry for her."

"I don't know. Odessa has her bag."

"Yes, it's her. She's from Philadelphia. Her grandmother keeps calling. I need to locate her. Please. Jules said her aunt was Vera Gold."

Art's other telephone lines were ringing. "What do you want me to do?" he asked, slightly irritated.

"You have to find her. She's in trouble."

"Listen, my secretary is off today. I'll look into it tomorrow."

"She may be dead, Art!"

"Let me get back to you. Someone's at my door."

A white man peeked through the blinds on the glass door, then walked away, then returned to pace in front of the plate glass window.

"Sure, sure." Rita Jane felt let down. She poured another glass of liquor. She looked out the window at the garden.

* * *

Art opened his door to see a thin white man in his fifties. The man stood with his shoulders hunched, hands in the pockets of a brown tweed overcoat. His nose was red and his face a puffy pink. His medium brown hair was mixed with gray and uncombed.

"Can I speak with you?"

Art looked at him gingerly, not saying a word.

"You are the lawyer, Art Strickland?"

"Yeah, but my offices are closed."

"I saw a light on in the window, so I thought you might be open. I want to talk to you about the reward I read about in today's newspaper."

"What are you talking about?"

He pulled a newspaper from under his arm. "Today's paper says they are opening up the Walker death. I worked with her. Miriam was killed about sixteen years ago, found in the James River. You see this guy?" he said, pointing to George Stevens on the front page, the local prosecutor. "I know him. It says he's behind reopening the investigation."

Art took the paper and looked at the photograph of George talking with a group of police officers, Blackstone among them. The headline read, "New Leads in Cold Case."

"Can we talk? I don't like the cold."

Art let the man enter. He flipped on more lights in the front reception area.

"My name is Earl Smith. You see, I worked at Gene's Brown Derby. I was a bartender when Miriam was a waitress. A lovely girl. Her death was rough on me, on Gene, on everyone there. Read the article. They're offering the one thousand dollars again. A reward for any information regarding the death of Miriam. I knew her."

There were several photographs, one with Miriam in a white mink coat, smiling like a movie star in front of the Brown Derby awning. It was the same coat that Penelope had worn to the toy drive that sparked Blackstone to speak to George about reopening the case.

Art became curious. "Seems everyone knew her." He motioned the cautious man to a chair near the plate glass window painted with lettering of his law office. "Have a seat." He pulled the blinds slightly open to see any passersby. Then he sat on the edge of his secretary's desk, wondering whether George was looking for higher ground, or getting heat for a second murder of a prostitute.

"Again. What do you want or know?"

"I came to find out how to collect the reward money," Earl said.

"What makes you think I have it?" He took a harder look at the man.

"I called around. And they said your office knew who has the money. Just after Miriam was killed, a reward was posted everywhere. They grilled Gene for information. But he was dead quiet. Most were too afraid to tell what they knew. About what happened. I was afraid too. Kinda afraid now, but I'm older, and honestly, broke. Working as a bartender, you can develop a serious drinking habit."

"Do you need one now?" Art asked. I've got some Jack Daniel's in my back office."

"No. I can make it. I heard the police were interested in someone named Rhoady. He was an old man who kept pestering her for a date. We kept an eye on him because sometimes he would say angry things to her when she ignored him. She didn't like him, but she wanted to keep her job. She enjoyed the music, dancing, drinking. A real good-time girl. Yesterday's paper says they're offering the reward money again."

"Who's offering the money? The police? The police wouldn't put a penny out for her," Art said.

"I called and they told me some black lawyer had the funds. Well, I found out that Rhoady has a lawyer in D.C. I thought he had it. He's been in the papers lately with those school cases. I called and he had no idea. He told me to talk with you."

"Me?"

"Then I started asking around. I knew she had an aunt named Vera Gold. Her lawyer was your father. It says

right here in this old news article. Your father's name."
Earl pulled out a neatly folded newspaper article, tainted
and worn at the edges, dated February 14, 1939.

"Can I see the paper?"

Earl handed him the fragile news article. It had a
few pictures of Miriam floating in the water, and one as a
teen smiling with a strand of pearls.

"See my underlined words regarding the reward."

"Mr. Smith, if there is a reward, I can't guarantee
payment. It may no longer exist."

"It does. George says it in the papers."

"The stipulation is that it is paid to a person who
provides information leading to the killer of the woman.
Do know the killer?"

"I know the restrictions. She had just turned twenty
years old. Gene gave her a surprise party few months
earlier, in November. Anyway, I remember a New Year's
Eve raid. She left out the back with a gang of fellows. One
was holding onto her the entire time. Later, I was told it
was Jules LeNoire, and she was up there with him on a
regular basis. Hugh the driver would pick her up a block
or two from the club."

"Hugh?"

"Yes. And get this. George was gambling with
them that night. After he became a prosecutor, I
recognized his face in the papers a few years later. Off and
on for this and that. Social stuff."

"George the prosecutor?"

"Right, he left with Jules, the girl, and three other
guys."

"The raid and the death are weeks apart."

"The two of them spent a great deal of time with
her. George started coming to the club after that night. I
think he was in law school then."

"This is hearsay."

"Well, I am here for the money."

"You'll say anything."

"No. There are a few other people who saw them together in the back of the club on a regular basis. Taking up the bathroom or smoking cigarettes in the alley real close. Then after her shift, she met up with Hugh down the block to go sleep with Jules. He bought her jewelry and new clothes. Whether Jules knew about George, I don't know, or whether Hugh knew, I don't know. A few weeks later, she kept calling in sick. George stopped coming. Then one night he comes by to talk to Gene privately. Gene then told everyone Miriam was too sick to work. Then he fired her. A week later she was dead."

"What about the guy Rhoady?"

"Some say he killed her out of jealousy. Mr. Art, I came for the reward, not to get whacked. It's supposed to be anonymous, right? All I said is confidential. That's your duty, isn't it? Never to repeat what clients say."

"You aren't a client yet. Let me look into the reward. Come back next week."

"I'm not coming back next week. I want to leave town."

"Hold on. What good is this information if no one will testify?"

"That's the problem, nobody will, especially if George is heading up the case. He's hushing it up. Anyway, the paper says 'information leading to the arrest.' It doesn't say it has to lead to a conviction."

"Well, I'll look for this reward that you say exists."

"I'll come back on Monday."

"What's your address and telephone number?"

"I don't have either until I see the money. Just have cash. I'll sign a receipt for it. Thank you, sir." Before Earl left, he and Art looked outside at the surrounding area to see if there were any parked or suspicious cars or persons passing. It was quiet. The man left with his hands in his coat pockets, his collar up around his ears.

Art was floored to learn that George had even known the Walker girl. Let alone playing around with her in public. The man is thinking of running for a state office. Fifteen years ago he was a budding nothing. Probably full of himself, behaving with indiscretion with a lonely wild woman. *Who cares,* Art thought. *Why does he have to sort it out?* There is no way he was going to pass around some strange man's words if he wanted to continue working his half-assed cases in this city. He turned off his office lights, intending to go play tennis. Calculating whether this was a high-profile case or a cover-up. Did he need the publicity? It wouldn't hurt. The school cases with old Senior had gotten him a few steps out front, but a big murder case? How can he ignore it? Where was he when this went down? Then he remembered Memphis. Traveling the tennis circuit full time. Drugs, women, and Rita Jane. He flipped the lights back on and dialed his dad.

* * *

Rita tried to phone Philly again, but couldn't focus to figure out the numbers on the telephone dial. When she saw Hugh leave the carriage house, she rushed out to persuade him to call. He always helped. He waved but did not stop. This made her suspicious. She had to steady herself down the back steps to catch his attention.

"What's going on, Hugh? Tell me." She called out.

"Tell you what?" His left eye twitched.

"Where is Jules?"

"Packing," he whispered with gravity.

Her brows knitted with surprise; Hugh was normally steady with trouble, a rock when it came to emotions. Her brown eyes widened. "Packing? Why?" She kept her distance, afraid he might smell her alcohol.

"He's leaving tomorrow. He told me he needs to make it to New York real quick. I told him it was closer to go from Florida. He said the ship out of there was not leaving for a few days. New York was leaving sooner. He wants to be out on the sea for a while. I can't say any more."

Alice pulled up in Talbot's station wagon. Hugh signaled to her that Jules was upstairs, then continued onto his cottage.

"Alice, aren't you off this week?"

"Mr. Jules wants me to help with a party."

"He didn't mention it to me," Rita said.

Alice squinted her eyes and held her hand over her brow to shield against the morning sun. Also, to prevent Rita from reading her eyes if she lied. "I think it just happened. Some old friends and him. Not many."

"Do you need help? I can call Ella."

"He doesn't want a lot of help. Just me."

Rita Jane sensed it was a clandestine matter. She'd heard of favors Alice's grandfather, a former overseer, had done out of loyalty to the LeNoires that no one would discuss. In return, a sizable parcel of land was given to him.

Jules confided in Alice that he'd been nervous and unsteady since Rita Jane wrote that Miriam's suitcase was found. He'd played upon Rita's *naïveté* and persuaded her not to ship the suitcase to Philadelphia but to invite the girl to Virginia during the time he was in the States for the holidays. He'd love to meet the girl, he'd said. It was a lie in order to gather his letters, which he knew were in the suitcase, and to destroy anything associating him with Miriam. He knew Rita wouldn't have destroyed the suitcase or sent it to him. He had hoped to arrive before the girl to retrieve it.

Jules pressured Alice to help but she did not want to volunteer her son. Jules had heard that Talbot had an interest in the girl and he wanted Alice to find out about the suitcase through her son. She thought he was being ridiculous.

Today, Alice got up enough nerve to tell him to do it himself. The land tenants were saying that the letters implied he'd had her killed. She was not going to get involved with it or have her only son framed.

Jules appeared in the carriage house window. Impatient, he began tapping the window to get Alice's attention.

Rita persisted with Alice, who kept avoiding questions.

"I'm also here because Esther Mae couldn't get the mail today. Talbot said he'd fetch it. Then the phones keep ringing for reservations. You know with the holidays, people look for a quick place for sex or parties. We have to be careful about the reputation of the place, especially with Miss Penelope's election hopes. I don't think Esther Mae can tell the difference in the customers we give bookings."

Rita understood the last statement to mean that Alice was afraid Esther Mae might book a colored person. Reservations had been low for three years straight until Penelope joined the resistance against desegregation. Now she hummed, pleased when the mail arrived. A new clientele had shown interest in the old plantation. Fellow Southerners wanted to enjoy the lifestyle of a period slowly fading. Or northerners who traveled south to see family and friends wanted to stay in a home setting instead of a sterile hotel room. The telephone rang regularly now.

"I'll leave you be." Rita turned to go into the house.

"Miss Rita. There is something. Jules wants me to go down in that pit and find the wine his daddy or granddaddy made. He believes that because his daddy and mine drank together, I should know where it is. I swear. I do not like the basement. Not with all of Polly's things hanging around."

"Ain't no dead bodies down there, Alice."

"After Miss Penelope frightened me the other day about blood, and with Jules talking about old wine that must be nearly poison by now, I refuse to go down there alone. And you knew where everything was kept, and all of Polly's goings-on."

"Only if you tell me what Jules is planning."

"I already told you." Changing the subject, "Oh, did you see the Sunday papers? There's a wonderful picture of Penelope at the toy drive. They talk about the Velvet Gardens with fine words. She'll be proud of the story. Read what they say."

Alice handed the paper to Rita. She stared at the front page, gripping it so tightly her hands shook. Then the screams began again in her mind. It was Miriam.

12

Miriam

The economy was gaining strength against the Depression. Little bars became big nightclubs with live shows, restaurants, and dance floors. The government's WPA program put extra money in pockets. More and more young men were drafted for a possible war. Living in Richmond gave Miriam stability. Except she did not feel alive.

During the day, Miriam read detective novels or helped Aunt Vera collect rents or do church work. At night they listened to mystery or comedy shows on the floor radio. Eating lots of chocolate cupcakes with orange soda became tasteless. She wanted to drink, and have spending money for fancy clothes, especially tight dresses.

Nightlife was exciting to her. She'd stand outside clubs smoking cigarettes, dressed in high heels and no panties, pretending she was part of the crowd, watching cars dispatch the well-dressed in front of flashy lights. Sometimes she was able to get someone to buy her a drink. She liked drinking, liked being around older folks that drank to find relief. Her life experiences made her a grown woman at fourteen who understood the drinking crowd.

Gene, the owner of the Brown Derby, a big bar restaurant off Canal Street was hiring, but he turned her down each time she asked. He'd seen her a dozen times outside smoking and laughing with some of his regular customers, men who dropped in for a few Friday-night drinks before taking the paycheck home. They liked her but she was too young to work in a liquor joint, not twenty-one yet.

One Saturday morning, at 8 a.m., a time she knew he brought in kitchen supplies, she put on a wide flouncy skirt, black-and-white oxfords with socks, and a tight pink sweater over her braless breasts. As Gene pushed a cart of supplies down the alley with one of the cooks, she dropped a thick book of detective stories, then bent over to pick it up as the wind blew through the alleyway. Up went the skirt above her waist. She rose with a pout and said, "I lost my undies. Do you see them?"

The man laughed and offered her a job, on paper as kitchen help. He picked girls who were not shy to rub their bodies against customers when serving drinks or food. She was very good with pressing her hips against an admiring customer's shoulder. Her skirts were shorter, her blouses lower. Some waitresses complained that she was going home with customers. It was none of their business, Gene would say. She slept with him too.

Miriam liked money. Who were they to criticize? She was dealt a bad hand of cards in life. Only money made the difference. With an eighth-grade education, half her family dead, physically abused, her father calling everyone Marie, his favorite dead daughter like a lunatic, there was nothing wrong with using what she was born with and what others wanted. This was not a sin.

Gene was not stupid about money either. Each Saturday night, he allowed blacks—mainly hustlers, daddies; not pimps, just guys who wanted to drink and rub against pretty girls—to enter the club through the front doors, allowing them to wander around the front bar and dance floor. If they wanted to sit and drink, they had to go to the back area of the restaurant near the kitchen. Sometimes they came with whites but still could not sit in the front area around the dance floor with them.

All the girls raced to serve them because they tipped big. The white waitresses competed for laughs by teasing the black customers until they drooled, beating out the black waitresses for the biggest tip. What they didn't share was when one went home with the guy. Gene didn't mind what they did after work. And he didn't ask for a cut of the money as long as the club stayed packed.

Gene was secretive about a private party one New Year's Eve, asking certain girls to work and to wear tight red dresses. No jukebox that night. A big band was hired to swing. The dance floor was packed. To add to the scene, a muscular man of color wearing a tuxedo, top hat, and gloves was hired to open car doors. Actually, to blow a whistle if police arrived to bust the place. He was cute, so Miriam decided during a break to smoke out front to get a good look at him.

As she lit up, Rhoady, the old man, stared at her from across the street, smiling in satisfaction that his concentration of desire had lured her from the private party. He couldn't get in that night, even though he was a regular. He often sat in the back of the club until closing, quietly watching her from a corner seat, always ordering the same meal and drink each time. Sometimes he came with a woman, but most of the time he was alone.

Miriam avoided him while others raced to serve him because his tips were a day's pay. He was a railroad porter along the East Coast, servicing white passenger cars. She'd overheard that he'd been married for more than twenty years but had no kids. He suspected his wife was barren, but he couldn't leave her.

Each time she passed his table, he'd say, "I can give you what you want. I have what you need. I'll take care of your kid. You won't need to work." She suspected that because she already had a child it made his desire stronger. But he was forty-four. She didn't want a poppy.

When he learned she liked orange sodas, he ordered them to leave on the table with her name on a napkin. Sometimes he left extra tips for her even though she did not wait on him. They were just for being good-looking. He constantly asked her to sit and talk to him in his blue four-door Chrysler. Then letters from long rail trips began to arrive, suggesting they were lovers. Writing how much he missed having her next to him.

He began accusing her of fooling around with customers. Wondering if she smiled or talked too much with another man. He was jealous. Fearful she had a taste for strangers. His imagination was unbearable and insulting. She complained the old man was harassing her. Gene needed him as a regular customer and the other girls liked him. "As long as he doesn't touch you, ignore it," was all Gene said. She should expect that from men now and then.

But Gene and the bartenders watched him. Gene even spoke to him in a friendly way to feel him out. Let him know he was being watched. It was too much trouble for the club to worry about one waitress. Fearful of losing her job, she endured the constant remarks.

Then this night, strangely, after weeks of not coming to the club, he stood across the street smoking a cigar. He was dressed for a ball, watching the parade of cars full of laughing partygoers. "Something in my heart told me to come tonight," he yelled.

Miriam coldly threw down her cigarette, stamping out its fire as if it was Rhoady. It was close to midnight and she wanted to be inside when champagne bottles popped, and the balloons and streamers floated over the dance floor.

As she was about to retreat down the alley, she noticed a group of young white men, twenty-ish, in fine wool overcoats, dark suits, and new shoes, joking and laughing as they left a black town car. They followed her. Their cologne was intoxicating. She tried to wiggle her butt in a cute fashion while walking fast to make it to the kitchen ahead of them. One reached her in time to put his hands on her hips so he could wiggle along behind her, whispering in her ear, "I like red."

Gene was at the door waving them in quickly. "Miriam, come on, let them by." She stepped aside to allow the young Latin-looking man past. His smile caused her to flush with a flash of heat. The group was ushered into the private room behind the kitchen. No one ever spoke of who and what they saw go in and out of that room. It was always locked.

Miriam stood near the open door to watch their manners. They were pleasant and respectful as they took off their jackets to choose lucky seats. Their gallant and measured speech captivated her. Their clean faces and polished bodies signaled they were still babies looking to taste the dark side of street life. Trust-fund babies whose debts were paid anonymously.

A blond guy noticed her attraction. Peering directly into her eyes over the shoulder of the dark, wavy-haired young man who'd wiggled down the alley with her, he said, "Jules, where did you find this place?" *Jules,* she repeated to herself. Now she had a name to remember.

Gene rounded up the girls wearing red dresses in the alley. "I need special service for a group of nice young men. The guys want girls to serve who have a special knowledge of card tricks. Who's in?" Miriam was puzzled as to what he meant by special knowledge. Blackjack, Crazy Eights, and Rummy were all she knew. She was not interested in tricks, except Jules had fascinated her. *How much of a trick is he?* she wondered.

Bottles of liquor never seen before came out of a locked cabinet, top brands, even some moonshine. When Gene opened the door to deliver the bottles, Jules pointed to her. She reminded him of the first woman he'd had in France, the lover of an expat writer. In order to have his friend's girl, they'd engaged in a *ménage à trois*.

Gene was reluctant, but he nodded her into the room. Miriam was overwhelmed by the masculinity of the men. How well they knew each other since grade school. They teased and talked about their family's business ventures.

They were comfortable with all the girls who were picked to serve, taking off their expensive watches. Smoking, drinking, tossing money slips with lots of zeros. Rubbing the backsides of the girls for luck. Their empty drinking glasses were quickly filled.

Many girls were exchanged for a set of new faces. But Jules kept her from leaving, holding up his hand of cards for her to see. There were five players. She didn't know how to give signals. So she just circled the table, pretending she was sending him luck. Really, she was just gushing inside to be with wealthy men. Jules won three hands in a row.

She lit his cigarettes. Refilled drinks, dropped ice into glasses. The blond man tried very hard to catch her eye whenever she moved behind Jules. He was George Stevens. Sensing a threat to his claim, Jules handed her a half-empty glass. "Please empty it." She took and placed it on a tray. "No, drink it for me." Jules held her hand as she drank from his glass, letting others know that she was his. The others looked over their cards, surveying her movements from then on.

Gene rushed into the room. "Miriam, your aunt's on the phone. It's urgent."

"Tell her I'm in the bathroom." But the bathroom was locked with another waitress and customer in a tight embrace inside, against the door. Then she got a knot in her stomach, like the time Grandma Philly had twirled those chicken bones. "Okay, okay," she said.

"Come back, Miriam." Jules smiled, as she left the smoky room into the busy and noisy kitchen. The dance floor music was loud. She felt like she'd left a world of love but she didn't want her aunt to show up.

Aunt Vera was in tears, "Dear, please come home. I received a call from a friend on the police force. He said there will be trouble."

"What does that mean? There is always trouble."

"He can't tell me everything. But he knew you worked there. Said to tell you to get out of there, come home now. It's the black hand, Miriam."

"I will, I will," Miriam lied. She was not leaving without Jules. Her aunt had a way of interfering with whatever she was doing. Seemed like she was the one placing bad luck on her. Miriam began to believe the closest person to you would do the most evil to you, knowing what hexes to place. Now her aunt wanted to scare her. She hung up the phone.

It was twelve o'clock. Everyone yelled, cheering. Horns blew. Not wanting to lose her way with Jules, she rushed to the small back room, hoping to be kissed by her prince. Then there was a boom. *Had a car crashed into the front of the building?* Old man Rhoady was at the back door where kitchen workers were running out the exit. Screaming police. He waved to her to follow as Gene ran into the private room to alert the players.

Jules called to her too. Shaking with fear of being jailed, Miriam looked to the old man, then to Jules. The police had poured into the front bar-and-restaurant area. Yelling and lining people up against the walls. Women screamed, men moaned. The lights turned from blues and reds to bright white.

The back door became blocked with bodies, all pushing to get out. She no longer saw Rhoady. Gene tried to shut the door to the back room, but Jules stepped in front of him, holding the door open to reached out for Miriam, who took his hand and was pulled inside before Gene put a wooden board across it. More police rushed into the kitchen, searching for Gene.

Police began to batter the door, while Gene hurriedly stuffed paper slips and cards into large food cans with lids. Then he overturned the tables, chairs, cabinets, and supplies into a big shamble in the middle of the floor. The well-heeled men left their watches and jackets, running down wooden steps and through an underground alley, then up a set of iron wrought stairs to a back street.

Holding Jules's hand, Miriam ran laughing with the young men around a few buildings. The earlier black town car swerved to the curb for the young men to jump. Then the bubble burst. She stopped. She realized was unlike the laughing men who crowded the car.

Jules was smitten and oblivious to his friends. He pulled her arm. "Get in, get in." She was hesitant. He put his arm around her waist, lifting her into the air, smiling at her pretty face, then carried her into the car. She sat on his lap as the car sped up Main Street.

Miriam was uneasy, detecting an artificial jovial sound in their voices. She listened carefully for clues. Were they going to have their way with her? Sensing her thoughts, Jules squeezed her hand to reassure her that she was his, and that he cared in another way.

13

A Long Way Home

Josephine rose upright on a bed of white sheets. Dazed, she moaned, "Where am I?" She had a sharp pain in her cheek. Her swollen right arm ached as did her wrists due to the tight cuffs now gone. She realized she was in a hospital ward filled with women of different ages who were either reading magazines, dozing, or passing time before their release. The bedding was clean, but the ward was old, with dingy walls and broken blinds at the window.

"Nurse, nurse!" cried one woman. "She's awake!" The patient pushed open the swinging double doors to find a nurse in the hall.

An older lady sitting on the side of her bed next to Josephine spoke. "The nurse is on rounds. You were in a coma for two days. They didn't know if you were going to make it. I think they wanted to kill you, but too afraid. A cop kept checking with the nurses."

Josephine softly cried from a dry throat, "Nurse!"

A young nurse in starched whites, shoes, and little cap, marched into the room. "Welcome," she said as she moved toward Josephine's bedside near the window. "You had a terrible fall."

"Fall? No, no, who said that?"

"You blacked out in the street and were asleep for two days. We were worried."

This set off moans from Josephine. Her hair was tangled and sweaty. "I want to go home. My face hurts. Is there a scar?"

"Just some bruising. It may not keloid; if anything, you'll have a little dark spot across the cheek, which should disappear in time. Skin with melanin reacts differently to trauma. You can discuss it with the doctor. We need more information. What's your name? Where are you from?"

"He hit me."

"Who?"

"The officer." She pushed herself to sit up straight.

"I can't verify that. But we do need information for the records. Your name is--?"

"Josephine Walker."

"Age?"

"Twenty." She fell back onto her pillow, exhausted.

A pregnant woman cradling her stomach interrupted. "Nurse, when is the doctor coming? I think my pains are getting close together."

The nurse admonished the woman. "Lady, back to bed, before you cause your baby to fall on the floor."

"Where is the doctor? I want to talk to the doctor!" Josephine moaned as she touched her cheek.

"I am the only doctor you will see today."

"Where are you from?" asked another girl. "This is the colored ward. Ain't no special doctor for us."

"Hush over there. Y'all are well taken care of here. And stay in your beds," the nurse ordered. Turning to Jo in a more soothing tone, "I will bring you some ice water. Are you hungry?"

Odessa entered with the suitcase and a newspaper. The nurse was surprised. "Who are you visiting?"

"My niece."

Josephine was too tired to object.

"Okay, just a few minutes, and please stop at the desk so I can get more information about her." The nurse left.

"Hello, I'm Odessa," she said, standing next to the bed.

Josephine barely whispered, "The lady in the street. You saw it. You saw him beat me. I want to sue."

"No one will be your witness. I tried to make a complaint with the police but they refused to acknowledge anything."

"There was a crowd. They saw."

"Even if you find them, they will not risk their jobs, their safety. They don't know you. They didn't know if you were a criminal."

The faces of the silent unmoving crowd flashed in the girl's mind. The pain of the assault surged. "There was a guy. He saw it. And Rita Jane, she must have seen it too. The cop pushed me into the car."

"Rita Jane from the Velvet house? We attend the same church."

"I stayed there. They had my suitcase." Recalling the toss of the suitcase. "My bag!" she yelled, remembering the bums yanking at the bag from Odessa, saying *"Come on, darling, you know it belongs to me. The cop gave it to me, you saw him throw it my way."*

The patient in the next bed said, "Why were you there? You know what they do up there. No wonder you're in the hospital."

Josephine stiffened as the women began to banter across the room about her. "Were you really at the Velvet house? They don't let coloreds up there."

"I don't know why," said another. "They're all trash, pretending they're white. Everyone knows their history. They married white, and kept marrying white."

"Mercy, mercy," another woman said, shaking her head.

Odessa kept a smile on her smooth face, bristling inside from hearing others express her opinions in a low way. She held up the bag. "Here it is, sweetheart."

Josephine was overwhelmed with gratitude. "Thank you."

"Nurse! Nurse!" a woman from her bed. "My baby's coming!"

A different nurse briskly entered. "Missy, if you holler one more time, I will move your bed down to the basement ward. And ma'am, your time is up," she said to Odessa. "She's not to have visitors without the police's say-so."

"I'm leaving," she replied. "Where should I put the bag?"

"Give it to me." Josephine shifted up and placed the bag on her lap. Opening it to check the contents, she said, "I still want to press charges."

"The truth is, even if you were killed and your family had a battalion of lawyers, you still might not get into a court. I brought a newspaper. There's nothing in it about your arrest. That's a good sign. Do you want to read it?"

"No, ma'am. But can you contact a young man who works at the Velvet Gardens. He witnessed it."

Odessa realized the girl did not understand the futility of pressing charges against a cop. "Do you have people you want me to call? Let them know where you are."

"No, no. Well, my grandmother. Never mind, I'll call her. Tell Rita Jane I'm okay."

"I will, and I will come again tomorrow. If you need a place to stay, I have a room."

Josephine pulled from the case a string of pearls with smudges of lipstick.

"Here is my telephone number," Odessa continued. "If you need anything, call me." She wrote in the side margin of the paper and tore the number off to place on the side table.

Another patient stood at the foot of Jo's bed. "Look at that suitcase. And it's real pretty inside. Look at those pearls! I haven't seen any like that since I was a young girl."

Two more women slowly walked over to Josephine's bedside. "Ummh, the suitcase smells good." One woman sniffed. "What else you got in there"

Josephine quickly closed the case and gave the women a look of distrust.

"Oh, don't be stuck up," said the first one.

The other two returned to their beds. One said, "It ain't none of our business anyway."

"Can you take it, Miss Odessa? I don't have a place for it here."

A nurse appeared at the door. "Ma'am, you have to leave. The officer is waiting to see the patient."

Odessa put on her gloves and took the bag. "Take care of yourself. I will call tomorrow." She put the newspaper under an arm.

One woman called to Odessa as she passed, "Missus, missus, can I have the paper?"

"You may," handing it to her.

The nurse stood in the doorway, waiting for Odessa to leave.

Odessa waved good-bye, then entered the hall and saw Blackstone standing at the nurse's station, his back to her. She hesitated, wanting to confront him but quickly accepted that it would cause a big disturbance. Seeing an exit sign across the hall, she move quickly to the doors before she had a change of mind.

The woman reading the newspaper said, "Listen, y'all. Speaking of the devil, that LeNoire woman. Here's a picture of her giving out toys. Got a big white mink on. Supporters of a manifesto want her..."

"What's that? Manifesto?" another patient asked, walking to the bedside of the reader.

"Can I see it?" The woman handed the paper off the new reader. "Hey, they got information on that James River girl." She read aloud. "'The young woman found in the James is twenty-two-year-old Evangeline of Hull Street.'" She mumbled to herself, then raised her voice again. "'Nude. She must had done someone wrong."

"Why you think just because she's dead she did something wrong? Apparently, someone did something wrong to her," said the older woman in the bed next to Josephine.

Continuing to read. 'Police have no leads, except the victim appears to resemble the last black woman found in the river...' She mumbled the rest of the sentence.

"They don't give a damn about a prostitute. My opinion, that river is filled with tears," added the pregnant woman. "Souls of slaves still crying down there in the bottom."

The reader continued. 'The killer has resurfaced since the last woman was found in the James River. Benjamin Blackstone leads the investigation and was on the Walker case.'

Josephine moaned.

"You all right, sweetie?" the pregnant woman asked.

Another woman looked over the shoulder of the reader. The two read in unison. 'The body was discovered floating in the river by a fishing crew. They called out but then they saw the dark blue rope marks.'

Now four women were around the newspaper. One said, "Might have been a lynching?"

"Could have been."

"I saw a hanging once," said the pregnant woman.

"No, you didn't," said the older woman with a stern eye. "Why lie?"

"Yes, I did. The body twists and twirls like a chicken with its head cut off."

"You didn't see anything like that here in Richmond. It's 1954. Maybe your grandparents did."

The young woman stood in the middle of the room to demonstrate, finding joy in describing the macabre. "The hands swell. The throat bleeds. Eyes bulge, the bowels empty."

"Lynchings stopped years ago, I said," insisted the older woman.

"No, they didn't." The pregnant girl held her swollen midsection as she paced the center of the floor. "It's that swampy river. Nothing but black tears, flowing down that river. Now we women are dying in it. Calling it accidents or suicides. Why is it that it has to look like we kill ourselves? We do get murdered too."

"Remember the Walker girl. Same river, same cop. Maybe he did it."

"Shut up! Nurse! Nurse!" hollered Josephine. The women stared at her as if she was crazy.

"Honey, they will tie you down. You're almost out of here," said the woman in the next bed.

Blackstone stood at the doorway of the ward, waiting for a nurse to give him clearance to enter. He'd requested a delay in her release, even though there were no charges pending. He'd learned that she was the daughter of Miriam Walker. A case he kept in his file cabinet, hoping one day to nail Jules.

Josephine put a pillow over her mouth and screamed, wondering why they didn't send the devil instead. Tears rolled down her face as she sobbed loudly.

The nurse entered. "Ladies, please pull your curtains, there's a male visitor." After helping some patients with their curtains and checking that all were pulled around the beds, she signaled the officer to enter.

He spoke cordially, "Ladies, happy holidays," to the few heads that stuck out from the drawn curtains as he moved quickly to the end of the room. "Hello, Josephine. I'm Officer Blackstone."

Hatred rose in her throat. She wanted to kill this man who leaned over to put his face in hers. "Do you hear me? I want you to know we are dropping the charges. Resisting arrest, solicitation, assault on a police officer." He winced at her bruised face when she lowered the pillow to her chest. He stepped back, thinking, *Why should I care that she was hurt? She'll make no difference in the world.*

She spit. "You're a bastard. Get out, get out!"

"Nurse!" Another patient jumped from her bed to call for a nurse. "Nurse!"

"Hating me won't get you far."

"I'll hate you the rest of my life. What right did you have to beat me?"

"I learned you may be the daughter of the call girl found dead in the James several years ago."

She turned away, *he'd killed her. He'd kill any woman walking the street. She seethed with hatred, watching him smile at her. Remembering his growling face in the car. How could he care about any woman dying?*

"Well, I want you to know I worked on that case. It's a cold case, but we may have some heat with this new death. I convinced the D.A. to open up your mother's case. It's under investigation again."

She pulled the sheet over her head.

He moved around her bed, looking under it, pulling out the drawers in the side table, continuing to speak. "Wondering if you recovered your things. The suitcase you had. Understand it means a lot to you. Do you know where your bag is?" He didn't want to plead or tell her why he cared. He surveyed the room to see if it was elsewhere. More women pulled their privacy curtains open to watch him. No one responded when he spoke loudly in the direction of the open floor of the ward, eyeing each woman. "I hope it wasn't lost. Captain said a lady came to the station with it. Do you know who she was? Come on! Speak up!"

The nurse arrived. "Officer, can I help?"

"No, no, I was leaving."

"Is she ready for release?"

"Whenever you think she's able. No charges." He wished he hadn't tossed the bag that was now crucial evidence. If she retrieved it from the Velvet Gardens, it may link that son of a bitch whore-monger playboy to the death. First, he had to find it. Anything to get them. He asked the nurse whether she'd seen it. Their voices faded as they walked down the hallway.

Suddenly there was loud talking. Some women jumped from their beds to find out who was causing the commotion in the hall. It was Talbot, holding a bouquet of flowers. He'd confronted Blackstone, who ordered him to leave.

"Hell, no. I saw what you did and I have a right to visit anyone I care to." He walked past the officer and into the ward. Blackstone watched Talbot, considering whether to arrest him. A nurse rushed after Talbot.

"Howdy," he said to the women staring at him as he entered. Josephine was full of surprise and glad to see him. He can vouch for her. He knew the truth. Two women pushed the double doors shut and leaned against them to prevent the nurse from entering.

"Don't worry. I won't hurt you. I came to apologize. Feel awful bad Blackstone arrested you because of me."

She listened with sleepy eyes. "It's okay," she said hoarsely.

One nurse pushed, and the women pushed back. "Move away from the door," yelled the nurse. She yelled to Blackstone, who was far down the hall, walking away. "Do something, Officer!"

He shrugged. "I need to get on." The nurse went to the station to call for help.

Talbot sat on Josephine's bed. "I live up at the Gardens in the back with my parents. If you need any help while you're in town, come see me."

"I need a witness. I need someone to tell what happened. You saw it all."

"Sure, sure."

Now a male orderly with two nurses rushed down the hall. Talbot knew he had to go but not before he kissed Josephine's cheek. She smiled.

Then he moved to the doors. "I appreciate you giving me a few minutes with her." He said to the women at the door.

"Small change." One patient said as she ran and jumped into her bed. The other moved away from the doors. "Hurry, boy."

He dashed across the hall into the stairwell.

14

Puff Puff Patois

Shortly after sunset, Jules and George Stevens were in Zackary's study playing cards through twirls of cigar smoke, sitting in high Queen Anne chairs before a square card table, drinking bourbon. Jules laughed at George's attempt to converse in French, speaking the most outlandish words.

Jules was happy a few friends were coming over to play poker. He'd wanted to reminisce about their youth and catch up on what was current in Virginia while gambling and sampling French cuisine. It was disappointing at first, when he made calls to the Holly Lawn golf club and the Aladdin, to see if any of his old friends still had memberships. The managers would not disclose phone numbers but assured him that if he left messages, they would have the parties call.

Of everyone, Jules wanted to see George the most. He gave him the warmth of friendship he longed for. George insisted on coming early to discuss Miriam Walker's death without revealing that Jules was a suspect. Equally, Jules hoped George would tell him about any evidence that might incriminate him.

Jules also wanted to ask for investments in a cigar and tobacco venture to export the goods to Europe. The countries were in need of new businesses after World War

II. George declined, not wanting to reveal his family's shrinking wealth.

"I'm moving more into the public sector. Government is becoming stronger after the New Deal." Although no longer a true member of the leisure class, he was still able to retain memberships in prestigious clubs and associations.

The phone rang, rang, and rang all evening.

"Aren't you going to pick up?" George asked.

"No."

"Where is Penelope?"

"Spending a week in upstate New York with one of Father's relatives. Uncle John, I think, though I'm not sure and do not care. Alice will answer soon. George, did you hear of the recent drowning in the river? Of course, you did."

"And?"

"There's a Detective Blackstone who keeps leaving messages. He wants to talk to me about it. Should I?" Jules took a long swallow of his drink.

"Why not?"

"I need an alibi."

"Hold on. I need to know why first."

"George, I was with a girl—only to wake up to read that another woman like the one I was with was found dead in the river. I arrived very late. Later than expected. I didn't want to wake up the entire house with all my things. So Hugh took me to the John Marshall. I spent the entire night there."

"With a black hooker?" George knew his friend could not wait to have an American Negro.

"Yes, yes, a black hooker, but she stayed the entire night. She left alive."

"What do you do in France? Can't be that many coloreds. I would think you would have cleared your system of those girls."

"There are enough. Many from Africa, but I prefer Americans. Now and then I meet a few on vacation or taking exchange courses around Paris. Maybe it's homesickness. Makes me feel Southern. Does it matter?"

"Only if they keep turning up dead. Your shuffle," handing Jules the deck of cards. "Who was the girl, what's her name?"

Jules shuffles the deck. "She was a street girl. And her name, well, she called herself Pudding. They all have fake names, addresses, and IDs. But I am sure she was not the one who died. There was probably a dozen just like her on the street last night. Mine can't be the one that was killed."

"What's the alibi for, then?"

"Blackstone keeps calling about Miriam. I refuse to speak to him without a lawyer."

"Good idea." George lit his cigar again. "You don't need me to stop him." George suspected that Jules wanted to involve him for an ulterior purpose.

"How? He'll blow up all my incidental affairs in the newspapers. Besides, Penelope has some notion to run for the school board. Anything like this could be harmful."

"Do you care?"

"No."

"Then it's an excuse. I assume no one else is in the house. No guests, no servants. Meaning this discussion is private."

"Everyone is off. Rita Jane is visiting with the laborers in their homes now, or down at a show. Alice is due to come shortly to help serve, but she will ring before she arrives. I made a *bouillabaisse*. We have liver *pâté* or hog's head cheese. Whichever you prefer. Alice has found some of Granddaddy's old wine. We have a plate of cheeses I brought from Paris. And of course, perfume for the wives. Not to have gotten off the subject, but I need an alibi or maybe a personal reference."

"Listen, I don't know what alibi I can give you. I was in bed with my wife. My in-laws were over. How can I change that?"

"It's not about the girl last night. It's for fifteen years ago with Mimi."

"Who?" He knew Miriam but hoped his pretense of ignorance would lead Jules to reveal what he was after.

Jules looked straight in his friend's eyes. "The girl at the raid. The girl we shared. New Year's Eve, the poker game in the back of the Derby. The cold case you announced you were reopening in the papers."

"Yeah, yeah. You were in Europe when that girl died, right?" George looked at his cards.

"Yes, but we were seen together for a few weeks before I left."

"Why do I need to provide an alibi then? Unless arrangements were made before you left."

"I had no desire or reason to harm her. I learned that you were involved with her—and had her picked up at the Derby---"

George throws his cards down. "Bullshit. I NEVER knew that woman."

"You had her.

"Are you trying to hang me with your imaginary guilt about a whore dying?"

"No. Just why are you opening up the case? Tying the new death to Miriam's? Knowing we had an affair."

"They turn up dead or missing on a regular basis. My advice is to stay away from the whores, and especially the black ones, if you don't want problems" George spit cigar stew from his mouth into a glass.

"Women. They are women. Very loving women."

"How much are you worth?"

Jules poured two more drinks. He knew George had become a working aristocrat. His family had lost much during the Depression years.

"Honestly, I really don't know, Jules answered. "I never kept the accounts. I received my monthly allocations on time. My lawyer is discussing the matter with my accountant this week to review the holdings."

"If this is a business matter and not blackmail, then payment for my services is necessary. I intend to run for the state house."

"Yes, yes."

"This is a delicate matter. Blackstone has to do his job. I can't just call him and say stop. I have to go above him. Your deal," George said picking up the stack of cards again. "This Blackstone issue is personal, isn't it?"

"He's a royal fool. He hates our family for something that happened before either of us were born, dating back to slave days. He sent letters to Penelope in the past seeking wrongful death compensations. All nonsense."

Jules wondered whether George would soak him for money. The all-for-one friendship was no longer. He picked ice from a silver bucket and clinked it into a crystal glass, swirling the drink slowly and pensively. Not wanting to say any more, he sipped his drink. Mulling over the possible ways he could trash George if he pressed for too much cash.

"Can you prove you were in Europe?" George was curious, but Jules thought the question was out of line. He'd known exactly where Jules was when Miriam was found.

"Yes, I did write letters to her from Paris, and there was a wire or two."

"If you can find them or proof of them, then there probably won't be a problem. But wow, the years have really gone by."

"Exactly why I question the reopening of the investigation into Miriam's death. George, I saw the newspapers this morning. Quite frightening how memories can go in different directions between people. I may have been away, but I have not lost interest in the local news. You made the headlines. 'Cold Case Reopened.' Yet you sit here speaking as if you didn't know Miriam. You had her too. You had her before me. I was too drunk to move. Last I saw, you two were laughing and dancing. Crashing on the bed. Then it became selfish. The lights went out and I was too drunk to do anything more than fall on the bed next to you."

George stared at him. "What I recall is that I was drunk that night. Too drunk to remember anything."

"Not too drunk to complain the next morning about her stealing your wallet. Come on, George. Own up to it. A private source said you continued to see her behind my back, sometimes right before Miriam visited me."

"You have no credible evidence or witness to verify that." He would never admit that he had been with Jules and Miriam that night or any night. One reason George had arrived early tonight was to determine if Jules had anything on him. He knew Jules suspected him. But if he could get someone in this house to talk, to tell about Miriam's nights with Jules or thereafter with Penelope, or Hugh. This case could catapult him into higher office.

"Blackstone may have leads. Possibility the same persons who informed me of your trysts with her," said Jules, hoping to motivate George to take him off the case. Blackstone had no loyalty. He'd eat George too.

George respected Blackstone's work. He was a strong man in difficult cases. Had a way of crawling underneath the skin of criminals. It was too bad, he'd gotten too excited trying to destroy Jules or Penelope. George was silent. Swallowed long on his drink.

"I will probably pull him off the case. I learned he beat up a young girl while in custody who happens to be Miriam's daughter. He said Penelope wanted her arrested. Any reason?"

Jules flipped ashes off his cigar. "I have no idea."

George picked up his cards. "You know, I got a call from Art Strickland, asking about a reward for information on Miriam's killer?"

"Wonderful. I shall add some money to it. Best way to counteract controversy."

George yawned. "Autopsy showed she was dead before she entered the water. The strangulation was a cover-up for loss of blood from a possible botched abortion. There was no baby, though."

Jules closed his eyes to prevent any inner sorrow from escaping. "She was pretty. Very pretty. So why are you opening it up?"

"Have to. The black community believes she was killed out of hate. Lynched. The mayor is getting calls daily. Saying they are not being protected. Case never died. More because of her aunt's reputation, Vera Gold."

The doorbell rang. It was Odessa with the white suitcase. Alice had arrived and was in the big house, arranging the dining room for Jules's guests. She answered the door. Upon seeing it was a black woman, she told her to go to the back door.

Odessa persisted. "I'd like to speak with Rita, please."

"She'll meet you in the back."

Knowing the white woman at the front door was not going to back down long enough to hear what she had to say, Odessa drove around to the back. Alice returned to the kitchen, where she was preparing platters for the party. Jules had peeked out the window in time to see Odessa with the suitcase, described to him by Rita Jane. He became nervous, anxious to speak to Alice.

George rubbed his friend's shoulder, trying to ease the distance between them. Then moved to the billiard's table in the room.

"We have far better memories than just Miriam."

Jules's mind was preoccupied with Miriam's suitcase. "George, you take the first shot. I need to speak with Alice." He picked up a wall phone and dialed the office. He received no answer, so he tried the kitchen. The phone rang and rang, because Alice was watching Talbot and Odessa out back. Jules wanted to find the woman who was at the door. "I'll be back."

After Jules left the room, memories of Mimi welled up in George. She was special to him, too, but he buried it hard for a long time. George examined his face in the mirror over the fireplace to see if one could find evidence of his true feelings when he said her name.

Feeling Jules's paranoia opened his own. He remembered the first night with Miriam. How she fell back laughing, pulling at him, laying there bare-legged. Her hair spread on the pillow, and her breaths short and quick. He'd stroked her hair, wondering if she'd been spoiled as a child. Or was she neglected? Was loving strangers an easy way to get attention? Or was she just wanting appreciation in a dark hour? She gave him a swagger that put polish on him as a prosecutor. He had been inside their world.

Mimi let him have his way. Any way. He'd met her many times after the raid, waiting to see her before her trysts with Jules, to steal what she would give his best friend. When they met secretly, she never dressed like a street walker, never wore short skirts or had smudged mascara or chipped fingernail polish. She was a lady. She was a seductress in bare legs and high heels.

Funny to think he'd asked her to teach him how to whore.

She'd said, "Everyone thinks it is easy, but it's not. First you have to lack something so deep inside that you cannot feel yourself. Something that only another can see and can satisfy." Then she kidded, saying 'Me, no stockings meant no underwear, meant free and ready for love.' And you George? What is it that you need?"

The game was about the predator and the prey. That the John and the girl were both. We switched back and forth. She was the John waiting to be seduced by a whore. Then there was danger. Who had the secret gun? Who was to die that night?

Her voice echoed in his mind, remembering her advice that gender didn't matter in interactions based on money. "Men and women were the same. So, let's play both, so you can learn." She said.

How much money? How much money will someone carry in their car? Not about pretty or ugly. Just adults with their own clocks ticking, free to use their skills and assets as they wished to satisfy desire. It was a struggle to keep their secret meetings from Jules who was open and unabashed with her, an easy fall guy, no one would suspect him. He thought.

He also thought he could forget Miriam. Only he couldn't. He hated to think he loved her more than Jules. Perhaps, dragging up the dirt of the case would cleanse him. Help him understand the desire he had for her.

* * *

Jules had rushed to the back, finding Alice staring out the back window. Talbot parked next to Odessa as she got out her car with the suitcase. He had been at the grocery store for his mother. When he spoke to Odessa,

Alice opened the back door to listen.

"Howdy, Miss. What can I do for you?"

"I'm looking for Rita Jane. I am a church member?" She had to speak loudly over the loud rock 'n' roll music coming from Talbot's car.

"Miss Rita? Did you see her car parked down yonder?"

"No, I didn't."

Unloading bags from the station wagon, Talbot said, "Well, can I tell her something for you?"

"I need to give her this bag." Odessa pressed her lips together, disturbed by Alice staring out at her.

"Yeah, I've seen the bag before. It belongs to the girl Josephine. She stayed a few days. I can give it to Rita."

"When will Rita be home?"

"Not sure, I heard her talking about a show downtown. Said Duke Ellington was playing. I'll keep the bag safe for you." He calculated that it might give him another reason to meet Josephine.

"Talbot!" Alice called.

Odessa was reluctant. "I have the right mind to keep it, but she knows Rita and believes it will be safe with her."

"No worries at all. I will be happy to put it in Rita's room. She won't be back until late. I am awfully sorry about what happened to her. I visited her in the hospital."

"Talbot, get in here!" Alice yelled again. Jules now stood behind her, peering over her shoulder, tense, wanting to approach the boy. Earlier Alice told him she would not tolerate him interfering with her son. She deeply believed Jules would try to influence him with his money, turning him against good moral values, that he would make him a womanizer, or drunk when Jules decided to drop his friendship. They were workers and that was good enough. She told him he should hire someone to get the suitcase, but not Talbot.

Talbot waved to his mother. Then said to Odessa, "Oh, don't mind her. She's one of those nosey workers who thinks she owns the place. She's waiting on these groceries. Here," he said, opening the car. "Put the bag in. It'll be safe as Fort Knox." The rock 'n' roll music continued to blast from the car.

Odessa handed him the bag, which caused Jules to brush past Alice to see, if in fact, it was the white suitcase. Her heart burned.

"Oh, it ain't nothing, Mr. Jules. Just another stranger looking for a handout." Jules couldn't find the words to ask for the bag as Talbot placed it into his car. Odessa was slightly curious as to why Jules was glaring, while Alice twisted her shoulders, peering angrily up at the man.

"Okay, I will be getting along. I'll call Rita tomorrow. Be sure to tell her that Odessa came with the bag."

"You're Miss Odessa?"

This surprised the older woman. "Yes, is something wrong?"

"I hear a lot of talk about you around town."

"I'm happy to be on everybody's mind."

"Sure are, with those school cases. What do you think is going to happen now?"

"The best. I do have to go."

"Let me know how I can help. I'm interested in that stuff," he said, leaning into her car window.

Jules gave Alice a strained command. "Get that bag. Alice! I'll hear no more about your son's innocence." Then left to join George.

Alice felt trapped. She yelled over the loud music. Then she began knocking on the kitchen door window, waving him to come in. He put a hand to his ear to indicate he couldn't hear.

She stamped her foot in the doorway. "What did you say to that woman? And what is that in your car? And turn that crazy music off!"

"Ma, will you leave peace alone?" walking with two bags of groceries toward her.

"How many times have I told you to stop talking to those people?"

"That's impossible, Ma. Absolutely impossible." He handed her the grocery bags at the doorway. Alice threw a hostile look at her son, who saluted her and returned to his car.

15

Going North

Two days later, Hugh stopped the black sedan at the front steps of the Velvet Gardens before sunrise as Jules, unshaven and in a dark suit, anxiously waited in the backseat with all his packages and luggage. He came to realize retrieval of the suitcase was out of reach. After seeing Talbot with the suitcase, he became embarrassed by his pleadings to Alice, a worker who now appeared on the verge of blackmailing him like George. She refused to give him a straight answer as to the suitcase's whereabouts, saying it disappeared from Talbot's car. It was better to leave and accept what may come his way in Europe.

"Hugh, why are you stopping? We have no time to waste."

"Yes, sir, but I forgot to give Rita Jane a package." He picked up a small gift-wrapped box from the passenger seat. "It will only take a minute. I see her light is on."

"Well, hurry up. Please."

Hugh, dressed for the northern weather, walked up the front steps to the big doors. He could count on one hand the number of times in his life he'd entered the front door of this house. It was sweet sadness to know it would be his last. He raised the crisscrossed iron knockers, banging them boldly as if he was the governor.

Rita Jane was on the phone with Ella who was crying.

"What's wrong?"

"Hugh has packed up. He's leaving us."

"No, he's only taking Jules to the station. He'll return." Rita tried to console Ella.

"No, no. He gave all his stuff away. I begged him to stay."

Hugh banged the knockers again.

"Hold on, Ella." Rita looked out the window and saw the black town car in front with the engine running.

"Miss Rita, talk to him. He doesn't have any kin anywhere but here. Don't let him go."

"I'll call you back." Rita hung up and rushed to the front door in her bathrobe.

"Hugh?" she asked as she unlatched the doors.

"Good morning, Miss Rita. You're looking mighty sad."

"Cause I hear you ain't coming back from New York. Is it true? Hugh, you can't leave. This is your home. Polly was my nurse, and, and..." She began to implore him. "There's nothing up North. Stay, please."

"It may be nothing but a dirt patch. So pray that it rains hard on me so I can grow with God's blessings."

"Come on, Hugh, come inside," she said, pulling his hand. "Talk to Penelope. Come. Let's call her."

He pulled back gently. "No, she already knows. I talked to Miss Penelope last night. Said she's coming back, but I told her it was no use. She can't turn me around about it. She was wailing so hard I hang the phone up on her." This was untrue but he wanted Rita not to hold bad feelings toward Penelope.

Rita began to cry, causing tears to roll down his cheek too, making him recall last night with Penelope.

Penelope had sobbed on the telephone. "Hugh, stop this talk, wait until I get back." Twisting and turning in her satin formal gown, sipping a glass of champagne. Pierre entered the oak-paneled library from the dinner party in the next room.

"I've been thinking about it for a while. Sharecropping to cover my expenses is hard on the back. Have to count the days I have left. My family has worked with this family a long time. I am getting too old to work the land and oversee your day workers. Yeah, I know it was hard during the last few years, and you tried keeping my salary going. But the pay you owe now is too far behind. I don't think you can manage to catch up now."

"It's absolutely wrong to make me cry like this, Hugh. I tried my best."

Her cousin touched her shoulders, concerned. "Is it money?" he asked.

She nodded her head up and down, her tears flowing. "Hugh's leaving," she whispered.

Hugh continued talking to Penelope. "I've thought about it for many days. Saw you selling the land, trying to keep up with the accounts, then watched you spend money too. I don't think I should wait around to see if you're able to pay me my five thousand that's due."

Penelope had hated selling the land, knowing she'd look out the window at a neighbor soon. Now she regretted holding back on paying Hugh his due. She was conflicted over paying her debt to him or keeping her land. It was selfish to think he would continue working on loyalty.

Pierre whispered in her ear, "Tell Hugh that the best I can do is have my accountant arrange some payments."

Hugh went on, "I have family too, and as you know they moved on for better work in the factories. Leaving me here, feeling I should be the one to show our thankfulness. So a lot of work fell on me. I don't want to wait until I will be of no use to you. There are others needing work."

"You will send your address?" She wailed loudly as Pierre rushed to shut the dining room doors to prevent the other guests from hearing.

"As soon as I can."

"Good-bye, Hugh. Please call me." She hung up the telephone. "What ingratitude," she said, whimpering. "Years and years of handouts to him and his friends. Never having to fear any white man because of our family name. Protected from insults. We gave his family dignity." She threw her glass at the large fireplace.

Now Rita Jane cried loudly in the cold morning air.

"Polly is gone, and now you. You are all I have left."

"No. Miss Rita. I am not your family, nor was Polly your family. I have this here box for you. My mother told me on her dying bed never to lose sight of this and to never let anyone have it but little Rita Jane."

He handed her the gift box. She hugged his fragile frame, feeling strength still in his bones, kissed him on the cheek and said good-bye.

Jules, tired of waiting, honked the car horn. Hugh and Rita held hands as they walked out to the portico. She stayed to see them off. Hugh hobbled down the steps to the car. Rita waved to Jules, thinking of the mess he'd created for others to worry over. Now he's leaving. He waved back.

Wondering what Polly left her, she unwrapped the gift box, thinking it was a book. Hugh had loved for her to read her schoolbooks to him.

It was one of the family's older fancy cigar boxes with the Velvet emblem. Inside was a baby's photograph with a date of birth. The same as hers. There was a note inside an envelope addressed to Rita Jane Porter.

"Master Franklin asked that I keep you from death. Now I am gone but I know that you are well and reading these few words. You were the last of Mary Margaret's children. The records said you died at birth. Master could not kill you. So I took you as my own. No need to explain why when you can see the difference in your skin. My word is not much, and disputes will be made. May God forgive me."

Rita Jane trembled, confused, flashing images of Mary Margaret and her husband, Zachary, who often stared at her as she played with the other children. The memory of Mary Margaret once begging Polly to repeat how the child had died. Polly only shook her head, then complained to Grandpoppa Franklin that it was none of her business to tell his daughter anything. She was fraught with fever then.

Rita continued to read. "This trinket was left upstairs on the big bed. Master Franklin kept it until the end, then he gave it to me to pass on to you." The outside of the locket was inscribed with the name Velvet. Inside was the picture of a fair woman. Polly had known that Mary Margaret had no need of a gold locket with Velvet's picture. She'd had plenty of diamonds.

Rita Jane rushed down the steps calling, "Hugh! Hugh! Hugh!" Yelling, grasping the locket as the car lights disappeared. She looked down at the locket and heard a car backfire, or maybe it was a gunshot. She looked over her shoulder at the plaque dedicated to Velvet.

16

Velvet

Velvet, a girl with sandy hair, bright skin, and dark eyes was born around 1849. She was considered a white slave. One with at least three white grandparents. She ran away from the Blackstone plantation, hoping to go north and pass into a white way of life. When she turned fourteen, she dressed like a boy, cut off her hair, and wore overalls and a cap in preparation for her escape. She was five feet tall and looked like a boy, which helped her to avoid questioning as to why she was walking around unattended.

She learned of the proclamation freeing slaves in Virginia by President Lincoln. She also knew there was a war going on and was afraid of being shot in the crossfire of a battle or captured by a slave hunter looking for runaway slaves and poor whites. But she was done with living in the small room with Lena. She wasn't her real mother, but she'd been the only one Velvet had known. Lena had two of her own children on the Blackstone plantation, both boys. A little girl was a joy to take in and raise.

Master John had brought the baby to her one night, only a day old. As she grew, some believed she was Master John's child with another slave woman named Sarah, who lived down the row of houses. She was seen to be pregnant.

Then Nannie, the cook in the big house, told her that a servant from twenty miles down brought the child in as a sale. Said she was the result of a love affair between a wealthy woman and a Union soldier. The baby was so cold and red in the face. Lena named her Velvet.

As a child, Velvet carried cups of water to the workers or ran full baskets of cotton back to the carts. Now as a young teen, Lena was concerned with Master John hanging around the cabin longer than usual, often until after sunset. Her mothering instincts feared the day he'd call the child to work in the house. Sure, she was white enough, but she was a slave, a white slave, and she would be treated as cruelly as a black slave. Color didn't define slavery as much as whether one had one drop of black blood from another slave.

Lena didn't like his long lingering looks, or that he gave her family more food to eat. One night he asked the girl to thank him with a kiss. She hated his smelly breath and rough whiskers. Then he touched her breast. She pulled away, not caring if he was going to whip her. He was angry. He had to devise a plan to get her away from Lena, who showed she would not tolerate him spoiling the girl. Velvet never left Lena's side thereafter.

While Master John was on a trip to Georgia, she decided to run away in the early morning while Lena slept. Velvet gently rose from the same bed she shared with the woman, taking some food from the table, and stuffing it into her pockets. She kissed the woman's hand gently, then crouching low, moved quietly away from the cabin.

Lena was not asleep, she just lay there with an aching heart, watching the child leave the cabin. Praying that she would live a better life than the one that awaited her with Master John Blackstone. The guard was asleep but his dogs awakened. They didn't bark because she had made friends with them. One led the way through the tobacco fields as she followed, crouching as low as she could. At the roadside the pet stopped and wagged its tail. She gave the dog a good hug, then scooted through the woods alongside the road leading to the city streets. She had to get there before sunrise and mingle in with a work crew.

Tired, she fell asleep behind some barrels at the back of a general supply store. Three brothers, around ages eight, eleven, and fourteen, whose father owned the store, stood over her, wondering if she had stolen anything. They asked her name several times. To avoid detection that she was a girl if they heard her voice, she pretended to be mute.

They laughed at her funny gestures, so she made more and more funny ones, each funnier than the last one. They liked her and felt compassion, so they motioned her to follow them. She became frightened when she saw men on horses with guns and dogs at the front of the store. Or when she saw carriages of chained blacks going down Main Street. Then there were the regiments of soldiers on guard throughout the streets.

The store had several workers to keep up with the high demand for goods by the Confederates. She learned the store also catered to bounty hunters stopping for supplies before riding north. Richmond was the second largest port in the South for slave traders, which kept the city bustling with men selling and buying slaves, in particular bounty hunters.

Velvet knew her skin didn't matter, she was one of the nearly one and a half million mixed white slaves. Even whole blooded whites were sold at premium prices, not for the quality of their work, but for their complexion. A captured slave could fetch four hundred dollars during a time when a year's salary was not quite one hundred dollars.

She believed by now Master John knew she'd escaped. And that her brothers hated her for taking pieces of their clothing. A strange feeling of danger overcame Velvet when a man in all black entered the store to purchase goods. He asked the brothers to help load his donkey and horse. The man had three guns. The boys gave her stuff to carry and load, instead she pretended she was too weak to help and kept stepping slowly backward out of the store to get away from the man. She didn't want to run down the street, so she walked slowly.

The brothers waved her back. One ran to pull her arm. The man became curious as to why the boy walked away, and asked about him, having never seen the boy at the store before. He was suspicious, even though he'd seen no notices for a runaway boy. Then it didn't matter. He asked who were his folks. They were not sure. Only that the boy couldn't talk.

He looked hard into her face. The eyes were dark. She looked down, which gave him a feeling that she was a nigger passing. He rode away because he didn't want to tie her up in front of the other boys who had taken a liking to her. He watched from a distance, waiting for her to separate from the brothers. Soon the boys went inside to the back living quarters to eat dinner. Two of them saved biscuits and slices of ham to take to her later.

Fear would not leave her alone, so she began walking down the road, looking for another place to hide. The hunter rode up from the back and roped her. She struggled to be free but it was hopeless. After gagging her, he made her walk next to the donkey, taking her to a slave trader he knew in Shockoe Bottom, not too far from the store.

She continued to pretend to be mute, causing the trader to reject her. It didn't matter. There were hundreds of slave traders along the river. Finally, one wanted to examine the boy for any other deformities. Pulling off her overalls, they discovered she was a girl. The trader began to bargain down the price. The hunter argued she was handsome enough to bring a good price, but it did not mean she could work hard, and the muteness made her cheaper than a blacker child. The two men haggled and haggled.

Finally, the man in all black took half price. He was anxious to move on to Maryland, around Baltimore, where he'd heard many runaways were being sheltered. Velvet spent the night in a large cage compacted with other slaves. The next morning at dawn, she was led with chains tied to ten other girls, boys, women, and men, all of different ages, to the sidewalk to be sold.

Master Franklin, a large plantation owner, was riding through the trading zone with his wife, Ann, to pick up a shipment of fabric she'd ordered from London. Once a week he walked through the merchant stalls examining the goods shipped from Europe, such as fine wine, cloth, furnishings, tea, and spices, taking time to talk with tobacco and wine exporters about the sale of his cigars and wines. Ann came at the suggestion of Polly, her young slave maid, who'd urged her to get some air to improve her frail health.

Ann had miscarried three times and took confidence in Polly, who prayed every night that she'd get well. Eventually Polly had to sleep in the room next to her, which caused the young mother to neglect her young sons living in a field house. Ann feared Franklin wished her dead and needed protection from the nightmares she was having. Polly prepared teas to help her conceive. Mostly to sleep at night or calm her nerves.

She often complained she was bearing a child and had to sleep alone until its birth. Franklin moved to a front room of the house. Her imaginations developed into a psychosis. Three years past and she still did not give birth to the child inside her.

When she saw Velvet crying in a sack cloth dress, she took an instant liking to the little girl and asked for her price. Velvet was bought. She rode to the plantation in the front seat with the horse driver, not entirely happy. Still a slave, bonded to servitude, she slept in the room with Polly, comforted and sheltered. Polly reminded Velvet of Lena's love.

Weeks past and John Blackstone continued to fret over the runaway girl with Lena. He put out flyers for her capture, and visited the slave markets weekly, asking if anyone had seen her. He could not prove ownership because he never logged her in his account books to avoid extra taxes. He had faith Lena could testify to one distinctive marking, a brown birthmark on the small finger of her right hand. She was a valuable good, and the loss was a loss of good money.

The slave traders up and down the row said they'd seen no one like her. She was common goods like all the rest, just another shade of a slave. Then the bounty hunter in black returned to the markets; and was told by the trader who'd sold Velvet that John Blackstone was down there looking for the girl.

The hunter rode up to Blackstone's plantation, and told the planter he might know her whereabouts. Master John said he would get back to him; he did not want to pay this hunter for information or to retrieve a slave he already owned. Slave hunters were known to be double-crossers.

The next week, Master John stopped in the supply store. There he started discussing his worry over losing slaves. Said he'd lost two slaves in the last three months. "Probably too easy on them," said the store owner.

Blackstone described Velvet, and the brothers, who'd been listening, realized the boy was a girl. The store owner remembered Franklin and the missus having come by with a young white slave girl about two months ago. "But you know there are so many of them now. It could be anyone." The boys listened as they shelved goods. They said nothing at first, but the eldest felt sorry for the boy/girl and wanted to say something to lead the man off her trail.

He knew Master Franklin was a good owner. She'd do better on his land than with this man.

The store owner continued. "You know, thinking back, a bounty hunter said he captured a girl pretending to be a boy right here working with my boys. Told me that Franklin bought her at a low price because she was mute. Well, John, I wish you good luck." The idea that Velvet would be at a nearby plantation infuriated John Blackstone.

He decided to visit his neighbor and see for himself. He took Lena with him, but Velvet pretended she couldn't speak. The girl's hair had grown long and she was well groomed. Lena said, "No, it can't be her. They all look alike, Master." She knew the girl was Velvet. The marking on the hand was proof. In her heart she believed the girl would be better off here because Master John was a drinker. He had other children he'd sold off. But John wasn't fooled. He noticed the mark too and began to argue with Franklin.

The next day he came back with a shotgun, demanding her return. Ann was crying. Polly was running back and forth from the kitchen to the front door hoping Master Franklin would pay off the man.

Velvet hadn't spoken around anyone except for Franklin. He'd discovered she could speak when he happened upon her in the basement inside Polly's cabinet pretending to read a book aloud, saying the words she thought were written. He had come down for wine and found her with a book taken from his library.

He was pleased but she was fearful of a wiping. He assured her that he would not punish her for trying to read. She then pleaded with him to keep her, after Polly told her that Blackstone had come for her. "He'll whip me." The older man could not bear the thought of John scarring the girl to mark her as his property.

Upon Blackstone's return, Franklin had to make a decision to keep Velvet or not. The cheated man stood out front with a gun contrary to warnings to leave. He stood there a long time with his gun raised, firing up in the air. Each blast made the workers in the big house holler. Having had enough, Master Franklin went to the porch with his pistol cocked. John Blackstone raised his rifle to fire. One shot was heard. Everyone ran to the front of the house to see who lived. John Blackstone was dead.

After the killing, Velvet stayed in Polly's room, sullen. She cried and cried. The gunshot sound echoed over and over. Franklin was afraid she would run and tell the truth of her ownership. He moved her sleeping room to the top floor, thereby hearing her footsteps should she try to leave the house. She had to have Polly's permission to come down and was always escorted by her to the kitchen and other parts of the house or fields.

The story told to the sheriff was that Master John had come to steal a farmhand. He was mistaken and confused. Drunk. Because Franklin was far wealthier, the story stayed that way. John Blackstone's wife and sons tried to keep their farm going but the Civil War and the occupation of soldiers devastated them financially. They had to sell and move on.

Soon thereafter Ann conceived and was indeed pregnant this time. She refused to leave her room. Franklin was happy. There was hope that Ann, who was only thirty-five and had lost babies before birth, could carry this one to term. Franklin was forty and childless.

Velvet tended Master Franklin's room while he was at breakfast in the large dining room. Soon he stayed in his room to watch her, skipping his breakfast. Polly thought she heard laughter and conversations about the war ending. Velvet was a free woman.

Then he kept her in the room all day, arranging things, even when he went out to tend to the land or had business in the city proper. He expected her to be there when he returned. She became his concubine. Eventually, she spent every night in the room with him. Miss Ann didn't care where the man went. She just wanted her child.

Velvet became pregnant, too. Master Franklin was even more proud. Velvet was a pretty child. To avoid too much conflict, she was to return to her room on the top floor while pregnant. Only Polly was allowed to tend to her. Polly heard the two talking when she walked up the stairs one afternoon. After Master left, Polly confronted the girl.

"You're a liar, little girl. Making trouble." Her anger was growing. "You come here acting helpless, now you lay up here wanting this man's house to fall." Velvet started to cry. She was sixteen now.

When Franklin returned to the room and saw Velvet sad and learned of Polly's harsh words, he explained to his servant that he was teaching the mute how to speak, and how to read and write. Velvet was a free woman. He'd freed her before the war ended.

"Then I am free, too," said Polly.

"Yes, and you may leave if you wish," he replied. "But I don't want you to go."

Polly was silent; she had no place to go. Her work was not hard here. They had other servants to handle the laundry, cleaning, and the fields. She liked to cook. "I'm fine where I am," she told him.

"Good. Let's be thankful."

Velvet was not. She refused to eat much. She didn't want Polly near her. She was scared the woman would harm her or the baby. Polly was too busy thereafter to worry about Velvet because Ann began to labor prematurely.

Days passed making Franklin frantic. He was also worried about Velvet who was due in a month. Ann smiled with joy when the child was born. She held the child tightly before falling asleep. Within an hour the child died and had to be taken away quickly.

When she awakened, she asked for her baby. Polly told her the child needed care and had been taken to a doctor. The child would soon be brought back. Ann was ill with a fever and too weak to count the days the baby was away. Polly was very sad. It would devastate the lady knowing she'd lost another child.

One night she heard a child crying. It was Velvet's baby girl, who'd just been born. Ann called, "Polly, Polly!" Polly was upstairs helping with the delivery. Master Franklin was drinking but rose from his library when he heard Ann moving toward the back stairway.

"My baby."

"Dear, you have to return to bed."

"The baby is here. Where is she?"

"I will bring her to you soon," he told her.

He escorted her back to her room. While upstairs, Polly swooped the little baby girl as soon as it entered the world from Velvet's womb, and wrapped her in a special blanket, then headed toward the door.

Velvet, tired and sore, cried out in a hoarse voice, "That is my child! Where are you going?" Barely gaining enough strength to get out of the bed, she fell, crawling to grab ahold of Polly's long skirt. "Let me see my baby. My baby!"

"This baby is Master Franklin's. He wants to see her."

Velvet was still holding onto Polly's dress when the man rushed into the room to separate the two women. He told Polly to go. Cradling the child to her breast, Polly rushed down the steps to Miss Ann's bedroom.

Ann rose up in her bed, her face full of joy. "My, my, there you are."

"Yes, ma'am, she just got back tonight from the doctor."

Ann took the child and lovingly embraced her while Franklin held Velvet, who was screaming, trying to comfort her. "You'll see the child, you will. Polly will have you nurse her. She'll need milk, your milk." He held her in his arms, and stroked back her long brown hair, kissing her tears. Then he led her back to the large white bed. Exhausted, she soon fell asleep in his embrace. He left, locking the door.

"Why do I hear screaming?" Ann asked.

Polly, feeling deep regret for stealing the baby, said, "I don't know, Miss Ann. I'll go see if it's someone out in the carriage house. I'm not sure."

Franklin rushed into Ann's room to see the child. Tersely, he said, "Polly, go to her. Help her, will you?"

"Who, Franklin?" asked Ann in the most pleased voice.

"Go!"

Polly turned, crying, wiping her eyes with her skirt.

He handed her a key. "Here, take this key."

Polly took the key with horror. Now the child was caged. The child he'd let romp through the house unchecked was now locked in misery. Polly was a part of the shame. But she had to help clean up and see if the afterbirth had come out.

He took two of Ann's dresses from the closet. "Here, take these to her. Make her decent." Then he lay next to Ann, who looked up at him, beaming with pride .

"She looks like you. The nose. The ears."

He was very happy because Ann's inheritance of the land they lived on depended on her conceiving an heir. He owned some land, but not the bulk of it. If she did not produce any heirs, her portion of the land reverted to her brother Daniel. At one point, he'd imagined her brother poisoned her at his family dinners to cause the miscarriages and deaths. He'd begged her not to visit him, but she loved her brother. Every Thursday she visited him when she was pregnant to prove she was fertile and could bear children. After each loss, Daniel sent her a lamb and rejoiced with his wife and children. It was finally settled. The worry was gone.

* * *

Franklin enjoyed watching Velvet nurse the little girl, christened Mary Margaret. As the child grew, Velvet accepted that the child was not hers. Mary Margaret was a prize who traveled often with her father. She had tutors. The best clothing. But she was extremely indifferent to Velvet. She often looked in the mirror and noticed her lips were shaped the same. She did notice their hands were very similar and that there was a mark on her left little finger, the opposite hand of Velvet's.

Franklin continued to teach Velvet her lessons every afternoon in the room above. Ann accepted his happiness with her. She believed the mute needed education too. No one told her that Velvet could talk.

Polly also kept watch, afraid the girl may try to steal the child and run. Eventually she taught Velvet how to sew in order that she could earn a living one day. Many of the clothes Velvet made were for Ann. It was fitting she would get them back after Ann no longer wore them.

Ann turned away from her husband. She was tired of childbearing, believing if she tried for another it may lead to her end. She didn't care where he made his lot. When she heard Polly was pregnant, she was suspicious, but she did not inquire much. She knew Polly had boys who worked the fields. And from time to time she would go out to pick vegetables or collect eggs, mingling with male workers, or take leftover food to the horseman's cabin. She trusted Polly would not lay down with her husband.

Polly bore the rumor because Velvet was pregnant again. The trouble was that Ann was not. So, Polly had to be pregnant too. This time the child was not blond. She was darker, pretty, but distinctively a Negro. Franklin was not going to allow the child to die. He still loved the child, but he could not raise her along with Mary Margaret. The new baby had to be Polly's.

Ann was satisfied that it was not her husband's, judging from the appearance of the child. She had to keep the reputation of a good moral family, even though many households were filled with an owner's illegitimate children. Now that slavery was over, one could not sell the child for profit. She did not mind another little girl in the house.

It took Franklin a while after the birth to climb the stairs to see how Velvet and the child were progressing. When he did, the room was silent. On the bed beneath the window, where the morning sun poured through the sheer curtains laid a note. She was free. With money he had given her over the years, and some from Polly, who'd known of the secret plan, she'd left the night before with her second child. Velvet was on her way north, where she'd dreamed to be all her life.

17

The Brooks Brothers, Please

Josephine was so anxious to leave the hospital, that she dressed and sat up all night, waiting for the morning discharge papers. But sleep overtook her willpower, and she was soon awakened by a buzzing in the ward. A young Dr. Brooks was making rounds today. They said he was handsome and unmarried.

Too tired to listen, she closed her eyes again. A nurse marched into the middle of the room to announce the doctor's arrival. A chorus of bed curtains zipped open quickly to watch him enter, causing a crescendo of sweet voices overlapping each other for his attention. The once trash-talking women softened into little birds, tweeting sudden ailments for medication, a sore arm, blood pressure, or any complaint that would make him touch them. They combed their hair and put on a dash of lipstick.

"Good morning, ladies," he said. Then she heard him say, "Patient Walker." Josephine threw off the cover to see a tall, athletic man with a smooth-shaven face. He was strong, assured, and muscular under his white coat.

"Good morning," she replied with the barest of breath.

The young resident smiled. He had the most perfect teeth.

"I am happy to see you made a full recovery." He pulled the curtain around the bed. "I am Dr. Brooks. How is your arm feeling?" Josephine nodded her head back and forth.

"Meaning?" Forcing her to speak. "Any pain?"

"No."

He leaned closer to look at her cheek, causing her heart to beat faster.

"Looks okay. The nurse says your vital signs are normal. If you experience headaches, or a rise in temperature, either go to a doctor of your choice or return to see me. My number is on the discharge papers."

Overwhelmed by his presence, she could hear his words but couldn't comprehend them. Then she heard Odessa ask for her. The nurse motioned her into the room. Dr. Brooks pulled back the curtain and said, "I am finished, nurse."

"Pasqual!" Odessa cried. She was surprised to see him. "How are you, young man?" She hugged him.

The doctor smiled. "Fine."

"I just spoke with your dad this morning."

"You're luckier than me."

"Doctor, you're needed in the emergency room," interrupted the nurse.

"Odessa, glad to see you." He moved to the door quickly.

"Listen, we're on our way to see Art Strickland," Odessa said. "Then we will be home for the evening. Please come by and bring that brother of yours. I have a homesick young lady here who needs a little cheering up about the South."

"Actually, I'm meeting Lorenzo at Art's after my shift. He's working on a case with Dad. Maybe we can have dinner tonight?"

Josephine smiled.

"Wonderful." said Odessa.

After all the discharge papers were completed, Odessa and Josephine drove away from the hospital. Odessa was ashamed and apologized for not having the suitcase. She explained that she'd left it for Rita, but the woman was not returning her calls. Something was mysterious about the bag. Mint was still in New York, and she couldn't figure it out by herself, nor did she want to get too entangled. She'd noticed Blackstone sitting outside the house when she left for the hospital. "Let's call Art's office. He knows Rita pretty well." Josephine was not satisfied with the explanation.

"I want to go there now. Take me to Rita Jane so I can get my bag. The other day the officer was looking for it around my bed. There must be clues to who killed my mother."

She hung her head, unhappy with the advice that they should get Art Strickland to help. She wanted to go back to the Velvet Gardens by herself, no matter what Odessa said.

Odessa changed the subject to avoid further worry and guilt for leaving it with that boy.

"If we are going to dinner, you need to have your hair done and some fresh clothes. You'll want to look presentable when we meet with the boys."

The thought of seeing Dr. Brooks brightened her. She was attracted to him. Odessa stopped talking when she saw a car in her rearview mirror, following her lane for lane, turn for turn. She grew silent, cautious. But she gabbed away, trying to keep Josephine occupied.

"The boys call me Auntie because their mother, Marguerite, dated my husband's brother, Ron, who was once a minor league baseball player in Baltimore. The boys adore him. He took them to practices and into the locker rooms. They got signed balls from all the players and even some from visiting teams. Dr. Brooks' younger brother is in law school, his third year, in New York. Their grandfather is a prominent lawyer in D.C., Lorenzo Brooks, Sr. He worked on the desegregation cases, on the national level. We call him Senior. Their mother, Marguerite, is his daughter and she's a very, very successful doctor. Marguerite found her husband, also a doctor, in bed with another woman. No way was he able to continue to practice around here. Not with Marguerite on every corporate board in a hundred-mile radius. Divorced. He relocated to Chicago. After a while Ron realized she was never going to marry him. He felt used. He did love her. But his money didn't have the right manners attached, as we say. The boys stayed in touch. They saw their father often, but they made sure they got to see Ron too. He eventually married. Meaning nothing to Marguerite, who calls him now and then for a little touching up, as they say. No one gives up anyone up in D.C."

They arrived at the La Chic hair salon in Jackson Ward, and the shadow car sped past as the two women parked. A hanging bell tingled over the glass door as they entered. The salon was busy for a weekday. New Year's Eve was tomorrow and no one wanted to be sitting in a chair. The four stations were lavender with chrome trim. Pictures of models graced the walls. Two overhead fans whirled the smell of pomade and hair spray, mixing with the heat from the pressing irons and dryers throughout the room. Big band music played on a tabletop radio.

"Hello, dear," Odessa said to Ruth, the owner of the shop.

"Good to see you, Odessa. Have a seat," replied the hairdresser.

"This is Josephine. Can you fit her in today?"

"Yes, ma'am. Come, missy, sit at the sink for me. Take your coat off first, dear," she said. To Odessa she continued. "You know Esther Mae left me. Haven't found a new washer yet. I know how you helped Esther too. She was that kind, always out for herself. I gave her a job right after beauty school. You know she went to school with Rita Jane. Then lately, she started working a few days washing hair over at a white salon in the Fan district when it was slow here. Said the tips were huge. More than pressing hair or doing nails at my shop. They like strong hands running through their thin hair. She said one woman liked her manners so much she asked if she wanted work with her, typing."

Odessa sat there, listening to the hairdresser, holding back her own feelings of betrayal by the woman.

"Now she thinks she's better than her own kind with that new typing job. Thinks she's like that Rita Jane up in that big house." Talking nonstop, she wrapped Josephine in a flowery plastic sheet to begin the shampoo.

"You know, I was wondering; you got some clout. Since I paid my poll taxes to vote this year. Can't do it each year but this year I did. Seems the mailman stopped delivering the mail." She sprayed water over the girl's hair. "Sometimes for a week or two. I'm thinking of hiring a lawyer. You think Art can help?"

"I'll talk to him." Odessa looked out the window to see if the shadow car had returned.

"Shame, the amount of money you have to pay to vote in Virginia only to be harassed. Who has money for lawyers to fight the government? You think you can look into it for me?" She scrubbed Jo's head so vigorously, to the point the girl feared the woman would wash her scalp away.

"You know I will, Ruthie. We need every vote." Odessa assured the woman.

* * *

In the last few days Art had made several calls around the city, gathering information on Vera Gold. He was impressed with her reputation and the work she'd accomplished in the 1930s. A time when he was away, unconcerned about Richmond and its residents. Since the reopening of the Walker case with the reward announced in the media, his office had been flooded with drop-ins and calls.

The telephone rang off the hook with all kinds of leads, which he directed to the police. Today, his secretary, Niecy, had asked him to speak to a nurse friend who appeared to be very credible. Mamie sat in the front office waiting for Art. She applied lipstick every five minutes.

"Lovely color, and your nails too," Niecy complimented the sullen woman.

"Ruby red in memory of my sister." Her nails were long and well-manicured. "It reminds me she's gone but near. The holiday time is rough for me. I can't sleep; that's why I'm here. To see that justice is done. After reading the papers about that girl in the river last week, it just set me off. It's like the same thing that happened to the girl Ruby was dealing with, all over again. Ruby was frightened for her life. She didn't kill that woman. It chokes me each time I ask why. Why? Over and over. Why is my sister gone? So young."

"Well, you know Ruby had no business in the first place..."

Mamie darted her eyes at the secretary and lashed out. "She was helping women the best way she knew!"

Niecy stood to file some folders in a cabinet to avoid her sting.

"Left behind by some man leaving you knocked up. Don't want to take care of his kids. She helped them be free of raising a fatherless child. Anyway, I believe it's all Hugh's fault. Ruby loved that man. She'd do anything for him. Why he killed her fills me with pain."

"You need to stop talking that way before you get yourself in trouble."

"We all know what he did with that Walker woman. You see this ring? It was Ruby's. Hugh gave it to her. I wear it all the time to remind myself of the no-good nigger he was. He brought that girl over there bleeding. Ruby told him to take her to the hospital."

"The one in the river last week?"

"No, the one years ago. Wish I had caught the chicken crap leaving town. He probably killed that new prostitute too. Looks the same to me."

"Art may be able to track him down. We got a lot of calls about the Walker girl. Seems fifteen years later the entire city knew the killer."

"Damn right, they knew. That's why Ruby had to run. Went down to Raleigh only to die in her sleep. She was healthy, only thirty-four years old."

"The Lord calls us when he feels it."

"Killing ain't God's calling. Hugh came back to live in Richmond after it all happened, and no one touched him for it. I bet those white folks had something to do with it. Ran her out. Said he was going to take care of her. Then one morning he calls the police saying she died in her sleep. How do you die sleeping next to your man? Who cares about a black woman dying in her bed with a black man in North Carolina? Then he came back to Richmond and kept driving around those folks in a big black car. I wonder how much blood is in it."

"Let me knock again. He usually doesn't keep people waiting so long."

"It's okay. I can wait. Lawyers are always late with you."

Turning from the filing, Niecy said in a hushed voice, "A few calls came in saying Ruby was trying--Well,

people believe the blood in the car is on Ruby for trying—"
Niecy abruptly stopped when Mamie's face turned into a
volcano, ready to erupt to defend her sister.

"No, she didn't. She told me. She told me the girl
had a lot of money. She told Hugh to take the Walker girl
to the hospital. He refused. Said it was a hush-hush thing.
Someone else did something to the girl." She repeatedly
shook her head. "Ruby helped women. She knew when it
was wrong. She killed no one." Tears swelled in her eyes.

"You're getting yourself upset. Let me get Art."

"I know, I guess it's around that time of the year
when she left. Then that Hugh leaving town now, makes
me even angrier."

Niecy knocked on Art's door, then opened it to
give him a look of exasperation. He was on the telephone
with Rita. He hung up and called. "Come on in, Miss—"

"Mamie Harris," said his secretary.

18

Art's Office

The day was finally winding down for Art. Easing out of his chair, he moved to the front office to look over the telephone messages. Five were from Rita Jane, three from Ella. 'Urgent, please call as soon as possible.' *Everyone's problem is urgent when they call a lawyer,* he shrugged off Rita's problem. Odessa, smiling, entered his office.

"It's Miss O.D. in over drive as usual. How you doing?"

Tickled, she gave him a hug. "Stop, Art."

"Just an overdose of love and strength." He hugged her.

Josephine stepped in quietly behind her.

"And who do I have the pleasure of meeting?"

"This is Josephine Walker. The young woman—"

He cut her off excitedly. "Yes, yes. You're Vera Gold's niece." He held out his hand.

"Yes, sir." Taking his hand.

"Has Pasqual or Lorenzo called?" Odessa asked.

"Lorenzo should be here shortly. Went to the coroner's office and the police for some records for Senior. And Pasqual, there he is."

The young doctor could be seen crossing the street, approaching in a suit and tie. Josephine smiled adoringly.

"Good to see you, Doctor," Art said as he opened the door. "Glad to see you're staying fit."

Affectionately, Pasqual said, "Auntie," as he leaned over to kiss Odessa. He turned to Josephine. "And hello again, to my dear patient."

"Thank you," she replied, not knowing what else to say.

"How long have you been in Richmond?" Art asked. "Working at the hospital and not calling me?" he jabbed.

"Just a week. The hospital is short staffed. Not enough black doctors. I was lucky to get the residency in an inner city. Black hospitals are sought after by ob-gyn guys. You can get a lot of experience. The number of births is greater in--"

"In poor black neighborhoods," Art finished. "You don't have to be polite with me. Hey, I spoke with Senior this morning. Not sure if I can make the New Year's gig."

"Art, why not?" Odessa asked. "You need to go."

"We can talk over dinner. First, I'd like a few words with Miss Josephine. You said she had some legal questions." Seeking confirmation from Odessa.

"Yes. Go ahead, Jo. We'll wait."

"Follow me, young lady. Can I get you a soda or water?"

"No, I'm fine."

They entered the back office where photographs of Art in tennis gear, some with his dad and mom, some of him at his tennis academy, many as a young tournament winner lined the wall. A few trophies sat on a bookshelf while rackets and tennis balls were all over the place. He eased into his large leather chair.

"You are a mighty loved child. I don't mean it the way it sounds."

"It's okay. I am blessed."

He began to tell the young girl, who sat straight and proper, impressed to be in a lawyer's office, about a reward for information leading to her mother's killer. "Give me a few days. I am not sure what it's about. I believe the reward was a thousand dollars. With interest it may be more."

"What about the killer? Will you work on my mother's murder case too?"

"No, dear, I defend people, I'm not a prosecutor. It's up to the district attorney. Odessa asked me to speak to you about the officer who assaulted you. As to whether your civil rights were violated. After some thought, I do not find it's a case I can manage."

Upset, she asked, "Why, because I'm not twenty-one? Is it because I'm from the North?"

Blackstone was his inside contact in the police force, who often helped him when there were police cover-ups. He wasn't going up against the man. He believed Blackstone was sincere about finding Miriam's killer, even though he had problems with anger and was set on solving the case as a personal vendetta against Penelope. He'd told Art the Walker woman was given belladonna or hemlock up at the Velvet house and that Hugh had taken it upon himself to try and rescue the woman, but she'd died. Sounded like rumors to Art. He was not going to explain what he knew or how he knew it to this rash girl.

He continued, speaking assuredly, "You may have a case, and should consult another lawyer, but it's not my type of case."

Josephine thought he was trying to get rid of her. Scared like all the other black people she'd met.

The office door behind her opened quickly, and in stepped Lorenzo.

He interrupted. "Thanks for the advice. I got the—" Then stopped suddenly.

Josephine turned, and their eyes locked. They were unable to stop looking at each other.

"I am with a client, come back in a minute," Art said.

But Lorenzo remained motionless. Josephine, in turn, couldn't believe he was just as good looking as the young doctor. Tall, athletic, confident. Wow, she felt like she had become engulfed by a bubble of delight.

"Lo, have a seat outside. I'll get to you," Art repeated. He waved his hand to break the connection between the two. "Go! Shut the door!"

Lorenzo backed out of the room, leaving Josephine and Art alone again.

Art told her that he had some legal documents concerning her great aunt, Vera Gold, but he hasn't read all of them yet and would contact her as soon as possible. Art noticed she was inattentive, turning frequently toward the office door each time the brothers laughed with Odessa.

"Let's wrap this up," he said.

They rose, and Art stepped out the office with Jo following, to avoid eye contact with Lorenzo. But the young man refused to stop looking at her with a deep desire.

"Come in, Lorenzo." Art returned to his office, but Lorenzo stood still. He was worried that Pasqual would steal Josephine away from him.

"Where do you want to go to dinner?" Pasqual asked her.

"I know a great Crab Shack nearby," Odessa answered.

"Lorenzo." Art called again, understanding that the young man was nervous over losing the girl to his brother.

"Hey, that sounds like fun. I'll be right out," Lorenzo said still watching her every move, studying her thoroughly.

"Hurry, Lo. It's getting late," Odessa said. "I'm hungry."

Attempting to thaw Lorenzo's heat, Pasqual said, "You can meet us there, Lo."

Josephine touched her newly pressed hairdo, and said softly, "We can wait." Lorenzo's face brightened as he stepped backward into the office.

Art reached for the papers in the young man's hand. "Let me see what you've got. You know that guy, Rhoady, called me a few days ago."

Lo sat down but continued to look out the door, watching Pasqual and Josephine in the front office.

"Shut the door," Art said.

"It's okay. It's a little stuffy in here."

Art rose and shut the door. "The problem is the information on Rhoady relates to that young lady's mother. Do you want her to hear it?"

Lorenzo was surprised. "Wow. That's great."

"She's looking for the killer and I don't think you should be involved with her. You need to focus on your client's needs. Once you get sidetracked or do favors you set yourself up for slaughter from the unexpected. It all unravels. Take my advice."

"Sure. But talking with her could help my client."

"She knows nothing about her mother."

"I can help her."

"Suit yourself. Let me see if they gave you all the documents." Art looked over the coroner's report, the police interview lists that included Vera Gold, Hugh Porter, Penelope LeNoire, and Rita Jane Porter. He scanned the list of twenty names, including the club owner's girls. "Where is Rhoady?"

"The cops never spoke to him. He told Senior he was out of town on a train to Boston. Now they want to interview him. Nor did they talk to Jules LeNoire, who was in France."

"Means nothing," Art said. "Let me read through the rest."

"Can we do this tomorrow?" Lorenzo asked, turning repeatedly to the closed door.

"Okay. Your mind's somewhere else." Art handed the file back.

Lorenzo lunged from the back office to see Pasqual sitting next to Josephine at the front glass windows.

"I haven't had this much time to myself in days. Always rushing from one floor to another. Lorenzo and I have tickets to a show. One reason I'm off tonight."

"Okay, let's go. My treat," Art said.

"Hold up," Lorenzo said. "We have tickets tonight to see the man himself. 'I got a woman...She's good to me.' We can't waste them."

"That's right." Pasqual smiled tightly. "I forgot. Why don't you take Odessa." He suggested to his brother.

Art and Odessa laughed. Then he picked up the messages about Rita Jane to reread.

Josephine became suddenly anxious. "I'm sorry to interfere. I'm not too hungry. You can go to the show."

"No problem, because one of us is going to take you, and not the other," Lorenzo said as he punched his brother in the arm.

Lorenzo handed her a quarter from his pocket. "You decide. I got heads."

Pasqual, annoyed, said, "No. We can arrange another dinner date. Let's go, Lorenzo."

"Nope," said Lorenzo. "Now or never. Here." Holding out the quarter, he suddenly realized that he didn't know her name. "Miss--Miss?" He looked to Odessa.

"Josephine," she said quietly. "I have a bad wrist. I can't toss the coin," she explained, not wanting to hurt the brother who may lose.

"You can," said Pasqual, wanting it to be over, went outside to get some air. He wanted to avoid showing his disappointment if his brother won the coin toss.

Josephine lifted her hand. "Close your eyes," said Lorenzo.

Up went the coin over her shoulder, hitting the window, then falling to the floor. Odessa retrieved the coin. "Heads." Jo bowed her head to hide her joy.

"Thanks, Art, Odessa." Lorenzo took Josephine's hand, and saluted his brother as they passed him standing on the sidewalk. Pasqual pretended that it wasn't a big deal, holding back his pride that as a doctor he could not swing the girl. The couple left the trio who walked to a seafood restaurant five blocks away.

Josephine was shy at first, but when she saw the canary-yellow convertible Thunderbird sports car, the coy Miss Manners disappeared.

"Do you like it?" he asked. "Senior was happy with my grades. Drove down in it."

"I'd rather ride in it than think about it."

"You got it," he said, smiling. He was glad that she was easing up a bit. He didn't want to come on too hard, too soon. She seemed shy, not aggressive like some of his favorite girls.

"So where are you from?" he asked.

"Philadelphia."

"I *am* lucky. Pasqual told me about the cutest girl he had seen in years at the hospital. You must be her."

She watched him put a file marked HOMICIDE 1939 MW on the backseat. Sadness overcame her. The suitcase, the few clothes, letters, and telegrams of her mother's came to mind.

They drove off, top down, and the night above.

19
Midnight Run

After Hugh's departure a few days before, the nights were not kind to Rita Jane. The contents of the cigar box put Rita in a frenzy. At the Velvet Gardens, she paced around Mary Margaret's room. The room where she believed she was born. She'd lie down for a while then pace to Polly's room. Only in this room did Rita Jane's anger subside.

In spurts of anxiety, she pulled Mary Margaret's clothes from the closet and the dresser drawers. Finally finding a large locked trunk. She'd pried it open to find family albums, photos, deeds, and an entire album dedicated to Angel. Notes and cards of condolences. A photo of Velvet, the slave girl with Polly. Photos of the entire family. She held the sepia photograph of Angel to her chest, the same photograph as the one in the cigar box.

The trunk's discovery unhinged her mind. Whiskey was not able to wash away the denial, the betrayal that preyed upon her heart, that she was unwanted. She was unable to sleep until she knew for certain whether a baby was buried next to Mary Margaret.

She drove to the Hollywood Cemetery to speak to Mary Margaret's grave. There she began to scratch circles in the grass and dirt begging for answers from the departed woman. The cold grave plots made her shiver. Angry, she scratched harder and deeper, scraping away the grass, clawing rapidly, soiling her well-manicured nails, upward to the heavens she prayed for forgiveness, prayed for answers, then pulled the rotting baby box from its burial place.

Holding the box, the exhausted woman kissed Mary Margaret's headstone. Her mind was flooded with memories of Mary waiting with arms open at the front door when Hugh brought her home after running away. She'd hugged her tightly that night, telling her stories of her lost loves, and wanting to marry. She'd told her how Ann and Franklin had been against it. She understood Rita's wanting to elope and marry. It was the only time Rita can remember being held by Mary Margaret.

Now, she at the tombstones of her mother, praising the hand with the dark birthmark. The mark that she covered with gloves. The mark she constantly washed, hoping to rid her hand of the stain. The hand she baked with incessantly, watching the white flour cover the dark mark, imagining it turning white from the dough. Now she rejoiced. It was her birthright. The same mark as the little Angel in the photographs. The same mark on Mary Margaret's hand.

Before returning home, she visited Polly in the black cemetery. She wanted to forgive Polly and to thank her for her love. But why hadn't she told her the truth before leaving this earth? It bothered her. She knelt with Polly, asking her if she was Angel. Polly was not to be disturbed.

Rita was afraid to open the box. Afraid there would be remains of a child in the box, that in fact a child did die after birth, and she was not Angel. She wanted to take the box into the house but Alice stood strong as a wall at the back door. Rita decided to wait in the carriage house until Alice left.

Alice was not leaving. She felt duty bound to watch over the big house. She witnessed the crazed woman ramble between Penelope's room in the attic and Mary Margaret's room, then down to Polly's room in the basement. Back and forth. Alice sometimes stood in her way to force Rita Jane to acknowledge her, but Rita was often in a trancelike state, never blinking as she brushed past.

Tonight, Alice's presence sent Rita into a panic. She held the burial box close to her chest, hiding it as best she could from Alice when she left her car to run into the carriage house. She stumbled up the dark stairway, panting out of breath, mumbling Angel over and over. The noise frightened Talbot, who was in bed with a girlfriend.

"Who's there?" he called.

"Talbot?" Rita asked.

"Yes, ma'am."

She turned on the overhead lights. He gasped at her pale, gaunt face and wild hair.

"What's happened, Miss Rita?" he cried, scrambling for his jeans on the floor next to the bed.

"What are you doing up here?" she asked.

"I was working late on the cigars downstairs with my friend. Becky, this is Miss Rita. And I, well, it got late, too late to take her home." He looked at her closely. "Are you okay? Did something happen to you?"

Without responding, she clamored back down the steps accepting she would just have to face Alice. To her surprise she found Lorenzo and Josephine parked by the garden circle.

* * *

The couple had intended to go to Odessa's home after the show. A show Lo was unable to enjoy, worrying that Josephine would discover he was in Richmond to gather information about her mother. It appeared impossible to find sixteen-year-old records, but the case became hot after the second murder. Art told him it was a clean-up job to clear some important people rather than solving a murder. Which meant he probably get nothing more than misinformation.

He tried not to pump Josephine about Miriam, but he couldn't control the thought of solving the case. Eventually he realized she knew nothing, still, he listened attentively about the beautiful suitcase with the scent of her mother. When she said it contained pictures, letters, and telegrams and Rita Jane had it, he became excited and proposed they drive to the Velvet Gardens and confront Rita until she gave it back. Senior would be proud of him.

* * *

"Miss Rita, it's me, Josephine," she yelled from the convertible.

Rita looked at the girl, wild-eyed.

"I came for my bag."

Rita felt trapped, twisting in her spot, turning from the girl, to Alice. So, she locked the little coffin in the trunk of her car. Too many were watching. "I don't have your suitcase, child. It's late. Leave me be." She rushed to the house with the girl following.

Lorenzo remained near his car. Gently, he said, "Jo, let's go."

"No!"

"We can get it tomorrow."

Alice still on the porch. "Rita Jane where have you been? What are you going to do now? Set the house on fire. You're ruining this property. Ruining it with that girl there!"

Talbot ran toward Rita. Upon seeing Josephine, he waved. "Jo!"

His mother called from the porch, "Leave her be, Talbot."

Rita scooted past Alice as if she did not exist to Mary Margaret's room where diaries and other personal things were scattered across the bed.

"Now, Rita Jane, you need to get ahold of yourself. Otherwise, I will call the police," Alice warned.

Outside, Josephine was having a temper tantrum, yelling for her bag. She wanted to call the police because Rita had stolen her suitcase.

Talbot took her hand. "Hush. Quiet. I have your bag. Follow me." He led them to the back of the carriage house and opened his car trunk.

Surprised that it was not there, he moved his hands around, as if he could make it appear. "It's here somewhere," sticking his head in to see more closely.

"There's nothing in there. Is this a joke?" asked Lorenzo.

"Nah, it's here." He got a flashlight from his glove compartment and shone light into the empty trunk.

Alice called from the porch. "Talbot! Talbot! I don't need to call your dad, now, do I?"

He ignored his mother's calls. "I'm sorry. I mean, it was in my trunk. I put it there after Miss Odessa brought it for Rita to keep. But Rita Jane was locked up in her room for days, so I kept it in my car until I saw you or Miss Rita come back to her senses."

"Who else uses the car?" asked Lorenzo.

"It's my car. No one."

Becky joined the group. "I want to go home, Tally."

"Josephine, give me a number or something where I can reach you," Talbot said. "I'll find it."

"Please find it. I don't have Odessa's address. Lo, what is it?"

"Look, why don't you call me at Art Strickland's law office tomorrow. Maybe we can nail down what's happened with the bag," Lorenzo said, using an official tone.

"There ain't no reason to have a lawyer get in on it. I'll find it. Jo, you can call me tomorrow. Here's my card." He dug in his pants, pulling out a business card that had his name, telephone number, and CIGAR SALESMAN on it.

Taking the card, she said, "I'll call tomorrow."

"Sure, sure, maybe I can take you to lunch or something. I owe you one for the trouble I caused you with the police," he said.

"That's nice. I'd like that."

Becky took Talbot's arm and snuggled up to him, while Lorenzo took Josephine's hand. Both feeling insecure after the exchange between their dates.

"It's late. Odessa is probably worried. Let's go, Jo."

Josephine was amused by Talbot's attention as they drove to Odessa's. To break into her thoughts, Lorenzo invited her to Senior's annual New Year's Day affair in Washington, D.C.

"I don't think I want to go."

"What do you mean? You owe me for the show. And what about lunch tomorrow? I'll be in the library, researching old news articles. Am I wrong to ask you to meet my family? It's as rooted as a three-hundred-year-old oak, wide as a two-hundred-year-old magnolia. Or would you rather date Talbot?"

"Yes, if he finds my mother's bag."

20

D.C. Cocktails

It was New Year's Day and memories swept over Odessa as she drove across the Memorial Bridge, through the bottom of Georgetown toward Dupont Circle. Two years ago, she had been invited to every ball the city could masquerade. Tonight, the memories made her uncomfortable, wondering where were the parading people who gathered around the newly elected or the old political stalwarts empowered by the Supreme Court's ruling. Where are they now, to enforce the change? To make it a real social policy.

Odessa stayed in touch with Senior, a lawyer deep in the epicenter of power brokers in Washington D.C. who made things happen with a telephone call. It bothered her that she was only attending the affair because she needed his help. For all her hard work, she was still just an unknown soldier in the field.

It was sunset when Josephine, Odessa, and Mat, one of the high school walk outs, whom she invited to surprise Senior, arrived to see a line of limousines double-parked. Jo had a sense of the family's prestige but had no relevant experience to gauge their social status until outside their brownstone.

A pang of being too poor and uneducated caused her to hide behind Odessa as they climbed the steps with fright. Odessa reached for her hand to lend confidence. Josephine wore a peach chiffon cocktail dress with rhinestone earrings. Her hair was swept to one side with a matching rhinestone comb.

"You're adorable and the prettiest of them all," she said.

They rang the doorbell just as Marguerite walked into the entrance hallway wearing a full-length off-the-shoulder gown. She approached a group chatting under the art deco chandelier, which had been updated with a slew of crystals. The group was discussing the large oak front door.

She informed them that her lovely son, Pasqual, loved artists and had insisted that a former fling in need of money carve various motifs into the frame and door to protect them and welcome ancestral energy. The doorbell rang again. She excused herself to open the door.

Odessa with arms open cheered. "Happy New Year!"

"My dear, you look lovely," Marguerite purred.

"It is my pleasure to be here, to see you again."

"Tat, tat." Marguerite leaned to hug Odessa as she stepped into the foyer with a timid Josephine following.

"And this young lady is...?" Marguerite managed to say while pulling away from Odessa.

"I'm Josephine Walker," as she extended her hand to the slim statuesque woman.

Trays of wine and tasty tidbits glided around the guests gathered on three floors as well as the back deck. Odessa was anxious to approach Senior before it became impossible to say a word to him. But Marguerite held the group while she inspected Jo further.

Mat, who was not wearing a tuxedo as required, caught Marguerite's eye, fascinating her as he dreamily drank her up. She smiled, appreciative of his lack of inhibition. Moving aside to allow Odessa to enter the larger room, Marguerite grabbed the lapel of the teen's suit. "Young man, you look handsome. It's not a tux, but suitable to me."

"Thank you, ma'am."

"It's Marguerite, to you."

She tried not to dissuade his youthful admiration, nor encourage it. Often her encounters with young men were awkward because they wanted so much attention from her without having the social skills of seduction, she was accustomed.

"Odessa, Senior has been asking for you. Something about someone over there he wants you to meet." Pointing to a circle of men near the baby grand.

Lorenzo shouldered his way through the crowd to reach out for Jo's hand. They kissed cheek to cheek, then he pulled her through the room to avoid his mother. He was still angry over a conversation they had that morning.

"Lo, that wasn't polite, you know. Who is she?" Josephine asked.

He whispered, "The queen of hearts, Marguerite, my mother. She already knows who you are."

Holding hands, they stood next to Senior, a short robust man distinguished by gray hair and mustache who was happily chatting with the trio of musicians, telling them of his fondest party, when Sammy, although a guest, was happy, to sing a few songs. Senior had continuously begged him to relax and enjoy himself, but the singer insisted. Thereafter he declined future invitations unless he received a limo and an appearance fee.

Breaking away, he noticed Odessa, eagerly standing next to him, and Lorenzo, whom he purposefully ignored as he welcomed Odessa.

"Odessa, my dearest, rock me," he said, holding his arms out to her. She inhaled deeply and pasted a smile, hoping the embrace would end quickly. Often, he held a woman to the point where it was no longer cordial but personal.

Breaking away, he said, "And where is Art? Is he coming? I have a few folks he should meet."

"Art apologizes and sends his regards," she said. "He looks forward to working with you on the next round." This was a lie. Art told her over dinner a few nights ago that Senior had called, extending a personal invitation. He'd refused, even after Senior suggested Art may find sponsors for his summer tennis camp tonight. Art declined because Senior often wanted him to do all his pro bono work for all sorts of folks crying the blues.

Art spent long hours with field workers needing directions, housing, and escorts on past legal cases. It took a lot out of his private practice. Odessa tried to soothe the beast of it by saying they changed history.

"Senior got national credit for our work. Even the name of the court case ignores the hundreds of students in Virginia who started the movement. Where is your name on the list for coordinating families to sign petitions, getting press interviews?"

Art's sourness churned up her last four years of endless and tiring work that was now a ball of blur. She was unable to recall the number of people she had housed or fed while they were in town. Even so, it was rewarding to be recognized for the small triumphs that survived the turmoil she'd faced back then.

"We can never slip into the past, Art," she'd told him.

She'd hoped he would attend tonight's party because she wanted him to support her in getting a recommendation from Senior for the governor's commission on integration of the schools. Art was against it, asking what good is a token, who will do what? Be a spot of color for the sake of saying the report was fair.

She'd remained quiet. He didn't mean because she was a woman. Still, he was putting her down when he suggested she save her marriage, going on about rocks and bottles thrown into her windows. But the meaning was there. It was worthier of a woman to keep a marriage than fight an unjust society.

Odessa could not convince Art that her drive to sit on the commission was not about power. He said she was lying to herself, believing that she could whip the entire South in one big selfless act, by jaw breaking those white men on that commission into swallowing her appointment as the true crusader for integration.

Having some sort of competition with Penelope LeNoire was a waste of her energy, he'd said. She needed to accept that public life was not for everyone. Bottom line, where are you going to get votes? he'd asked. People still had a hard time registering to vote. She'd heard it over and over. A problem that was not going to be solved overnight, or in one election.

She now told Senior, "Art has a winter tournament next week, but he truly sends his regards." He'd been anxious about the calls he was receiving about Rita Jane and didn't want to leave town.

"He did an extraordinary job in Virginia," Senior replied. "I need to send a check down for his summer youth camps. Excellent man. We couldn't have succeeded without his legal help. Change can never happen without people like you either. Especially your hospitality, opening your house to our staff, so many briefs before the courts in Richmond there." Senior continued, drawing a larger group around him.

"What is most dangerous are the coiled snakes in the Southern legislatures. I hear they are writing new Jim Crow laws across the entire South. Virginia is using taxpayers' money to form a commission to determine the feasibility of desegregation. In reality it's about how to keep the schools segregated. Once the schools go, then bus stations, then restaurants. Governors will stand at school doors. But we will not be turned away," he went on, very pleased by the gathering around him.

Thankful that he'd opened the conversation up, Odessa jumped at the opportunity. "I like to be on that Jim Crow committee," she said.

Senior looked at her in disbelief. He coughed.

"I need letters from you and other supporters to get my name recommended to the governor."

"Odessa, they're looking for racists. Are you one?"

"If that means promoting equality for black people, then yes."

"That commission is to save those politicians in the next election. They seek to justify segregation. My connections are no greater than yours in Virginia."

This irritated her, because Senior had been on the front pages of national newspapers for weeks at a time. Whereas the mass protests of students and civil rights workers gained them little notoriety, just the grace of God. The two stood quietly, neither one knowing what to say next.

Lorenzo jumped into the dead space. "Senior, this is Josephine Walker."

Senior nodded. He wanted to console Odessa, realizing his words had stung. "It ain't because you're a woman," he whispered in her ear. "Mint called the other day. He's worried about your safety, your life."

"Senior, this is the girl we talked—"

He raised his hand to shoo Lo away. He was not happy that Josephine had captured his grandson's heart, and he wanted her to know it.

Meanwhile, Mat canvassed the room for his black Venus. Marguerite, sensing the heat of eyes on her bare shoulders turned to meet swollen eyes filled with desire. Although she was normally reserved around people who easily expressed their emotions, she could not prevent returning his look of pleasure. He was moving toward her when Odessa grabbed his arm to hold him in place.

Odessa tried to be cheerful. "Senior, I brought Mat, a student from Prince Edward County."

"My pleasure to meet you, sir. You may not remember me. I was one of the students who testified at the initial civil trials," Mat said.

"Yes, yes. I remember."

"Thanks for pushing us. We were lost after our walk-outs. But when you encouraged us to resist the building of a new separate black school because we should do better, I was, well, I was ready to fight." The young man held his hand out to Senior.

Senior shook the young man's hand vigorously, avoiding Lorenzo look of rejection as he ushered Jo away.

"If I never try another case in my life, I will cherish the fact that children will not have to tolerate being forced to suffer denigrated schools while another group is educated with the same tax dollars, who have better classrooms, books, and better paid teachers. I appreciate your coming. I do remember the sacrifice you and others made, studying at home and church basements until we won the good fight. Stay in touch."

"I will, sir."

"Odessa, please give me a call next week, and bring me up on what you see coming at us. I will discuss with my defense committee about how to approach your letter. Can't be as foolish as dashing courage in someone."

Bursting with delight, she grabbed Senior and hugged him tightly.

Millie, the head housekeeper, dressed in a maid's uniform with strands of pearls and her hair in Marcel waves, rang a silver bell to alert the guests that the buffet was ready in the adjoining dining room. A man in his mid-fifties moved quickly through the crowd until he stood directly behind Josephine, who was waiting in a food line. He had watched the young girl during the cocktail hour, which caused Marguerite to watch him.

He leaned forward and whispered in her ear. "I miss her." He was thankful Senior kept his promise.

She shook her shoulders to make him leave her alone. The older man stepped back.

He leaned forward again. "Please, forgive me. Can we talk over lunch?"

"No, she's busy," Lorenzo was annoyed.

"We are all busy, but we take time for friends," the older man said.

Lorenzo wanted to leave the line, but there wasn't enough room to ease away without making a scene. Instead, he whispered in her other ear, then kissed it lightly.

"Miriam was my dearest friend," continued the old man in her other ear.

Jo turned excitedly toward the man, upsetting Lorenzo.

Marguerite moved quickly toward them. She squeezed in between the groupings, stopping on a few occasions to say a few words to colleagues who tried to engage her in small talk. She persisted, wondering who the man was.

The whispering man saw her coming and decided his invitation was over. He waved his hand toward a young woman in heavy makeup, with piled hair, in a slinky champagne gown whom Pasqual escorted around the party, and pointed to the front door. Then another young woman dressed in the same champagne dress joined the two in the foyer, waiting for their furs.

Josephine tagged along with the older man, making Lorenzo question whether she liked him or was more obsessed with her mother than anyone else. *Maybe she's using me,* he thought.

"Mister, mister. I am her daughter. Who are you?"

He stopped, sensing several people were watching. As gentlemanly as possible, he took a business card from his jacket.

"I'm Rhoady Johnson," pleased that she took the bait.

Reading the card. "Thank you, sir, I will call you tomorrow."

A limousine pulled up in front. Rhoady bowed and exited with the two twin dressed women following.

Intrigued, Marguerite asked, "How do we know him?

"He's Senior's client," said Lorenzo, now calm enough to speak. "He asked me to put him on the guest list to show him how D.C. can turn a trick."

"Lo, I have to see him. We can't go back to Richmond tonight," Josephine begged.

"You can stay here if you like," he replied.

Marguerite turned away to prevent Josephine from seeing her disapproval.

"Millie can fix a room for you," he said.

"What is his business?" continued Marguerite at the front door watching the group enter the limo.

"He says he may be framed for a murder that happened some time ago," Pasqual said, hoping to expose the fact that Lorenzo was working Josephine's mother's case, as revenge for his brother winning the coin toss. Lorenzo stared at him to shut up.

"Murder? Is he dangerous? Tell me, Lo." Josephine seemed happy. "Where is he from?"

"Come with me." Lorenzo took her hand and walked toward Senior, who was chatting with a House representative, the president of the National Women's League, and the police commissioner. Senior shot him an iceberg that spun Lorenzo around. She was too preoccupied with Rhoady's card to notice. He rushed with

Josephine in tow past Odessa, who was dipping her wrapped stuffed shrimp in Cajun black-eyed pea sauce. Jo wanted to speak to her, but he pulled her away to get their coats, then rushed out the front door.

21

Part of the Job

The couple drove around the Washington Monument, down Constitution Avenue, then to the Lincoln Monument. Nothing Lorenzo said interested Josephine.

"When are we going back? There's a party, and your family is there. I didn't get a chance to speak to your mother."

"What for, aren't you having fun?" he asked. "You said the last time you were in D.C. was on a junior high trip."

"Odessa must be worried. I need to go back to Richmond. Then I have to see Mr. Johnson before he disappears. I think he knows what happened." Josephine was getting anxious with Lorenzo. She suspected he didn't want her to meet Senior or Rhoady.

"Geez, you've got a lot on your mind."

"And *you*, because we went around this block three times already."

He was trying to understand why Senior ignored them. Lorenzo desperately wanted Senior to meet her, not because of Miriam, but because she was different from the other girls he dated. Aware Marguerite had no interest because of her lower social class, he'd hoped Senior would be receptive. Instead a big row at the breakfast table happened when Senior learned he'd invited her to the party. Unbeknownst to Lorenzo, it was all a charade.

With great distaste, "Is she a hooker?" said Senior. He knew she wasn't but wanted to jab at Lorenzo about his hunger for street walkers and their uninhibited lifestyle. It was one of the reasons he believed the young man could get information from the sex workers in Richmond. Death of their own kind didn't go unnoticed.

* * *

Senior had been irritable that morning because he had to sit at a round table with no corners to stack his papers or books. The dining room table for family meetings was set for the dinner party. Lorenzo looked at Senior thinking how stoic he was, as ancient as an Egyptian in a pyramid. Shuffling a stack of papers. His usual habit was to push the stacks from the corner's edge to the center of the table and back when he spoke. Lines intersected at the corner, symbolic of crosses, or disasters intermingling. They reminded him to be cautious of ideas put forth in discussions at a table.

He was equally upset that Lorenzo had taken up with Josephine, making his client's case complicated. He knew there were no ethical rules against it, but it was wrong to lead the young woman to believe love was involved. He moved back and forth a set of documents dealing with a proposal for the city to study the placement of police officers in schools where neighborhoods had high criminal activity.

Their morning gathering was constantly interrupted with Senior answering telephone calls from police or leads and tips on cases.

While Senior took another call, Marguerite said, "I understand you have a very special girl. Please be careful with sex with her."

"Meaning?"

"Besides not making babies, try not to give her gonorrhea every other week. I'm sure you have not stopped spending money at 118 G Street."

"That sucks, Mom," he replied with a sneer, setting him on a tirade of how out of touch she was.

Senior held his hand up to quiet the noise. Silence fell. After the call, he returned to the table where Marguerite and her two sons ate without saying a word.

"Any suggestions? Module, budget, methodology, administration, findings? Anything. Submission is Monday."

The silence continued.

"This girl, Lorenzo, we—" Senior began.

"I don't want to hear it."

"Yes you do, because I have to say it. This new murder investigation in Richmond is political. Years have passed and now the D.A. sees a way to ooze the festering crime out of the public's mind. People are upset about the second black woman in the river. Shabby police work and a bunch of two-cent wannabe detectives crawling with tips. We have to be careful who we talk with or about the case. The client has paid a large retainer. We have to be meticulous. Make sure I meet her tonight."

Lorenzo was confused. First it was why did you invite Josephine. Then he wanted to meet her. Senior didn't want to let on that it was to impress Rhoady Johnson by having Miriam's daughter appear. It was about the money not a daughter-in-law.

* * *

Lorenzo's anger subsided as they drove up Georgia Avenue. *Why did he dismiss us like that?* he kept asking himself. He'd had to leave the house before they hurt her feelings with a degrading look or word. He stopped in front of a greasy spoon, Freddy's Kitchen. "What do you say, dinner for two?"

"You can't be serious in these clothes," she said, looking at the tired people in work clothes sitting in booths or at the counter.

"Why not? They've got great ribs and chicken. Or do you think we should go muddy our clothes first?"

"I'm not trying to be better. Take me back so I can go home with Odessa."

He pulled away, laughing. "Okay, Okay."

He drove downtown and pulled up to the valet at the elite Hays Adam. She looked at him wide eyed, totally impressed.

"Let's do it Princess, said the frog. Kisses are free."

A valet drove Senior's Mercedes into the parking garage, while Lorenzo escorted an astounded Josephine into the lobby to register.

"Dinner now or later?"

"Later."

"Smart choice. We could have stayed and talked crap with my folks. Or allowed me to be with you alone. To know more about you." As soon as the elevator doors closed, he pressed her against the wall, kissing her long and deeply as they rode to the penthouse suite.

* * *

The cocktail party is over. Odessa and Mat gathered their coats worried as to Josephine's whereabouts. "I don't feel right just leaving her like this. Her grandmother is expecting her tonight in Philadelphia."

Overhearing, Marguerite is surprised. "Oh, doesn't she have parents?"

"No." Sensing Lorenzo did not tell Marguerite about Josephine's upbringing. And she was not going to either.

Senior rushed to Odessa. "Do you know where they have gone? Lc has my new Mercedes."

"No, but I have her bags in my car. She's staying over, so, I guess they will return soon."

Mat looked sheepishly at his new love. "I hope we meet again soon." He kissed her cheek.

"I do too," she replied. Calling her housekeeper, she said, "Millie, find someone to help Odessa bring Miss Josephine's things in. Take them to the bedroom on the third floor."

"I'll bring them in," offered Mat quickly.

Senior said, "Have a safe trip. Call me about the letter, Odessa."

"Thank you." She couldn't wait to get home to tell everyone about the score. Her mind raced over the people she'll need to contact, lots of people to form a committee to raise public awareness of her quest. She knew it will turn her house inside out but it was worth the trouble.

Senior saluted her and returned to the few guests left as Odessa and Mat left. Marguerite took the back stairs to the lower level of the brownstone, through the kitchen and pantry to a door leading to the street to wait for Mat in the dark area outside the building underneath the main stairs. Odessa pulled up front and stopped to let Mat out with Josephine's overnight bags. Marguerite stepped out of the shadow to wave to him. Mat smiled. Odessa adjusted the heat, lights, and mirror, not noticing Mat's direction.

Under the stone steps Mat lowered the bags to rub Marguerite's shoulders as their eyes filled with passion.

"So young and full of love," Marguerite whispered.

He kissed her lips lightly, then she embraced him and kissed with fire.

Odessa sat shivering in the car, waiting for the heat to kick in. After two minutes she looked up at the house to see if Mat was at the door. She beeped the horn causing Mat to pull away, but Marguerite pulled him back. Odessa put on the car flashers and went up the steps.

The couple could not stop caressing and kissing. When they heard the doorbell ring above, Marguerite pushed him away.

"Call me." She gave him a business card. "You're perfect for Senior's next project." Then she turned and entered the lower level of the brownstone. Mat hopped up the two steps from underneath and stood on the sidewalk.

"Odessa, let's go."

"Okay, kid, I thought I lost another one."

* * *

In the penthouse suite, Lorenzo lay next to Josephine pleased he had her heart. Rolling over to see the time, his pleasure turned into panic to find it was two in the morning. He called Pasqual, knowing Senior was probably mad, which was okay with him.

"Pasqual, wake up."

"Yeah."

"I'm still in town, tell Senior I will see him in the morning."

"Yeah."

Josephine mumbled half asleep, "Let's go now."

He hung up. "Not yet." Then kissed her all over her face.

"My things, Lo. My bag. Odessa has it. Let's go," she begged, sitting up in the bed.

"Why? I finally have you all to myself."

"I think you're keeping me from your family on purpose."

"Come on. Why do you think that?"

"Because we are here."

"It's beautiful here, classier. Why sleep in an old stuffy guest room in that old house? Besides. Remember the building I showed you, the Capitol. That's my dream, Josephine. One day, sitting in there."

"As?"

"As your honorable one." He hugged her.

Josephine smiled. A feeling of warmth and calm swept through her. Nothing could disturb the peace she felt inside. She closed her eyes and fell back to sleep. He brushed her hair, kissed her, and fell asleep until room service knocked at the door.

Groggy, he called out, "Yeah?"

"Breakfast."

"No, thanks."

"It comes with the room."

"It should."

Josephine awakened. "I'm hungry."

Then the cold reality of his grandfather splashed across his face. He jumped out the bed frantically, "We need to leave. I've got to get the car back. We can stop in Freddy's Kitchen, it has the best grits in D.C."

* * *

At 7:30, they parked in front of Freddy's, who was happy to see Lorenzo.

"Senior in town?" asked the potbellied man in a red apron.

"For a minute before he flies out to Alabama. Can we sit? We'll take the deluxe."

"Take them away." Freddy tells a waitress who ushers the couple to a red leather corner booth with windows facing Georgia Avenue. "Watch out for that Benz. I've been having a small problem with the police ticketing my customers." Just as he mentioned it, a squad car pulled up behind the Mercedes. Lorenzo leaped from the table to stop the officer.

"Is there a problem, sir?" he asked the officer.

"The car's been reported stolen."

"Really?!" Angry Senior would do this.

"Do you have a license?" the officer asked.

"I am Lorenzo Brooks. This is my grandfather's car." He showed his license.

After looking over the card the officer returned it. "You need to take it home."

"Sure, Officer. Thanks." Lorenzo returned to tell Josephine he had to take the car back to get his T-bird and she should order.

"It's okay. I'll wait. Don't rush into an accident." She smothered her happiness that she had a chance to call Rhoady. After he drove away, she rushed toward the waitress, asking where the telephone booth was. She casually pointed to the far end of the counter near the restrooms.

Josephine scampered to the booth.

"Hello."

"Mr. Johnson? Rhoady Johnson?"

Rhoady held back his joy from hearing her voice. "Yes, muffin."

"Can I talk to you today?"

"Where are you?"

"I'm still in D.C. Right now, I'm at Freddy's Kitchen. I can meet you."

"I know the place."

"Don't come now."

"Why not?"

"I'm with Lorenzo. He doesn't want me... He thinks..."

"It doesn't matter what he thinks. I'm paying him. I'll be right over."

Oh, boy, she thought as she held onto the receiver. *It's done.* She scurried back to the booth, hoping the old man would come and go before Lorenzo returned.

* * *

Senior was irate as he blocked the front doors watching Lorenzo park his Mercedes. Speaking from the top of the steps, "What has come over you? You said you were going for a short ride." His white shirt was open, no tie, looking as if he'd slept in a chair all night. "She's not worth it!"

Lorenzo stopped at the bottom of the stairs, hurt. "Meaning, who I love is worthless, my choices are worthless, and I am worthless."

"I didn't say that. I said *she* was not worth it! You know what her mother did for a living."

"She was a lost young woman." He ascended the steps, handing over the keys as he past the older man. Millie and the other cleaning workers stopped their vacuums to hear Senior roar.

"You have a future that will go far higher than hers. She's not even in college! Is she dull too!?"

"Stop. She's a little naive, maybe overprotected because of her grandmother."

"Nonsense. What's wrong with the girls whose names I sent you? Sophisticated, educated, with reputable families. Their social groupings will take you further than any court win. Instead—"

Pasqual interrupts the two. "Senior. You got a call. It's Rhoady on the line."

"Tell him I'll call him back! And you, Pasqual, your taste in women needs to improve too. Any talk of marriage means you get nothing from my estate." Pasqual exited quickly to escape Senior's rage.

"I guess she is better than the whorehouses you can't stay away from. What good will those places do you as a lawyer? I hope you get them out of your system." Senior walked down the steps to check his car.

Millie moved to hug a despondent Lorenzo. "If it's good loving, you keep on loving her."

He bowed his head.

"He doesn't know her, Lo. She looked like a good girl." She added.

Pasqual waited until Senior left to return. "Lo, to be honest, I'm sorry I lost the toss."

"Thanks. Got to go." Lorenzo raced to get back to the diner.

* * *

Dressed in a nice business suit, Rhoady spotted her, still wearing the chiffon cocktail dress. Everyone watched him out of the side of an eye.

"Hey, Rhoady."

"Yeah, Freddy. Coffee for now."

At the booth, he asked, "May I sit?"

"Yes, yes, of course."

"Still look as pretty as last night."

"Thank you. I called because you said you knew my mom."

"Yes, we met at a club called the Brown Derby. She was a waitress. We were in love. I gave her everything money could buy. I loved her. When I heard she died, it blew me away."

"If you were dating, why weren't you with her the night she died?"

"I was on a train headed to Boston. When an assignment came, I had to take it. I was a conductor back then. Now I am a businessman. I own rental properties here in D.C., and a taxi-limousine service, to name a couple of my enterprises. She loved me. I know she did. It broke my heart when they told me she was dead. I cried and cried a mighty storm. I've been looking for her killer ever since."

"Is that how you know Senior?"

"Sort of. I'm a client."

"Client?"

"Didn't Lorenzo tell you? He's on the case."

"Oh?"

"You mean my man said nothing. You think he loves you? Listen honey, he's been working my case since some cop named Blackstone got wind I was in D.C. I didn't kill Mimi. I need protection from that bastard. It's all political now. I hired Senior 'cause he can shake a raccoon out of any tree."

Josephine hung her head, trying hard not to show her hurt and shame that Lorenzo was using her. "Did they find anything, I mean, did Lo find anything?"

He pulled out an envelope. "Here are some police reports they got. Photos."

Surprised, choking back tears that Lorenzo had had all this information, but never mentioned it, knowing how desperate she was to learn what happened to her mother. She silently stared out the window.

Rhoady felt sorry for her. "I didn't mean to hurt you. I know how young love is. But the boy is into hookers. I know you are too good for that, even though they keep telling me your mother was a whore. And the cops have nothing on me, so don't worry, no charges are being pressed against me."

"I need to go." She jumped out of the booth, bumping into the waitress holding Rhoady's coffee causing it to spill onto the table. She rushed to the front door.

He jumped up and caught her arm gently before she left the cafe. Feeling bad, and fearful he may lose track of her.

"Hold still. You might want to see the rest of the reports I have. We dated regularly. She was a lovely woman." He pulled a gold hairpin from his jacket pocket. "Here, this was your mom's. I picked it up off the floor at the Derby one night."

The hairpin brightened her mood. It was precious.

"Come back, sit with me," he said.

He put the pin in her hair. The two walked slowly to the booth, which had been cleaned by the waitress. She pitied Josephine, for being tricked by Lorenzo. She'd seen him get rough with many girls late at night. "Watch out, honey," she said.

"Is everything alright there, Rhoady?" asked Freddy.

"Yeah, man. Send me over some more coffee."

"I don't want any fighting in here. Lorenzo is a good kid."

"I'm a client, friend of the family," he said.

Quietly holding her hand, he continued. "I know this is upsetting but I don't want them to use you for my sake. Understand?" She shrugged, too heartbroken to say anything. "Now, here are a few photographs." They showed Miriam floating in the water, outside on the ground, and in the morgue during the autopsy. Tears began to roll down her eyes. In a comforting voice, "Listen, now, I can take these back."

"It's okay. I want to see the rest."

"They say in this report that she was probably killed by poison. There are punctures to the uterus, and the rope marks around her neck were staged to look like she was hung. They think she was trying to abort a baby, at six weeks."

Jo looked at him stonily. "Was it your child?"

"No." He realized that he'd put himself in hot water. He was not sure if he could have children, but he knew he'd never had sex with Miriam.

"You said you dated."

Lorenzo parked his car a block away because there were no spaces in front of Freddy's.

"The best I can say is I didn't kill her. I put money on the ground, and it came back with Hugh's name on it. I don't think he did it, but he probably dropped her into the river." She had heard of Hugh.

Lorenzo entered. He was shocked. Angrily he stormed over to Josephine. "What are you doing? I told you not to call him."

Rhoady stood. "Whoa, buster."

Josephine started to cry. She struggled out of her seat. Lorenzo grabbed her, but she pulled away to rush outside.

Rhoady said, "It was nice seeing you, Lo. I called this morning to speak to Senior to okay meeting with the girl. He never got back to me. Thought it was okay."

"It was not!"

Freddy rushed over. "Anything I can do to help, Lo? Rhoady?"

Lorenzo ran after Josephine, looking for a cab. She kept turning away from him as she tried to get her attention. She didn't know what to do or where to go. Rhoady went to the telephone booth and called his limo service to have a car take her wherever she wanted to go.

Lorenzo tried to calm her. "What happened? What did he say?"

"You're a liar! You knew all the time about my mother. You had all the stuff, all the reports!"

"It was confidential! He's a client."

"You used me! Easy lay, right? While everyone watched. Thinking I was a poor-ass wench!"

A taxi looking car pulled to the curb. "Got a call, you needed a ride, missy?"

She jumped in and slammed the door in Lorenzo's face as he leaned over to speak to her.

Lost for a fix to win her back, Lorenzo glared at Rhoady talking to Freddy. He wanted to go inside and beat the old man.

Freddy sensed Lo's anger. "I don't want Senior coming down here getting on my back about his grandson."

"He won't," Rhoady promised, holding a steady eye on Lorenzo who continued to glare at him.

Rhoady hoped he had not ruined his chances of seeing Jo, again. He wanted to tell her how elated he was when Senior said he had found Miriam's daughter. He desperately wanted to meet her. So much so, that he paid extra for Lorenzo's expenses to court her and bring her to D.C. Not to disgrace her, or con her, but to express his love and grief for his Mimi.

Josephine went to the brownstone to retrieve her bags. Millie answered the door, telling Josephine that Odessa had left last night and her bags were locked up in Senior's office and he was at a meeting.

"Can you get them?"

"No one has a key."

"That makes no sense."

"It's his house, his rules. If it burns down everything goes with it."

Fuming, she hurried down the front steps as Lorenzo pulled up behind the car waiting for her in the middle of the street.

"Jo, wait! Listen!"

"Go away!" She jumped into the car, slamming the back door in his face again.

"Driver, take me home. Take me to Philadelphia."

Yes, ma'am," the driver said. "Compliments of Mr. Rhoady, he said to take you anywhere you want to go."

"Just take me home." Tears rolled down her face.

22

Rita Gone Mad

Art called several times to get Rita on the telephone, but Ella wasn't able to coax her to leave Mary Margaret's bedroom.

"Miss Rita, please talk to him."

"Tell him to stop calling me."

"Do you need a doctor? Are you hurting?"

Ella's constant knocking annoyed her. "Leave me be, Ella. Don't knock again!" She growled.

At night, Ella could hear her opening and shutting doors of various rooms as she walked the halls. Haunted. The older woman hadn't planned to sleep in the big house but she couldn't let the younger one suffer alone. She stayed, begging the woman to eat food she'd leave on a tray next to the door, only to collect it untouched.

The telephone messages from Ella and other day laborers at the Velvet disturbed Art. Rita Jane was acting strange, possessed, delirious.

Ella retreated to the yellow wall phone. "Mr. Art, she don't want to talk with you."

"Does she have a coffin?"

"A coffin? You mean the kind you get buried in?"

"Yes."

194

"No, sir, I didn't see her with one."

"It would be a little one."

"I really can't say. She hasn't come out of that room for days now. Except sometimes in the early morning she checks her car. Then runs back into the room."

"Is Penelope home yet?"

"Due tomorrow. But I hear a snowstorm may keep her longer."

"Okay, thank you. Wait. Tell her... No. Ella, are you spending the nights there?"

"Yes, sir, I'm afraid to leave her alone."

"Can you see in through the windows?"

"No, she keeps them shut and the curtains closed."

"Thanks. I'm going to see if Dr. Miller is available to make a house call. If he is, I'll get back to you."

"Please, Mr. Art."

Art sits in his office remembering a few nights ago, before this episode began. He had just gotten into bed with a date when Rita Jane rang his doorbell, drunk. She knew he was home because he'd left his new Jaguar in front of the garage doors. It was 1:00 a.m. and there was no stopping her from leaning against the doorbell.

"Can I come in?" she asked, wobbling into the front room.

"Sure, sugar."

"Art, I found her. I mean, I found me."

"Rita, it's late. Can we talk tomorrow?"

"No. Kiss me. Aren't you happy to see me?" She hugged and kissed him, holding his cheeks in her hands.

Pulling away, he said, "Not now."

"I want to dig up a grave."

"Tonight?"

"I need a witness." Pacing, she continued. "I need you to see what we find. What's inside the box? There's a body, no, a child, maybe nothing. I want to see. I need to dig up the coffin."

"You need a court order. And stop pacing."

"Honey, is something wrong?" Art's date entered the living room, wearing a wrapped sheet.

"Doesn't she know about me?" Rita slurred. "Cheat," she yanked at the front door.

"Not my fault, you let me go." He smiled.

"You never had me."

Art watched the backside of the woman he still loved walk with effort to her car. He felt like a coward because he didn't want to be involved anymore. It worried him. Was he responsible for her alcoholism? Wearily his high school days came to mind.

* * *

Rita did not attend private schools like Penelope and Jules. Instead, she was the royal bee at the city's all black high school. And one of the biggest teases. Art could not get near her except in the school halls or lunch room. Eventually he was able to penetrate her elitism by inviting her to his parent's lavish parties.

They understood each other. They had food on their tables when others didn't. They were the beautiful ones always in new clothes and shoes.

Hugh never liked him. Always kept watch over her, made sure that no one mistreated her. Hugh warned her that Art had nothing to offer.

"Love," she'd pout.

"Marry him. Go to Miami. Come back when you tire of sleeping in cars. Tennis is not a career to support a woman. Where has a Negro made money playing tennis?"

"It's a dream. You have to try your dream. His father will help."

"--til he works like his father, you will want. Appreciate what you have here."

"I will not be a maid."

"It's home."

Rita Jane tried beauty school but quit after a few months. She hated the gossip in the beauty salons. Sometimes it was about her. She had an air about her that made others think working on other women's heads was beneath her. Washing and pressing hair was too hard on her hands and feet. She was not used to work. Polly had taken care of her, dressed her like a little doll all her life. Now Hugh and Polly were gone.

Seemed they were grooming her to be like Polly, but she'd insisted she was not going to follow her footsteps. She'd intended to leave the Gardens but where to was still a blank. Art was traveling throughout the country and Europe, playing tournaments, attending camps. Rita Jane became very attached, forcing herself on him when he returned home, keeping up with his whereabouts, collecting news clippings on his achievements. She was his number one fan. She was obsessed.

Eventually Rita Jane left home to travel with him from tournament to tournament. It was exciting at first, new rooms, new people, new cities. Soon it became weary and tiresome sitting on the sidelines. Drinking became a cure for the loneliness and confinement of hotel rooms, or to ease her fear of other women sitting and waiting next to her on benches. At first, she thought they were waiting for other players because they were white.

When she realized they were waiting for Art too, she stayed back and drank. He came later and later to their rooms, then stopped. She returned to Richmond and cried for weeks.

* * *

After Rita left his home drunk that night, Art heard talk that someone was out to get the LeNoires. One of the cemetery workers whose son attended the tennis camps was telling everyone the LeNoire family plot had been dug up. It needed new flowers and grass covering. It was dismissed as a prank, more than likely hate against Penelope's campaign. Art knew differently. Ella was worried something new was wrong and called Art almost every hour for two days.

It's the first week of the new year, and Alice insisted Ella keep Rita in her room while she showed potential clients around the gardens. She agreed to conduct the tour when Penelope became snowbound after a blizzard blanketed New York the night before.

The freckle-faced woman, suited and perfumed, arrived early to meet the tour group. She brought Miriam's suitcase to have Ella burn it in the cellar. It was causing trouble between her and her son.

Talbot started spending nights in the carriage house alone, fretful after arguing with his mother about the missing suitcase. She told him she didn't know what he was talking about. He learned from his father that Alice had taken it from his car. Now he watched her from the carriage house carry it into the big house. It made him angrier than a tree snapped by lightening.

Promptly at 9:00 a.m., Alice dutifully showed the Kansas tour company's representatives around, leaving her office door slightly open. She encouraged them to return and spend a night before leaving the city. At the front door as usual, she gave complimentary cigars and bade them to have a good day sightseeing.

Returning to her office, she found Esther Mae shifting papers and envelopes on her desk.

"Excuse me, what do you think you're doing?" Alice asked.

"Miss Penelope called to say I should take the tithing money to the churches. Rita had not delivered them, and she's afraid the pastor—"

"No, she didn't tell you anything. Go. I'll find out what she wants."

"Ma'am, I know what I am saying. She also wants to know if a letter from the senator came for her."

"You're mighty demanding, aren't you?" Esther backed out the door. "And where is the suitcase I left on the chair!?"

"I didn't see any suitcase."

"Why not? I put one right there! Now it's gone!"

Esther stepped into the hallway. "I'm sorry, Miss Alice but I ain't a thief. That's why Miss Penelope trusts me here. So please don't yell that way."

Hearing the loud talking, Ella left the kitchen to approach the two women in the hallway.

"She's right," Ella said. "I heard her talking to Miss Penelope yesterday. There are envelopes for the church in there. Miss Penelope wanted me to take 'em, but I couldn't get down there 'cause of Rita. So she asked Esther to take the tithing envelopes to Pastor Poindexter and Pastor Whittington."

They were annual contributions to Mary Margaret's and Polly's church. Of course, it would seem like she was trying to buy black votes with the envelopes going to the black church, but that was for others to reconcile. She had to continue the tradition of her mother.

Taking a deep breath, she decided it was better to let it go. *Keeping tradition is important*, Alice told herself. She thanked Ella, though she was still upset over the missing suitcase. What bothered her the most, was the idea that the house would soon fill with campaign workers, calls, and hate mail in the next few days. Nothing but empty pockets.

She had a feeling the church money was doubled this year. Money that was needed to pay bills. Money taken from other parts of the budget, just to keep black people from being so angry, they'd vote against Penelope.

"And I'm also supposed to take the baskets to the tenants because Rita forgot. Miss Penelope doesn't want her near them now." Esther Mae continued.

"And why not!?" Rita Jane stood at the end of hall inside the kitchen doorway. "They're my basket. I'll take them when I'm ready!"

The three women were petrified by the face of a ghost with streaked lipstick, muddy hands, bare feet, in a dirty wedding gown. Rita was unrecognizable.

"Miss Penelope wants you to stay put," muttered Ella. "I'll see if the pastor will come talk to you." Ella moved toward the anxious woman, who retreated hurriedly back to Polly's room, slamming the door before Ella could reach her.

"Esther, I'll look around in my office. You go on and do what you have to do. The money will get to the churches somehow today or tomorrow," Alice walked into her small office.

"Thank you, ma'am." Esther stood in the hall, thinking about Rita Jane. She'd always been so well-dressed and sociable, invited to all sorts of civic events because of her association with the Velvet Gardens. Anyone in need of money called Rita. Esther heard she volunteered for the ladies' tea and fashion shows and the book drives for schools, only to show up for the photo shoots, taking credit for the grunt work of others, or things she never did.

Esther Mae knew deep inside she did not like her. She didn't want to admit it was jealousy though she knew it was. She knew that this Negro woman had enough money to ignore anyone she chose. All she had to do was write a check and her snub was forgotten.

Esther advanced toward the kitchen, curious, wanting to see the woman in her depraved state. Then again, she didn't want to witness how money can drive a person mad. She stopped and leaned against the wall, thinking Rita Jane had always been mad. People talked about her all the time. The good side of her wanted to reach out and pray for her, but the other side of her wished the worse. She did not deserve her help. All she did was drop in at church now and then, leaving large sums of money for the pastor, establishing herself as a pillar of the community. Yet she was nothing. Esther realized a different world existed inside this house. Esther wondered whether working at this house would cause her to go crazy, too.

The telephone rang in Alice's office. "Morning, Officer Blackstone. Benjamin. Okay. Benjamin. I had the darn suitcase here in my office. It disappeared. It's somewhere. No, I don't want any money. Just keep my boy from that black girl. The girl's nothing but a boll weevil. Got him excited. No. Miss Penelope doesn't know. Why you ask? You sure this won't hurt Miss Penelope? The Gardens is all I got now, and the reputation is important. Land won't mean much if it fills up with buried scandals. I hear what you're saying, but I have to trust you will keep my son out of it. And me. The suitcase is here, somewhere. I'll get it. Had the right mind to burn it this morning." She paused to listen. "Inside. Some clothes? I'm not sure," not revealing she saw the letters and telegrams from Jules. "Okay. Just watch out for Talbot."

Alice saw a shadow move outside the door. "Let me go now. I have some duties. I'll have my husband speak to you at the lodge tonight. Yes, sir, my pleasure."

Alice walked to the door to see Esther turning into the dining room. She spoke to her back.

"You ain't heard nothing. Did you?"

Esther didn't answer as she sat down at the dining room table to sort out the mail. Alice returned to her desk, wondering if Esther had taken the suitcase, but she wasn't too worried about her overhearing her telephone call, confident her denial of wrongdoing was better than Esther's truth, if it ever came to it. She had a right to protect her son.

23

All God's Children

Penelope had a buying fever in New York City. She shopped and shopped and shopped for tailored suits, shoes, and handbags to replace her simple homemade dresses. She wanted a stronger business style for speaking engagements.

But not one piece wiped away the gloom of missing Hugh. All during her train ride home, she longed to hear his voice. A voice that would shake away any demon working itself against her.

Calls from Ella and Alice stirred an ugly feeling. She cared and didn't care about Rita. She'd tried hard to talk to Pierre about it but he was dismissive, even hostile. It made her even more depressed because he was always kind and loving during her visits. Visits she looked forward to each year. This winter he was cold and critical.

Harping about why she thinks black people should continue to be educated in log cabins. She tried in vain to explain the state will build new schools. There was no need for blacks and whites to intermingle. They'd have the same quality of education.

"How do you know, Penelope? Did you attend a segregated school?" He sat on the sofa next to her before a large stone fireplace, with his long legs intertwined with hers. She tried to ignore his arguments, wanting only his warmth and gentle touch. But his criticism was unbearable.

"Of course not. I know from—." Although his eyes reflected the glow of the fire, she saw ice.

"--From your workers? From Rita Jane?"

She untied their legs and jumped up. "Damn it, Pierre. Believe in me. I know. I saw the schools. They can read and write."

"Learning from old books in cold, run-down, overcrowded buildings."

"Hugh showed me around."

He laughed. "You mean he drove you and Jules to the front door of Rita's schools. Only privilege she had was being chauffeured like you. Did she ever let on how it was?"

"Sweetheart, please don't shame me. I know. You don't have to be like someone else to know what is good for them."

"They are using you."

"Don't say it. Don't say I will be no more than a hawker for ignorant fools. Change is the only thing that defines life. Life is not philosophy. It is real day-to-day living, surviving. People's living standards are being eroded by the government. Next it will be our neighborhoods. We have to show that mixing and mingling makes no difference in living. They have theirs and we have ours. Simple. Why do we need to sit next to each other?" She paced before him.

"We need people. I have workers in my plants. Like you have on your farms. Why, because they need wages to take care of themselves and their loved ones."

"That's different. Working for money is one thing, but to socialize with people who are less educated and poorer is not necessary. How would you like it if a black man bought your factory and was your boss?"

"If the pay is good, does it matter? Anyway, it seems a disgrace to me, knowing you were raised with blacks, fed by Polly, and cared for by all those families who lived at the Velvet Garden for years."

Penelope stopped her pacing. "They knew their place and they were provided for and rewarded for their loyalty. Suddenly, they want what we have."

"A better life above servitude is a noble goal."

"Pierre, you sit there as if you aren't lord of the lowly. You thrive off cheap laborers from abroad. This mansion was paid with their sweat."

"Yes, but they can vote, sit in schools with other whites, ride buses and trains in any seat. Hotels rent to them. Why? The color of their skin means less than the color of money, the true equalizer."

"Stop!" She stamped her feet angrily. He laughed. "We will not let the federal government trounce on Virginia! We can't let the federal government tell us how to live. It cannot be tolerated. What will happen to our culture if, if, all sorts of people tell us what to do? And—And—"

"Recognize people as equal? Hopefully, a loftier-minded civil society. Humanism." He rose. "Let's have tea. Maybe I should tell you the story my father told me. A story about Mary Margaret and how her last child was black."

Outraged that he thinks she's a fool, she shouted, "Your father knew nothing but how to steal money!"

He laughed again, louder. She began to pound him with her fists.

"Penelope, Penelope! Stop!" he said, grabbing her small fists. Shaking her brought her back to the moment. Bursting into tears, she ran to the second-floor bedroom, wishing she was home, home in Grandpoppa's room. For once she felt like Velvet, captured and scorned by love.

Sulking, she tried to remember their first moment in love. It was Christmas. She was fifteen. Pierre's father, John, and his mother, Nancy, had visited Virginia for the holiday to reconcile the family feud over the financial affairs of the cotton and milling business started by their grandfather.

While everyone was toasting each other's great achievements, happy to end decades of strife between the two brothers, John and Zachary, over the estate's distribution, Pierre and Penelope began necking and petting in Grandpoppa Franklin's upstairs room. Only Mary Margaret noticed their absences.

After high school she moved to New York to live with Uncle John and Nancy to learn the business, but really it was to be near Pierre. After the stock market crashed and the crops began to fail from the boll weevil infestations, Mary Margaret pleaded she return, make herself known to the sharecroppers, and develop loyalty so they would stay and keep the land going.

Penelope had not been moved. Not until Mary Margaret threatened to cut her from her will. The subject irritated Penelope because her mother's will didn't provide specific names of the beneficiaries. A will that was so vague, anyone could inherit. *I leave all to my descendants.*

Descendants could mean anyone. Her mother insisted on using the words of her mother, Ann. Penelope knew this would cause unfounded whispers of other children in line.

After four years living near and loving Pierre secretly, she became despondent that they had not married. Then it was certain not to occur when Pierre went on a business trip to Europe and met a Dutch woman whom he brought home as his wife. Penelope was heartbroken. He loved her and pleaded she stay.

But she returned to Virginia to listen to Mary Margaret tell stories that burdened her soul. Penelope knew her mother had had many suitors and wanted to marry young, but her father, Grandpoppa Franklin was against it, never telling his daughter why. Secretly he feared the children she might bear. There was the possibility her heritage would be destroyed if there was any sign of Negro blood, causing the marriage to be annulled. Virginia laws forbade marriage between the races, even if it was one drop.

Mary Margaret was petite with long straight black hair with white facial features. As the only child of wealthy parents, she was a desirable, privileged young woman at the turn of the century. Her mother, Ann, never questioned Mary Margaret's desire to marry. Her concern was that her only child would elope.

She worried over the passing of the estate. There were responsibilities of land management and sales of the goods that she wanted to see Mary Margaret handle while she still lived.

Slavery was over and the workers who stayed became sharecroppers. They were given a small parcel of land to work for themselves, but had the obligation to work the vines, the chickens, hogs, and keep the horses, and cultivate and cure the tobacco. It was necessary to keep them working on a quota for their shelter and food.

Tired of the restricted life imposed by her father, Mary Margaret began a series of love affairs with younger men and some married men, many with northerners or foreigners she met while traveling abroad to protect her reputation, but the number of affairs grew as she grew older.

Ann, often bedridden, began to complain of chest pains, ailing more frequently. Franklin acquiesced to giving parties at Velvet Gardens in hopes of attracting a husband for Mary. With all the strength she could muster, Ann planned a social tea to raise funds for the beautification of Monument Avenue. There was a convention in the city that week and an open invitation was sent to the young men to attend.

Zachary LeNoire, a merchant from Alabama, was there to sell cotton goods. He was the grandson of a lesser known Confederate General and son of the biggest producer of cotton in the South. The family's business expanded under the management of his uncle in upstate New York along the Erie River, where two mills were built. The area was a hub of manufacturing goods for export.

Zachary was the sixth child with no independent money of his own. So Mary Margaret had to provide a dowry. She had an elaborate wedding at the Velvet Gardens at the age of thirty-seven. Soon after the wedding Ann died, leaving her share to her descendants, which meant Mary Margaret and her heirs.

Each time Mary went into labor, Zachary was told he could not be present at the birth. It was a family tradition. Actually, it was a precautionary window of time for Grandpoppa Franklin to inspect the child. First born was Penelope, then Jules. Penelope was blond, and Jules's scalp was nearly bare, with strands of brown hair.

Polly was elderly but mobile. She was the unofficial mistress of the home after Miss Ann died, leaving her active in the affairs of the household. Mary Margaret was very dependent upon her as was Franklin, who was nearing eighty.

He relied on her for his food and care as well as the births of his grandchildren and the supervision of their growth. He trusted her quietness, her ability to hold a secret without harm to self or others. Zachary continued to travel, selling goods across the country.

At forty-two, Mary Margaret had the last girl, two years after Jules, but she was darker than expected. No one dared to question Mary Margaret's heritage, instead, the focus was on Zak, the young man from the Deep South, who must have had mixed blood. Or was Velvet's blood appearing more and more in each child. This troubled Polly.

Quickly the little girl was swaddled and swooped away by Polly before Mary Margaret could see her.

She asked, "Let me see the girl."

"Hush, you need to sleep," Polly said. Taking a damp cloth stained with an herbal mixture, she wiped Mary Margaret's face. Slowly the tired woman drifted to sleep. Polly whisked the girl away to Master Franklin, who was sitting in an easy chair in the front parlor. Upon seeing the darker skin of the wailing child, he said, "You take her, Polly. Do as you please." The child continued to wail.

"I think I'll keep her. I had all boys. And she's too little to let go."

Zachary was in New York as instructed, visiting his family's mills, as well as meeting foreign exporters to sell cotton goods. There he received a letter from Franklin stating the child had been deformed and stillborn. It had to be taken away before Mary saw it.

They had no more children.

The child was named Rita Jane by Polly. Whenever she heard the child cry, Mary Margaret became sad, reminded of the child she'd lost. She'd ask Polly to bring the girl to the house so she could see her. Polly was hesitant, putting her off by saying she had enough children in the house. No need to care about another little girl. She was fine.

But Mary Margaret continued to insist the girl be raised in the big house, not with the boys. She took a liking to Rita Jane. A liking that Penelope despised. Her dislike grew when Grandpoppa Franklin left her an inheritance. And so did Mary Margaret.

On the train, Penelope recounted Pierre's narration in her mind, concluding he only wanted to shame her. Which reinforced her will and duty to fight harder to uphold the dignity of her mother. Pierre's retelling of an old rumor hurt. She'd heard about the lost child taken from Mary Margaret as she lay in her bed, demented, babbling about a child named Angel. How could Pierre discuss the subject now?

The rattle of the train was loud as it picked up speed in Pennsylvania, reminding Penelope that she was traveling home. Alone, old, and unmarried. Maybe Pierre had brought up the rumor as an excuse for not marrying her. Maybe he believed she was of mixed blood and he dared not to have children with her. Maybe he loved her because she was forbidden.

He'd apologized before she left, but doubts about his sincerity made his kisses stale. She couldn't wait to be home in Grandpoppa's room. The room Granpoppa slept in until the end. The memory of counting the steps to the top refreshed her mood.

She'd sat on those steps outside the door for long periods, waiting for Grandpoppa to come out of the room. She could see when the door swung open, a lady they said was black lying in the big bed. Then Polly would shoo Penelope down the steps. When Grandpoppa's time had come, everyone gathered around as he lay still on that bed, imagining the woman, Velvet.

The train jerked as it stopped in the station. She stared at her reflection in the window. Afraid of the growing lines on her forehead, the crinkle around the eyes, wondering if she is like Grandpoppa climbing stairs to lie in a bed where love was lost.

She looked at her speech, knowing she never saw Velvet, or Grandpoppa's lust. She could only imagine him climbing those steps every afternoon. Eventually laying in that bed to the end, refusing to rise, refusing to eat. Passing his last breath with memories.

Can she escape her longing for Pierre? Has she come to the same point of desperation as Mary Margaret?

She had doubts about her mother and shame about the fable. But it had to be a lie.

She tried to concentrate on the speech in her hand, underlining the important points while blocking out Jules' buy-out offer, and not allowing the idea of a crazed Rita Jane stop her. She had calls to make, a flurry of schedules to meet.

In Richmond, Talbot listened to loud rock 'n' roll in his Chevy while waiting for Penelope. The train was late and because Alice had a doctor's appointment, Talbot was sent. To make her arrival notable, Penelope had her name announced repeatedly throughout the station for pickup.

When the petite woman walked across the spotless granite floor wearing the white mink with two red caps pushing several suitcases, heads turned. She smiled at each. Pleased she had acquired some fame but not sure why they were gawking.

Talbot raced inside, flagging to get her attention. Melancholy swept over her. There was no Hugh who gently bowed to make her feel like a grand lady, while escorting her to the black shiny sedan, graciously handling the red caps and the luggage. Instead there was Talbot with his hair slicked back, in jeans and a leather jacket. He was cordial and tried his best to be pleasant as she sat in the back of the car while he managed the luggage.

Along the drive he watched her in the rearview mirror, wondering why she'd called the police on Josephine. He quickly averted his eyes if she looked his way. She requested he turn off the music and explain why his mother did not pick her up, and how his father was sowing the tobacco fields, and the improvement of his cigar rolling.

Then she whined about the loss of Hugh and how the new business calls made her anxious. How was she going to recruit help? The wages were going up. They want more of this and that, even more time off.

"What a difference a slight change in persons or events can make," she reflected.

"Yes, ma'am." Not knowing what she was talking about. "Change brings consequences that can be upsetting. Not always pleasant, is it, Miss Penelope?" In the car mirror, he saw her smirk at him. To humor her, he said, "Why, the federal government's attempt to change the South's laws is indeed wrong. Momma and Pop are right behind you on that one."

"How do you know what I believe?"

"People talk."

"Their talk is trash."

He drove quickly and silently the rest of the way. When they arrived, a gathering of land tenants whom Penelope rarely saw except at the top of the month during the accounting of crops and rents, were tending Rita's peace garden. Their faces brightened to see her but not with joy.

They were really there for Rita Jane. Holding a vigil for her well-being to ensure she didn't go off too badly. She'd been good to them with food, lending money when they were short, helping them with legal papers, or taking them to doctors.

The house was warm, and Ella was in the kitchen with her Bible open on the table. She had made some cookies.

"Welcome, Miss Penelope."

"Thank you, Ella. How have you been?"

"Well enough. Miss Rita Jane has been in the room for the last five days, so I had to try to keep the other workers busy and the cooking hasn't been bad. Can I take your coat now?" Penelope allowed the woman to help her out of the white mink.

"It must have kept you mighty warm up North. They have a nice picture of you in the Sunday papers wearing it."

Talbot brought her suitcases into the kitchen. He watched the mink being set on a chair, then retreated to retrieve more luggage from the car.

"Alice called. It's so exciting, isn't it?"

"Yes, ma'am. It has you downtown at the toy drive."

"Do we have the paper?"

"It's with the rest of the mail in the study," Ella wondered what Mary Margaret and Mr. Zachary would think about Penelope's politicking.

"Thank you, Ella. Give me a list of your work and the others' too. I need to hire new hands soon. Business is growing, right nicely." Penelope walked to her father's study with Ella following.

Talbot returned with more bags and saw the women walking down the hall. He began to believe Penelope intended to fire him or his parents. He didn't really care. So, he gathered a bundle of linens set for a laundry pick up, tucking the mink inside. Then left.

Ella continued, "You have several calls there too with the mail. Esther Mae has been good, picking it up at the post office. Lots of messages. Some not so nice, Miss Penelope. You have to be careful."

"Where is Esther?" Penelope asked.

"I think she and Rita Jane had an argument. I haven't heard much from her since yesterday. She took the day off."

"We'll work it out. Where is Rita Jane?"

"In Miss Mary Margaret's room."

Penelope stiffened and stopped midway in the hall. Then started again, stepping lightly to a forced hum to lift the heavy feeling in her chest after hearing Rita was in her mother's room. A sacred private place in Penelope's heart.

Ella slowed her gait too, not wanting to follow Penelope any longer. She wanted to hide her sadness over the change in Rita. She didn't want her eyes to reveal the discord and ransacking carried on by the disturbed woman. She was beginning to believe Alice was right about that girl coming here, turning the past upside down. Got Rita Jane looking for her mother too.

"Let me heat the water for the tea again. I'll bring it to the study."

"I noticed Rita's car not parked behind the carriage house."

"Cause she keeps checking on it. Something in it she's worried about. I stayed here overnight, Miss Penelope. I couldn't leave her alone. She kept going out there in the middle of the night. Two, three o'clock."

"It's okay. It's understandable."

Ella mumbled softly, repeating, "I stayed overnight, Miss Penelope. I couldn't leave her alone."

Penelope, preoccupied, no longer listened. There were telephone calls to return. She needed to find an overseer. Probably mail from Jules's lawyer awaited her decision, and an accounting of the cigars she needed to reserve for her campaign.

Penelope hummed louder as she walked farther down the hallway. It was a pleasant passageway. When the front door was open, the breeze swept away any onerous air. Her footsteps gained the swiftness she'd lost while away, gliding her across the familiar oak floors, soaking in the stability of Velvet Gardens. Gathering strength to deal with Rita's troubles.

Sitting at her father's desk, she flipped through the envelopes, paying attention to company names. "Wonderful! we have more reservations. Another company wants to schedule a visit of the house and grounds with prospects of booking several tours this summer."

She quickly opened one from Pierre, hoping he would be with her on election day. It was a check. "Five hundred dollars. Still stealing." She thought as she looked about the library feeling her father's deep betrayal by his brother, Uncle John. Zachary asked year after year why his annual distribution from the estate was late and lesser. Penelope and Jules took very little now that Cousin Pierre was in charge. The money was still late and in lesser amounts.

She picked up her telephone messages. Some were frightening with threats and foul language which she would pass on to the police. There was one message from George Stevens, who wanted to speak to her. Another was from her committee chair worried about the white mink. *Mink? My coat? Ridiculous.*

The corner of her eye picked up her photograph taken at the toy drive. It was positioned next to an old black and white of Miriam in a similar white mink standing in front of the Brown Derby. Gasping, she stared at the front page in disbelief. Was this a joke? "Ella!" she called. "Ella!"

Penelope rushed down the hallway toward the helper who exited the kitchen.

"Yes, ma'am?"

"Where is my coat? Where is it?" she screamed as she frantically pushed past Ella to the kitchen.

"Alice came. She said she would take care of it." But Ella really did not know where the coat was. She remembered placing it on a chair near the linen bag.

"Alice! Alice!" Penelope yelled.

"She left."

"Left? Where? Call her. Tell her to get back here." Penelope, stressed, pulled at her hair, pulling it up and away from her face.

"She went down into the cellar." Ella said, pretending she knew where Alice was. Hoping it would calm the streaking woman. Penelope pushed past her and rushed down the steps to the empty concrete bottom, calling Alice.

There was no Alice.

Ella spoke quietly to the little woman scampering up the steps. "Get rid of it, Miss Penelope. It's evil. I can feel it. I told Rita Jane you were home. She's waiting for you."

Penelope dialed Alice, but the telephone just rang and rang. She slammed the telephone down. Sweaty and tense, she climbed the back steps to the attic to her Grandpoppa's room to find solace. Upon opening the door, she was shocked into near insanity.

The room where her cherished ancestral spirits comforted her in her loneliest moments was vandalized. The bed was overturned, the dresser on its face, dresser drawers thrown, broken mirrors, and clothing scattered. Outraged and bewildered that Ella had not mentioned anyone entered the room, she screamed for Ella down the hollow staircase.

Ella withdrew inside, knowing there were no kind words that would reach any common sense in the woman. To keep her composure, she continued with the preparation of the serving tray for tea. Rattling the saucer and cup as she set it down.

She steadied her hand as best she could to pour the hot water into a teapot covered with roses, blocking out the woundedness in Penelope's voice. At the bottom of the doorway leading into the kitchen, Penelope was further enraged to see Ella quietly standing at the counter with her head bowed over the tea tray.

Screaming and screaming was all Ella heard. "What happened, Ella?! What happened to Poppa's room! Who did it!" Then it stopped.

She turned to see Penelope overstep and tumble onto the kitchen floor, twisting her leg under her body. She laid there, moaning. Ella worried, graciously lifted her.

"Oh, my ankle. Someone burglarized Poppa's room." Speaking rapidly, as if in a craze, "Did they come in a window? Did you call the police?! Was there a burglar? What happened?" She hopped with Ella's to a chair, moaning.

"No, ma'am. I believe Rita Jane was up there."

"RITA JANE!" she hollered. She was uncontrollable. "RITA JANE!"

Rita appeared in front of Mary Margaret's bedroom, with light haloed around her. The dark hall cast a pall of blackness upon her face.

"Why are you wearing my mother's dress? You're dirty. Your feet!" Penelope noticed dirt tracks on the kitchen floor, leading to the wing where Polly's and Mary Margaret's rooms were. "Why are you back there? Take me, Ella." Penelope tried to rush but found she couldn't. "Hold me, Ella. Hold me. Take me to the room."

Ella supported Penelope as they walked down the long narrow hallway, displaying portraits of the family. Rita, dressed in Mary Margaret's wedding gown, soiled with mud, cradled a bundle in her arms, watching Penelope limp toward her.

Penelope's mind was heated with killing Rita. Rage to kill over powered reason. There was on only one way to end this lie. End this lie. End Pierre's fable. Her voice became steady and cool. Whispering to Ella, telling her to get Poppa's gun.

"No Miss Penelope. No." Ella quietly tried to keep Penelope's mind from slipping.

"Get the gun, Ella!" she screamed.

Rita stepped backward into the ransacked room. Penelope limped quickly to catch a hold of Rita but fell. Hatred propelled her to grasp Ella to rise. She wanted to reach out and grab Rita Jane, who dodged her hand. Penelope fell again. Pleading with Ella to get Poppa's gun.

Ella helped her up onto the high queen bed with a red canopy. "Lay still, Miss Penelope. Lay still." Ella was very afraid.

Rita snatched the handmade quilt from the bed before Penelope could sit. The quilt was made of the family's clothing, the shirts belonging to Franklin and Zachary, and the dresses belonging to Ann and Mary Margaret. It was a quilt that Polly had slept under each night with prayers that the family stay safe. Rita hated the quilt because she believed no one should love anyone that much.

"Get out of this room. You're filthy, dirty. You've destroyed my mother's room!" Penelope wailed. "You've destroyed my mother's name!"

"It's my mother's room."

"You are insane?" Penelope looked at her with disgust.

"I know the secret."

"There is no secret, except you're a bastard child. Get out! Ella, call the police! In a low and deep tone, "And bring Poppa's gun."

Ella shook her head no. "I can't do that, Miss Penelope. I'll call the police though."

Rita Jane screamed back, "She was my mother. She *is* my mother. She IS my mother." Rita jumped to block the door.

Ella was frightened. "Miss Rita, let me go. Miss Penelope hurt herself. I don't want to fight you. Miss Rita, let us go."

"You go, Ella."

"I don't know. You'll be all right, Miss Penelope?"

"Call the police. Hurry. And lock the doors. No one is to enter the house."

She didn't want Ella to hear what she suspected Rita was going to say. Even if Rita Jane was acting strange, a rumor is like fire. Once it burns, there is no undoing the scar of people's tongues waggling about Rita Jane's breakdown or the secrets she learned about Mary Margaret.

218

"May I leave, Miss Rita?" Ella asked apologetically, afraid of the disheveled woman.

Rita stepped aside to allow Ella to leave, confident that Penelope couldn't walk away quickly. Ella ran to call Art.

"Why do you have Mama's doll?" Penelope asked Rita.

"Hugh told me. He told me that I am Angel." Rita continued keeping guard of the closed door.

"Nonsense. Angel died. Born dead. Hugh lied to you."

"Hugh gave me a box. In it was a photo of a baby. A baby with the same mark as on my hand. Look, here is a photo of the baby." She touched the locket around her neck. This locket had belonged to Velvet and inside was a picture of Mary Margaret.

"Can I see the locket?" Penelope asked.

"No! Hugh said Polly was to give it to Mary Margaret, but she didn't—she—she kept it." Pacing around the bed, she went on, "He told me that Mary Margaret had a child and Polly was to kill her or give her away."

"Hugh was lying to you. Lying because he left you. He's gone, Rita."

"I am that child. Don't you remember, just before she died, she cried and called for Angel. She cursed Polly for taking her doll. She searched—"

"Mother is dead. She was senile." Penelope was worn from hearing the lie that would not fade.

"She said Polly stole her baby doll and buried it. She buried it when I was born. When I was born. When I was born it disappeared." Rita was struggling to keep her thoughts coherent.

"Rita, stop! You're going insane. Mother suffered from dementia. She babbled about many things."

"There was a doll and they buried it as me."

Ella called Art but there was no answer. Penelope called for Ella but she didn't want to return to the room. She didn't want to call the police either because Rita Jane would be buried alive in the insane asylum if they came.

The workers out back waited in prayer around the peace garden. They could hear the yelling and cursing.

Ella's husband shouted, "Ella! Ella! Come on out of there. Before they arrest you."

Alice and Roy had rushed to the house. The land tenants who did not come to the back of the house, locked their doors and pulled their curtains, preferring to pretend they heard nothing and therefore had no answers for any questions that may arise.

Art pulled up around the circle. Everyone out back greeted him with relief. Ella let out a wail, crying as she opened the back door. "Mr. Art, thank you. Thank you. I was trying to call you."

He heard the women shouting, years of rage being unleased. Ella pointed the way not wanting to go back to the room.

"Rita!" he called. Rita!" He tried to break the intensity of the sound. He banged on the door incessantly until Rita opened it. In disbelief, he backed away from the shadow of a being possessed by a demon.

"Art, I thought she was going to kill me. Look at me. My leg is broken."

Finding composure to approach her, "Rita, come with me," he said.

She sneered. "I'm not going anywhere with you. Never again!"

"Please, Rita. It's okay this time." Touching her, he slowly put his arm around her shoulders. Art smoothed back her hair. It quieted her prattling. "Come with me," he said gently as he slowly walked her out the room with the bundle in her arms."

Penelope called Ella to come for her and to call the police. She continued to yell commands, but Ella stood in the kitchen until Art and Rita left.

Alice and her husband were in the kitchen waiting for Penelope and Ella.

"Miss Penelope, I told you this woman was going to betray you. It was coming." Said Alice, shaking her head, to shame Penelope.

"Where is my coat? The mink coat."

"The mink coat?" Alice pretended to be surprised. "You took it to New York, didn't you? I saw no coat here."

"Ella said you took the coat." Penelope looked to Ella to see if she was lying.

"Yes, ma'am, she did."

Alice could not contradict Ella, because she had taken the coat, not from the kitchen, but from Talbot who had gotten his hands on it. She was not going to put her son in trouble. "I'll find it, Miss Penelope. But I hope it's destroyed."

"No!" Penelope screamed. "Alice you get that coat back here, or I'll have you---".

Alice's husband asked Penelope to calm down as Alice ran out the kitchen to get away from the crazed woman. She was not going to be disrespected.

Roy said, "I apologize for Alice. She has some notion that the coat has turned on you. I saw her with the coat at home. We'll find it. I'll get her to turn it loose. Do you need me here for the police? We heard y'all yelling and called them for you."

Penelope couldn't make sense of anything. She started crying, then wailing, then screaming as loudly as she could. She was horrified that Rita Jane had caused a scandal.

Art was outside the house, holding Rita in his arms, wanting to take her away before the police arrived. She kept pulling away from him wanting to go to her car still parked near the circle garden.

"No. We have to take my car." He led her to his car. He wanted to clean her up before the police began questioning her.

More tenant workers gathered out back. "Thank the Lord, Mr. Art," one said.

Rita Jane had managed to hide papers in the bundle with the cigar box from Hugh. She also clutched a diary. "Art, are we getting married?" she asked.

"Sure, sugar, anything you want."

"This is not my car," she said, becoming agitated again. "My car! She's in my car!"

"Who?"

"Angel."

"I'll get it later. Let's go home first. We need to eat, change our clothes." After putting a tired and weary Rita into the backseat, she lapsed into a catatonic state clutching her bundle. He sped down the back road through the fields. He knew Penelope would file charges, anything to clear her family name.

Two police cars arrived to find Penelope, still leaning on Ella's shoulder in the grand doorway yelling, telling them to chase down Art out back.

They were unmoved. "Can we come in?"

She screamed again at them for letting a colored man get away. Art was too respected in the city for them to chase his car.

24

Arraignment of Angel

A week later, Rita, composed and well-groomed, sat in the courtroom waiting for her arraignment on charges of assault and battery, vandalism, and grand theft. She was arrested at Art's house and released on her own recognizance. Holding Mary Margaret's diary with well-manicured hands as an anchor, she silently reread the entry that was most touching and calming. *"Today, I gave birth to a precious little girl, Angel. As happy as I was, blessed by another of God's miracles, she was taken away. Never did I lay my eyes on her. They told me she could not breathe. There was whispering that she was blue or dark, I'm not sure. I asked to hold her at least once, before they took her away. I am sure I would have kept her in my arms forever. They would not have been able to take my child. I would have brought her back to life, I am sure. In my sleep there was crying. A baby was crying. It's my Angel calling me. God be with my Angel. August 14, 1910."*

The courtroom was quiet, but her mind was loud. Voices continued to bang against reason. Art was encouraging her to leave the Velvet Gardens. He'd even warned her that it may be a condition of getting the charges dropped. She questioned his sincerity. After years of their off-and-on love affair, it always came to her leaving Velvet Gardens, to wander in wonder as Hugh would say. She had money, but no dreams, no idea where to go or what to do.

Last night Art grilled her about who-what-when-where until she thought she was in a daze again. Rita wondered if George was trying to shame her with these charges in order to put her in her place as a black woman. Maybe it irritated him that she was raised under the roof of Velvet Gardens, making her less willing to be treated like other black women, or a servant, cleaning homes, watching other people's babies. Now he had an opportunity to bring her down. Art said it was more about building a scandal against Penelope.

She couldn't piece together Penelope's involvement in the school fight that represented hatred of blacks, with the woman whom she knew was a caring person toward her workers, or that she herself still cared for Penelope whom she had known all her life as a good person.

The judge's clerk entered the courtroom carrying files to place on the high bench. It was Rose Sable, one of Penelope's close friends from high school. She'd often spent weekends at the Gardens and now was working on Penelope's campaign.

"How are you doing, Rita? Are you feeling better?" Rose asked.

"Thank you. I am."

"Good. The judge will be out as soon as Art and George finish talking. They're out in the hall."

Rita nodded and smiled. The politeness ate at her. Rose reminded her of the girlish good times she'd had with Penelope and her friends in high school. Then she wondered, behind all the friendly talks she'd had with Rose whether she was like the rest of those people.

Double-sided people. Would she accept her as kin to Penelope if she knew?

"I'm sad to hear about you and Penelope. I hope it all goes away soon. Penelope told me all about it."

"What did she say?" Rita asked.

"Nothing much. Just how sorry she is. You know she loves you dearly. I'll leave you be. We'll be starting court in a bit. Take care, Rita." Rose retreated to the back chambers.

Rose convinced Penelope to turn the bed-and-breakfast into a part time campaign bull pen. The place was losing money until the noise of meetings gave the appearance that business was growing. It really was nothing more than messy papers scattered in every room and dirty floors scratched with sandy dirt tracked in by footsteps of optimism, believing that the federal government could be defied with local laws.

Rita was relieved to some degree to be away from the Velvet Gardens. Now that the holidays were over, the place would swarm again with those people. She couldn't stop thinking about their deceitfulness. Emotions were never one way.

Now, having to be tried by Penelope, she understood how it was to dislike a person and still like them. Sometimes the land tenants acted that way toward her. Still, Rita felt guilt over the harassment they suffered from George and the police who visited the Gardens several times, interrogating them endlessly.

They asked if they saw a white mink coat, which Penelope reported missing, or a suitcase that a colored child had owned. They asked if anyone had died in the house. Of course, family members and workers died in their homes, in their beds. Nothing unusual. The cleaning people and some laborers told about a runaway slave girl dying there. Ran up in the attic like a raccoon and hid. Died of suffocation. Now the place had spirits.

She knew as far as those workers were concerned, white folks were the real ghosts, invisible in their daily struggle to survive. They learned to avoid seeing them, speaking to them, and if trouble existed, they saw nothing. Saw no murder. Not when food and shelter were hard to come by.

* * *

Outside Judge Powell's chamber door, lawyers and clients packed the hallway, some leaning against the two-tone beige walls, talking in low monotones, posturing their bodies, with droll facial expressions to prevent revelation of their thoughts. Art awaited George's arrival.

They knew each other fairly well, having tried cases against each other. Art found George to lack ethical values, desperate to take on high-profile cases for self-aggrandizement. He was a son of an aristocratic family dating back to the early 1800s that was no longer independently wealthy. He'd changed his practice from estate planning to criminal prosecutions, looking for headlines. Lately he had become overly aggressive and zealous.

Neither disliked the other, often chatting at various legal events. George thought Art was lazy. Taking advantage of his father's reputation as a fighter in the trenches for the last fifty years. A tennis bum at heart. Problem was, judges danced lightly around him when he was on a case, making the prosecution work harder for a bite.

They agreed the charges could not be proven unless Penelope testified. She'd refused. Alice and Esther Mae seemed to be on the fence, but they wouldn't testify, more out of compassion for Rita. Even so, George was driving hard, which made Art dig for dirt to shake him.

"I heard Blackstone was pulled off the James River cases because he continued to accuse Jules LeNoire, a white man of killing a black wo-"

"It ain't always about race, Art," George cut him short.

"Why did LeNoire have the Walker girl arrested, then brutally beaten?"

"It's a different set of facts. It's not about the Walker girl, as much as it is to keep Penelope safe. She claims her life is in danger."

"Bunch of acorns. She's running for office and needs splash. So she gets the police on the hook about her victimization. Lack of police protection. Now she's using Rita, another black woman."

Studying his polished shoes, George said, "Rita Jane has credibility issues. She can't beat the charges. Digging up grave sites, talking to dolls. She's an angel. She needs hospitalization."

"She is Angel."

"You too, Art?" George smiled.

"Do we need to fight this one?"

"Here's the deal: I'll drop all charges except count one, reducing it to trespass. No fine. No time. Just a warning. The judge's clerk opened a door near where they stood. "Gentlemen, the judge is ready."

"We need a few more minutes," Art replied. After the clerk closed the door, Art stepped away from George.

"Come, let's walk. I know you're pushing this case to smear Penelope's family. Hoping she'll drop out of the political race, if at trial, you prove Rita's madness is connected to the LeNoire's history. And if that doesn't work, you'll keep pressing her workers to break and squeal on Jules or Hugh about Miriam Walker. Either way you win, as long as you get press. It's not about Rita Jane needing help."

Hesitant, George took a stance, not wanting to move.

Art continued, "Spoke to a source about your affair with Miriam Walker."

"Prove it."

"Don't have to when there are others who can." Art looked directly into George's eyes.

George decided it was time to walk the corridor. Art followed.

"Not worried about your sources, Art. What do you want?

"All charges dropped."

"No. She needs hospitalization."

"To keep her from talking about you, Jules and Mimi. Not going to let it happen. Even if you had nothing to do with her death, the fact she met you, found dead and pregnant, lends itself to irrevocable damage to an aspiring career."

George turned and looked at the wall to avoid eye contact. "There is NO EVIDENCE in the file that woman was pregnant."

"The only reason Penelope pressed charges was to have Rita Jane committed, jailed, anything to destroy the woman's reputation. She wants people to think Rita's insane. Insane to be talking about blood relationships. But the last thing she wants is a trial."

"You sound like the ghost she talks about. I have a reputation too."

"Come on, George. You know Penelope isn't testifying because it will blow up her family in the papers. No one else is going to talk. If you think Rita's going to rattle on about Penelope or Hugh or Jules in some murder plot, you're wrong. At best you'll get rambling about her birthright."

"Okay, I'll drop the charges. But if she is arrested again, we fight."

"Deal."

* * *

After the dismissal of the charges were read into the record, Art and Rita Jane walked the few blocks to his office.

He explained, "Part of the deal is for you to vacate Velvet Gardens. We'll have a civil standby while you collect and pack your belongings."

"Why? It's my home. I can't leave. All my life is there."

"It happens."

"Art, please. I own part of the estate. Here, wait." She stopped and pulled out a document from her purse, pointing to a phrase. "It's Mary Margaret's will, same as her mother Ann's will. 'All descendants of her body shall take...' I am Angel."

"Here we go again."

"You've seen the diary, the papers, and the gold necklace. Hugh told me."

"Polly is dead. Who's going to take a blood test? Penelope, Jules? At best you may get some similarities. Come on, let's get something to eat, Cinderella."

"If you don't believe me, then let's part company now."

Angry, he replied, "You need my company. Listen to yourself! You were born white, but look black, and killed at birth, then you found a buried Angel that you believe is you. Does it make sense? Now you want them to sell that big old house, if they fight you? You believe Hugh and Jules, or Penelope killed the Walker woman. So you invited her daughter down to set up a trap. They will bury you alive, smear you until you commit suicide."

"Who's scared? You or me!? I don't believe you. I know them. Is that why you're a lawyer? So scared that the best way out is to scare others?" Art ignored her walking faster. "Who? Who?" she continued.

Her words were like needles in a voodoo doll. Was he a coward to force her to leave, afraid of a loss at trial, afraid they'd commit her for life? Or was he acting out of reason.

Rita wondered if he was afraid of George, or any white man. Maybe his dream of Wimbledon was his way of surmounting it. Winning something they could not defy, negotiate. His refusal to answer, deflated the magic bubble that she once believed would allow her to escape with him to another world. She continued. "Who Art?"

"Anyone, Hugh, Penelope, or George."

"George?"

"Forget I said that. Let's put those papers in my safe. And George gave me the inventory from the search of your vehicle."

"Who gave them permission to go in my car?!"

"They don't need permission once you're arrested, but since it was on the property, they got a warrant to impound it. The baby coffin had no human remains."

"Exactly, because I never died. Polly killed a lamb. A sacrifice to God, instead of the child. She made a doll for Mary Margaret who grieved for the lost child."

She began to appear confused, dazed, and lost. Art worried that she was about to melt down again. She shook her head back and forth, rubbing her temples. He took her in his arms, holding her firmly, to stabilize her stance.

"I am Angel. Aren't I Angel? I showed you Polly's note and the diary. They treated me like a black, without family."

"You are black."

"I know, but they are too."

"They will put you away forever before they turn back to black."

"Then I am white."

"Not hardly."

"Rita, you were loved. That means more than anything.

"Means nothing. Nothing."

"I forgot, a letter from Jules came to the office yesterday." He handed her a blue aerogram from France.

Dear Rita, My sail was wonderful. Your troubles saddened me. A letter was at my flat when I arrived. Before the sun could set again, I dispatched a warning to Penelope not to try you. Hugh told me everything that night with Miriam as he drove me to the ship in New York. He cried his heart out about having too much loyalty to Penelope. What an awful night it was for him.

Rita Jane walked quietly, holding Art's arm as she silently read. *There are many expats and Southern soldiers still here after the war who long for American food. They will adore your cuisine, chéri. I know the perfect place to start a café in the left bank.* She stopped. Disappointed.

"Hugh didn't tell him about the box, about my being Angel. I'm not going," she said.

"Okay, stay and snivel. Let the entire city talk bad about your arrest? The tongues will wag a legend out of jealousy and envy that you went crazy in that big house, thinking yourself better than the rest. Or you can take your lovely fashionable well-bred self to Europe and write home about the French they will never know."

Blackstone passed by in a squad car. He made a quick U-turn. Yelling out the window. "Heard it was dismissed."

"Yeah."

"Too bad. I was looking forward to hearing testimony about that Angel child." With a sneer, "Always knew Penelope was a lunatic."

This rattled Rita, whose eyes squinted with distaste at the officer who waved and drove off.

Art continued walking briskly. "There you go. What are you going to do? Be a princess or a lunatic?" He hoped he'd been right in resisting the prosecutor's call for psychiatric observation.

25
Flip of a Coin

Weeks passed as Josephine spent days in her pajamas, miserably counting the Forget-Me-Nots in her bedroom's wallpaper. At times she played the radio loudly to drown out Grandma Philly, shaming her about leaving home for a suitcase only to lose it. Or hearing her talk on the telephone with friends explaining how Miriam's spirit got ahold of the child. Trying to ruin the little girl. Her mother was never worth anything to anyone.

"You can't bring your mother back to life. Leave it be. You don't need to know anything about what happened to that woman." On and on each day.

Lorenzo called and called. At first Grandma Philly was irritated.

"Why you take up with that boy, knowing he ain't your kind? It puts a bad feeling in you. Makes you feel cheap."

"Who is my kind?"

"Can't you see, you were used only for his pleasure."

"The truth is that it was right fine, mighty okay with me too."

She was sorry she'd even mentioned meeting Lorenzo, or needing money to buy the cocktail dress for the affair. Nothing she said made sense to Grandma Philly.

But Lorenzo didn't give up. He began to charm Philly. Soon she became irritated that Josephine refused to speak to him. When the phone rang, the older woman began to expect Lorenzo's quiet voice asking about her day. She appreciated the attention.

Then Vicky, a school friend who lived across the street, started stopping by every afternoon after work, or calling after supper to talk about the latest song or hairdos. She was about to split in two, waiting for Josephine to talk about Virginia. But Josephine stayed quiet. Never saying more than yes or no, contributing nothing to stop Vicky's questions.

Finally, having waited long enough, Vicky asked, "So where is the suitcase? I want to see the stuff your mom had."

"It's coming." Josephine was disappointed that Talbot had not called yet. Odessa did, to say she saw the young man while on an errand. He told her he was shipping it the next day. It never came. Then Lorenzo called to say he had the suitcase and could drop it off. Josephine didn't believe him.

"What's in it? What's it like?" Vicky pressed on.

"It's very special. It has a silk lining with little pink roses. Telegrams, some love letters. I think from someone who cared and loved her dearly."

Really excited, Vicky asked, "Who?"

"A man named J. That's all I know. Maybe an ambassador. He lived in France."

Then one snowy evening before dinner, while Josephine was watching television, the doorbell rang. Grandma Philly peeked out her bedroom window to see Lorenzo in the falling snow holding a white suitcase. She was as curious as everyone else about this suitcase. Josephine described it as holding the entire world.

"Answer the door, sweetie," Philly called, knowing it to be Lorenzo, arriving as they planned.

Depressed, still in her pajamas, Josephine went to the door. "Who is it?" Peeking out the door's window, her heart jumped at seeing Lorenzo standing on the porch of the two-story row house. After a few minutes lapsed, her grandmother called again.

"Did you open the door, Jo?"

Josephine slowly opened the door and stood quietly. Smiling, he said, "Hi. I bet you thought I would never find you." She looked down at his snowy shoes.

"Can I come in? I have your bag."

Philly had descended into the living room, standing behind Josephine. "Welcome him in," she said. "Come in, it must be cold."

"Thanks." He entered the small living room where one could lean forward from the stuffed forties' furniture and easily turn on the mahogany floor-console TV.

Josephine said nothing. She sat on the couch and reached out for the suitcase, which he gently handed to her.

He was very happy to see her. "Are you sick?"

"No." She didn't open the suitcase because she didn't want him to see her emotions. She just hoped everything was still in it.

"Can I get you tea or chocolate?" Grandma Philly asked, standing in the dining room doorway.

"No, thank you," he said. "Do you want to know how I got the suitcase?"

"No." She already knew; Odessa had told her that he'd made a visit to Talbot. Probably paid him.

"I was just preparing dinner. Will you stay?" Philly asked.

Josephine was shocked. "Grandma, he has to go."

"Sure, I would love to have dinner with you."

The older woman clasped her hands and smiled, then left for the kitchen.

Josephine felt trapped. She wasn't dressed and couldn't run outside, and if she went to her bedroom upstairs, Grandma would make a scene.

Lorenzo whispered, "I miss you."

"Miss using me, I bet. What do you want with me? I'm not very smart or Miss Snob Hill."

"I'm back at school in New York, not far from you in Philly. Why don't you come visit me on the weekends?"

"No."

"Then I'll drive down to see you."

"What for?"

He was silent. Biting his lower lip.

"Why didn't you tell me that I was just a job, Lo?"

"I apologize. My dad apologizes. It wasn't intentional."

"Sure it was, because how else could you get the inside on my mother?"

"Not the reason. Not to lie either, but I wanted to get inside you. Meaning I could have worked the case without meeting you—but I did. Then you were not her. You were you. Meaning you, I saw you as a very—someone I liked, a lot."

Her eyes closed, shutting out his handsome face.

"I asked you to the party because I wanted Senior to meet you, not because of Miriam, but because you make me feel so different from the other women I've dated."

Josephine twisted on the couch, trying to keep a firm resistance against his charm.

"And what was the excuse for taking me from the party? Too ashamed of me?"

"No. I wanted to be alone with you."

"You'll find girls your type."

"But you picked me," he said. "You tossed the coin."

"Your coin. Probably was fake."

"Even if it was, I remember your face was filled with so much happiness when the coin landed."

"That was then," she said.

Grandma called to them. "Come in, Mr. Lorenzo. The table is set. You, too, Jo."

"Thank you, ma'am."

Josephine sauntered into the small kitchen, warm and smelling of freshly baked biscuits, mashed potatoes, and roast beef.

"It's simple but the gravy is good," Grandma Philly said contentedly. "It's a pleasure to meet you. Josephine has spoken of you so much."

Josephine hid her smirk, knowing the woman has said the worst kinds of things about Lorenzo.

"She's my heart. I hate to see her hurt. I remember when she first returned from Richmond, crying night and day in her room. Glad you've come to heal that soreness."

Lorenzo bowed his head. "Thank you for inviting me." He watched Josephine as she sat at the table waiting to be served. She still would not directly look his way. He understood Josephine's innocence; she'd been so sheltered, it was why she'd never thought of going to college. He watched her grandmother prepare their plates, feeling self-conscious that she probably thought he was some fast guy who'd stolen her precious girl's cookies.

Speaking over her shoulder while filling plates with food from pots on the stove, Philly asked him, "You ever hear of a lawyer named Senior Brooks?"

"Yes, that's my grandfather."

"Well, he's been calling here."

"Really?" Lorenzo was both surprised and pleased that Senior was reaching out to Jo.

"He wants to talk about the police officer who beat up my baby, there."

"That's great," he said, truly elated.

"Josephine doesn't want to bother."

"Grandma, stop. I can talk."

"Why?" Puzzled, Lorenzo looked at her for an answer.

"She thinks you are involved," Philly said.

"I am not. It's a surprise to me," Lorenzo insisted.

"She would have to see you," Philly said. "Now you're here. So what can we do?"

"I can talk." Josephine pouted.

"Then speak up."

"I'll think about it," she said, picking at her food. "I have to go back to Richmond anyway to talk to Art about some papers about my Aunt Vera."

Grandma Philly became quiet at the table, uncomfortable after hearing Vera's name. "We can worry about lawyers later. They bring nothing but trouble."

"Dad's in D.C., call him," Lorenzo told Josephine. He ignored Philly's change of mind.

"Odessa wants me to talk to Art first," Jo replied.

Grandma Philly stood. "Excuse me, I have to go take some medicine before I eat. Please say the grace."

In her bedroom, she sat on her bed, head heavy with the idea that Odessa, some strange Southern woman, was influencing her baby girl. She opened her Bible and prayed that the child wouldn't go back to Richmond.

After dinner, the two washed the dishes and talked into the late evening on the couch. Before leaving, he reminded her that she'd tossed the coin. And there was no going back. She laughed. Standing at the front door, he longed to embrace her, but she kept a slight distance.

"I'll send you more reports when I get them, if you kiss me once again," he said.

"No, it's okay."

"I'll send them anyway." He kissed her cheek then walked down the snowy sidewalk, then backward to look at her as long as possible. She shut the door softly with a smile, then watched him from the window drive off.

The telephone rang.

"It's Vicky. Geez, who is that guy? And that Thunderbird. Wow, where did you meet that love? Was that the suitcase?"

Josephine couldn't get a word in between the questions.

"Why didn't you tell me about him?" Vicky asked.

She was happy that he'd brought her scrapbook too. Odessa had been impressed by it. It contained newspaper articles she'd secretly torn from the library archives. Bad, but she didn't care. Her train ticket. Wrapping from a perfume box from the suitcase. The hairpin. Flipping through the book, she told her friend about the news articles in the *Richmond Black Press* and the *Baltimore Sun* about Miriam. She read, 'The James River, winding like a snake into the heart of Virginia. Today it continues to be polluted with venom from murder.' Blah. Blah. And so on.

"It has a picture of her," Josephine continued, "in a waitress's uniform. Young. Pretty. Black, shiny, thick hair. Wavy and pulled up in a pompadour in front." Reading the clipping, she said, 'The police received more than one hundred tips but have no suspects yet. The Velvet Gardens owners were interviewed. No witnesses remember seeing her at the bed and breakfast.'

"I want to hear about the guy," Vicky said.

"Lorenzo? He's just a friend."

"He must like you. He came in the snow. And he was there almost three hours."

"I'm just an assignment."

"What?"

"There is no value or truth to him. I was an opportunity. I don't know if I like him anymore."

"Josephine, I'm coming over there now. He has a car. He's cute."

"And money. His family is well-to-do. They don't like me."

"So what?"

"Vicky, please!"

"I'll chase him away for you. If you really don't want him."

"I just want to concentrate on finding out what happened to my mom."

"You're not going to find the killer. You're wasting energy going to Richmond. You need to get that guy instead."

"I want to know more about her. You have a mother. I never did. I want to know who she was, where she went, what she liked. I am her. I didn't go there to find a boyfriend. Mothers are love. They teach you love. How can I love?"

"All mothers don't love, Jo."

"Oh, Vicky. Stop trying to win."

"You can't live all alone with your nose in some river. You have to find love inside yourself. Around you. That's what mothers teach."

"I'll talk to you tomorrow." Josephine hung up. Then she flipped through scraps of newspapers not pasted down. She picked up an article about the Velvet Gardens high-society women who went there for treatments. They paid lavishly to stay overnight. *What kind of treatments?* Josephine wondered as she closed the scrapbook.

26

The Boll Weevils

At 4:00 p.m. on a Sunday afternoon in late May, George Stevens entered the front doors of Velvet Gardens with his wife Lara. He balked at attending, but Lara insisted that a silly murder case should not come between them. Secretly, he toiled with pressing charges against Penelope for illegal abortion services, and murder of Miriam Walker.

His jaws locked tight when he saw her in the crowd chatting. He had tried to talk to her informally about Miriam, but she was always indisposed. Then retained a lawyer who accused George of harassment for his own political gain. It was a stalling tactic until after the primary election next month. She could not afford publicity about Jules' affair, Miriam, or Rita. He despised her ambition to enter politics.

Two of Penelope's campaign staffers graciously took their invitation and offered a cigar if they made a contribution. George declined, fearful of a conflict-of-interest.

"Lara has given plenty," he said with a false grin.

Pulling her husband further into the crowd, Lara was pleased to see the first floor filled with guests milling in and out of the hallways, dining room, parlor, and the library.

Alice was relieved to see the couple and approached with as much bravado as she could muster from the heavens to welcome them. She'd heard from Blackstone that there would be trouble.

George bowed his head to hide an urge to laugh at her freckles that seemed to be frantically jumping around her cheeks, betraying her alliance with Blackstone. Her eyes sought empathy for the secret pact she'd made with the officer. She had to protect her son.

Alice charmed Lara while George moved further into the crowd. Lara was pleased at the turnout. She'd tried to arrange for the luncheon to be held at the Jefferson Hotel's ballroom, but not even a D.A.'s wife could swing a hefty fifty percent discount for a good cause.

Nervous and upset over an earlier argument with Penelope, Alice confided in Lara.

She is overworking herself," Alice said in a solemn tone. "I'm afraid she will exhaust herself. The newspapers aren't letting go of Rita Jane's breakdown."

"Oh, lovey, I understand. It's shameful."

"What I mean is the cartoons and everything are making it hard for her to raise money. She weeps over the news coverage. Rita Jane is a scandal; the cartoons with the mink coat dripping blood is awful. You know, her lawyers advised her to file a libel suit if they continue."

"Lovey, I stay out of men's stuff, that's why I am thrilled that Penelope is running. She'll find a way not to be thrown out with the trash. How is your boy? George says he's making a name for himself."

"He's fine. Thinking of going to school out West.'

"My girls love him. His hair all slicked back and that crazy music. Hoo-ee! Can't take your eyes off him."

"Thank you, ma'am."

"Keep him from those black girls," Lara whispered, giving Alice a cold warning. "My girls are precious to me. Hate to be mixed up with that race stuff. He's always welcome to come over and visit with them. I want to keep them happy, too."

"Thank you for the compliments," Alice said. "I will tell Talbot how much you think of him."

"Thank you. I must join George." Lara grinned wide and long as she moved away to mingle in the full house. Alice stared at the woman who'd never said more than good morning to her. She vowed never to speak to her again after insinuating Talbot was no more than a toy for her three teen girls. She knew she was just trash to Lara, but Talbot was a prize to all the girls in the city.

Alice tried to tame her rage over the insult. But it only added steam to the morning argument she'd had with Penelope. Blackstone had called Alice to warn her there would be unexpected guests. So, she asked Talbot to stand watch for intruders. But Penelope was against having Talbot meet her guests whom she considered pillars of pristine society. He was not to stand out front. Alice took it to mean Penelope was firing the him. The mother hoped her son would take over the management of the farm one day.

"Just ain't right, Miss Penelope. Talbot worked here since he was a small boy helping with the harvesting of the crops. Learning to roll cigars, selling them downtown."

"I'm not firing Talbot. He can still handle the cigar selling. Just need someone who can handle my work inside. I need someone who will grow into being like Hugh. I need a chauffeur. I can't listen to that loud crazy music."

"It's because you saw him with that black girl. You think he likes black folks."

"It wasn't appropriate for a fine young man like your son to be sitting and talking with that girl down by the water."

They were referring to the day Josephine and Talbot were seen downtown along the river.

Odessa called several times urging Josephine to return to Richmond. Each time she called, Grandma Philly answered, then would turn up the radio to keep the young girl from hearing. Josephine promised Art for weeks she would return, then without notice change her mind.

One Saturday, Jo overheard her grandmother's voice yelling and cursing louder than the radio that they should stop calling. "She's had enough trouble down in Virginia. Are you trying to kill her like her mother? She ain't coming back. I know all about the money. We don't need it. They keep writing for her to come there. Why don't they come here? That money has been sitting there a long time. Let it keep on sitting."

Overhearing her rudeness to Odessa, Josephine picked up the extension in the living room. "Hello? Odessa?"

"It's me, dear."

"Hang up, Grandma."

The older woman was sore. She stood in the doorway, wringing her hands, watching her granddaughter cheerfully speak with Odessa. She wondered if she had lost her love to another. Oh, how long can she keep her from that money, and from leaving her?

"Art, remember him? His father was your Aunt Vera's lawyer. He's been trying to reach you since you left. He sent letters, and called a few times."

Josephine didn't know what to say, so she lied. "I didn't know."

"There is a trust set up for you to attend school. He is anxious that you get it. You have to be at least twenty-one and attending a college."

"Really?"

"Once you are enrolled you can get a lump sum and then monthly allotments. I think you are getting money now."

"No, it's from my father."

She looked suspiciously at Grandma Philly, who turned and walked back into the kitchen, to bang pots and pans on the stove to running water to drown out Jo's telephone discussion.

On her first day back in Richmond, Josephine went to the rapid rocky river to toss flowers in memory of her mother. Talbot was making his rounds, delivering cigars to a few shops when he saw her.

"Hey you. Hey, Josephine!" He yelled, "It's me. Talbot."

She waved to him as he approached. Happy to see her, he'd left his car running on the side of the road in park.

"You're back. Why didn't you call and tell me that you were coming again?"

"I wasn't meaning to meet anyone. Just come and go. I have business with Mr. Art."

"Yeah? Why are you down by the river?"

Holding a handful of flowers, Josephine said, "Flowers for my mother. I thought it was a good idea. And you?"

"I'm delivering cigars. How about lunch?"

"Lunch?"

"It's okay. We can drive out to a nice place, where black folks are welcomed."

"You sure?"

"Where are you staying and how long?" he asked her.

"Maybe a week. Odessa's trying to get me to enroll at Virginia Union."

"Did you get your suitcase?"

"Yes. Thank you."

"I was hoping I didn't do wrong. That guy you were with cornered me one night in the carriage house, snuck up on me with a gun."

"No!"

Laughing, he said, "Kidding. He paid me to hand it over. It was enough to buy new rims for my car. Hope you didn't mind."

"No."

"Unless you wanted me to personally give the bag to you."

Josephine looked away, not wanting to see if he was playing with her feelings.

"Look, I know it seems scary but I ain't like the rest. I feel really bad about how that cop treated you. I know good people here. I know Mr. Art too. Call me. If I don't answer, hang up. Easier if we meet here tomorrow."

"I can't. I'm to see Mr. Art tomorrow. Thank you anyway."

He backed away. "Okay, see you around. Hey. Hey!"

"Yeah?"

"Miss Rita sent a letter asking if you got your suitcase. I wrote that you did."

"I know. She sent Art a picture of her in Paris wearing a white mink coat."

"Really? Wow. Okay, well, call me." He waved, knowing it was he who had taken the mink coat to Art's office to protect Miss Rita after her arrest. He looked back, wondering if Jo would survive in Richmond. Ain't much luck here for outsiders.

This short meeting was watched by many passing cars. Some circled around a few times. It got back to Alice, Penelope, and Blackstone. Penelope went off into a tantrum of mistrust. She no longer wanted Talbot in the house or driving her anywhere. She was suspicious that he'd taken the mink coat, believing that anything missing was in his possession.

After Lara's comment, the argument she'd had earlier with Penelope played over and over in Alice's mind. It began an hour before the luncheon. Penelope had passed by the office and heard Alice talking very heatedly on the telephone. When Alice inadvertently said Blackstone's name, Penelope walked in filling the room with heavy perfume. Alice hurriedly changed her tone of voice and pretended she was calling about a linen delivery to the house.

"Any trouble, Alice?" Penelope asked, feeling mistrustful of Alice lately.

"No, no. Just the linen service bill is getting high with the stream of penniless campaign workers rooming upstairs." Every day she told Penelope they needed two cooks to feed them. They were also wearing out the cleaning staff.

"Oh so right, Alice, the house is filled. Full of life. Even if they aren't paying." Penelope shot back.

"The books show you're spending too much money for their keep. Going bankrupt pretending there's spare money for more servants, carpeting, drapes, and chinaware," Alice retorted.

"We will manage. We will turn all those ugly rumors around. The ghost scandal will die down, and the election will soon be over. I'll have you take care of the Velvet house more and more when I am handling my public work." Secretly she wanted to spend as much money as possible before turning over the accounting books to Jules's lawyer, and now Rita Jane's lawyer.

"Just moving the feast from one set of parasites to another set of boll weevils," Alice said. "Mary Margaret didn't raise you to be out there flirting with the government."

Penelope's friendly face paled. "You may think of me as a wilting wildflower of some kind, but I like what I'm doing. They will leave. Right now, the house must have people, living people. Talking, laughing, singing. At any expense. No ghost stories. Or Talbot stories."

"Penelope, that's my son, my only son. I'm not feeling comfortable with you using his name that way."

"Every child needs boundaries. I mean no harm to him. He should know what can't be tolerated. That girl is trouble. Rita meant well. Then that girl stirred Rita into delusions." Her eyes teared up. She turned and rushed out the room before Alice could say another word. She didn't get a chance to tell her what Blackstone said.

* * *

Alice, uneasy, now stood guard at the front door, looking over the front grounds, often turning to survey the guests inside the big house. She tried to persuade Penelope to hold the event elsewhere. Penelope insisted she show her home was not haunted. Worse was having the new man, Earl, pester her about supplies, the names of other workers, on and on. Earl had been hired without any references, appearing to be a good white man in his fifties, well-mannered, and dutiful in his job. But her intuition did not trust him. Penelope saw him as a boost to her credibility with working-class voters. Alice saw him as a replacement for Talbot.

Penelope mingled with guests in the dining room as George and Lara entered. She rushed over to them with arms stretched in a dramatic fashion for all to see. "Welcome! The event would not be worth talking about if you hadn't come. Oh Lara, what a lovely dress."

They hugged. "Thank you, dear."

"Praise the Lord, the Rita Jane affair is over. You can't believe a word she says. I'm disappointed treatment isn't required. Hospitalization would have done her well.

Then again, it may end well. The French are very adept at dealing with head problems. Gossip says she disappeared after being lynched out front. Another reason to have had her hospitalized. To show she is alive and unwell. I guess one must accept truth never gets its day in court."

He responded quietly, "The records are sealed, Penelope. It was part of the deal."

Fawn with her husband, Mr. Charles, the county school superintendent, interrupted. "Oh, I must say, you looked fabulous in the white mink. Front page and all with that Negro woman trying to copy your style."

"Good day, Mr. and Mrs. Charles." Not pleased but cordial, Penelope said. "That's old news, Fawn. Old news. Very happy to see the superintendent here in support of my campaign."

"It's our civic duty to attend. We appreciate like-minded Southerners who stand for quality education," said Mr. Charles. "We do not need Washington's help to manage our affairs. Do you agree, George?"

"It's my nature not to agree to anything."

"Come, now, you can't believe intermixing of the races in the schools isn't one step away from changing our entire culture."

"It could happen," George replied.

"It just cannot happen," said Penelope.

"Dear, let's have a drink," Lara pulled her husband's away not wishing to debate when George needed to circulate among potential donors for his future campaign. "Nice seeing you."

"Let me join you," Mr. Charles said to the dismay of Lara, as he followed the couple.

Fawn stayed with Penelope. She was pale and bone thin with cropped jet hair. Twisting her head upward as she sniffed and whispered, attempting to hide her lingering desire for her high school heartthrob and later extramarital lover.

"Jules sent me a wire. Begging forgiveness for not meeting with me during his short stay."

"Really? How charming," Penelope sniffed back.

"He asked me to handle some details as to his share of the estate. Of course, I have to be discreet. Otherwise most will assume our affair is still alive."

"Isn't it?" asked Penelope.

"Love can never be destroyed, Penelope. Isn't that what you wish of Pierre?"

"Never considered how fleeting the emotion is. But what is it that Jules asks?"

"Seems he is concerned over your impending arrest."

Penelope's eyes became steely, penetrating Fawn's soft face soaked with lust just from saying Jules's name. Because she was the daughter of the biggest publisher in Virginia and the Carolinas, undeserving cordiality was mandated. She tried to shield her dislike of her with a cool veil of disinterest.

Penelope continued, "I have been so busy with my campaign, I didn't realize a crime had been committed."

"Besides the impending investigation of your alleged acts some years ago regarding the Walker death, he is not pleased about his home being turned into a tourist dump."

"Strange, he never mentioned it." Penelope hated when he came and left. They'd stopped talking directly about the family trust after Mary Margaret became sickly and bedridden twenty years ago. Although father was still alive, Jules used others to deliver messages of his discontent. Penelope scoured Fawn's face, noting her resemblance of Mary Margaret, only with short hair.

Fawn's words were whispers, inaudible over the conversations around them. "I want the best for Jules. The best for Velvet Gardens."

Penelope refused to lean in to hear her words. Fawn had no shame screwing Jules every chance she could get in Mary Margaret's bed while in high school. The same bed their mother, in a demented state, had called only for her precious Jules and Angel to stay near during her last sickness. To stop the crying for Angel, a doll had to be swaddled and laid next to her, and Jules kept watch to soothe her urges to climb the servant stairs looking for Velvet. Zachary wanted nothing to do with her dementia. Penelope protested their use of Mary Margaret's bed. Jules cried it was the only place he could console his love and then grief for mother.

"He is under the impression you are wasting money on this campaign. His money," Fawn continued.

"His money?" Penelope repeated sarcastically. Memory of her disgusted father's face appeared. Zachary returned from his retirement in Spain to meet his dwindling group of older Southern stalwarts to protect the family name. The costly cover-up of Miriam's death had created demands for more money, leaving Velvet Gardens nearly bankrupt at his death, while Jules pretended a lavish lifestyle in Paris.

"Penelope, I am not interfering, but I have visited him in Paris. He lives sparsely. He misses home. I miss him so much. But with my marriage obligations it's impossible to leave. I really don't want to be a carrier of messages."

"Thank you, Fawn. The war is over. Pigeons aren't needed any longer." Then reluctantly said. "Perhaps you can be of help. The Richmond papers can do a few favorable editorials on my behalf. Surely you have enough clout with your family to make an endorsement for me."

Fawn sniffed. "We print what will sell, not favors."

Facetiously, "Oh dear, then Velvet Gardens will soon be gone" Penelope stepped away. "I must join my other guests."

George was at the bar, surveying the room over a drink. Something about the bartender held him captive. He'd look away but turn back to stare. He squinted at the face. Finally, "Didn't you work at Gene's?"

"Gene's? Yeah, long ago, sir." The bartender recognized him when he approached and avoided direct contact. "Closed many, many years ago." He began to think it was a stupid idea to take this job. When the catering service called for an experienced bartender, he took it, hoping he'd find clues, get paid the reward, then leave town. After Penelope offered him the job as overseer, he decided to stick around.

"Didn't you call my office looking for the money on the Walker murder?" George asked.

"I may have."

"What do you know? I'd like to solve that case."

"Nothing really. I thought I could lie and get it. A lot of people talked about the old man, Rhoady. Nothing came of it."

Penelope stopped a few feet away to eavesdrop. She noticed George's shoulders shrug nervously.

"Actually, I remember you too," the bartender said, hoping to fend off George's intense suspicions. "I saw you at the Derby a few times, as a matter of fact. Friends with Mr. Jules, aren't you? Mimi spoke of you." This was a lie, but he hoped for a reaction.

George was terse. "She didn't know me."

"Gene did, said you were a regular customer of the back room." The bartender was holding his gaze steady on the man.

"Gene's dead."

"Right-O. Miss Penelope, can I make a drink for you?"

George turned sharply to Penelope, who prance up to the bar with the biggest cat grin.

"No, dear. Well, what do you think? He'll make a good replacement for Hugh."

"Thank you, ma'am."

"George, I hear I may be arrested soon. Is that true?"

George stared, calculating what she heard. Before he could speak, there were calls from the foyer and hallway.

"Speech. Speech! Penelope."

Lara took her hand and swept her to the bottom of the grand staircase. George followed looking over his shoulder, wondering how much this guy knew. With a glass of whiskey in hand, Earl toasted George's intimidating stare.

"Up the stairs, Penelope." Lara cheered her on.

There was a commotion at the door. Alice tried politely to tell Reverend Poindexter, the black preacher from Rita and Odessa's church, to use the back door.

After reaching a step above the guests, Penelope stuttered at the sight of the black minister walking into the middle of her guests with Alice tagging behind, trying to persuade the man to leave. The murmur of the friendly crowd silenced. Only the reverend's voice, deep and melodic could be heard.

He walked to the bottom of the staircase, in front of Penelope, holding an envelope of money and a wicker basket. Alice rushed to lock the front doors to keep the reverend's escorts from entering as well. Some guests were angry, wanting to leave immediately. She pleaded they wait because there was a car full of Negroes out front. This caused greater alarm.

"Please don't panic, my fellow citizens," the reverend began. "We are not here to harm you. I am Reverend Poindexter. I know you all are here for a cause dear to your hearts."

"Reverend, please, can we discuss this later?" Penelope's pleaded.

"Let him speak," said George, standing in the middle of the crowded foyer.

"Thank you, my friend. I am here to thank Miss Penelope for the grand donation she made to my church. One thousand dollars, a mighty sum. She gives every year in the name of her nanny, Polly, a wonderful woman who cared for this family. Today, I find it fitting to begin a coalition in her name."

"Reverend, please." Penelope began wheezing for air.

Guests began to leave down the hallway to exit through the kitchen.

"I want you all to know how generous Miss Penelope has been and I want to dedicate this money to the coalition to save our schools. To build our schools. I know you all agree it is necessary to educate the children of our future nation. I have a basket here to take up a collection to help with this coalition."

"When are the police coming? Call the police!" a few guests yelled.

"It will be a mighty sin to shut our schools down to avoid integrating the schools. We must stand against the manifesto that is growing in the halls of our legislature."

Two male guests took the minister's arms to throw him out.

George stepped forward. "Let him, be. I'll handle it."

Rumblings of "hurry," and "please let us out of here" roared through the crowd.

George spoke, "Let me escort you to your car."

"Thank you, sir. The anger does not frighten me," the reverend said. "I'll be in touch." He winked at the prosecutor.

Lara followed her husband closely to their car parked in front of the portico in case he had to leave early for criminal matters.

"You mean you ain't going to press charges? And get those coloreds out of the drive!?" Alice yelled.

"It's okay, Alice. I'm handling it," he said.

Penelope was devastated as she sat on the steps, dumbfounded. Guests questioned her as to why she contributed to this man. How did she allow him to enter? Estelle stood on a step to speak.

"Hear me, everyone. Hear me. I know the reverend to be a good man. I believe in better education. There is no evil in giving money to the church. They will need books, and teachers, too."

The hallway was nearly empty.

One guest said, "Report him, Estelle. He's trespassing."

Realizing it was hopeless, Estelle sat to comfort Penelope, whose hands hid her face, crying, as guests fled.

Talbot was out front holding back the surge of cars trying to leave all at once, in order to allow the reverend's car to pull out first. George beeped his horn to let him know he was behind to assure his safe trip downtown. The reverend slowly drove down the long drive with windows down so all could hear the parishioners accompanying the reverend singing gospels with Bibles in hand.

Lara asked her husband, "Honey, did you know the reverend was coming?"

"Does it matter?"

27
Fire

Three days after Penelope's fund-raiser, Reverend Poindexter's First Baptist Church was on fire. Odessa got a call three in the morning that the redbrick building was engulfed in flames. Minton begged her to wait until sunlight, but full of tears, she could not let the reverend stand alone.

Minton asked Josephine who was still in Richmond to go with his wife. He needed to stay back to protect their home from any trouble that night. A rifle stood by the front door.

Odessa joined other church members who were arriving to pray. Josephine was overwhelmed by the excitement, and by the sharing of grief. People were praying for the power to overcome any hatred against their church.

We will rebuild. We will continue our fight. Was all she heard.

Some parishioners were angered over the reverend's visit to the Velvet house. They said he'd gone there to incite those white folks. All their prayers, all their beliefs in the almighty had been stepped upon. They were upset that he should have known it was coming. Others were rock solid behind him, supporting the push against segregation. They stood before the burning building until the sun rose.

Fire crews and police swarmed the area, allowing no one near the building even though the pastor pleaded to enter, to gather important papers. Then the mayor arrived to give his condolences. As a favor to the reverend who brought the vote out, they were allowed in with a photographer trailing for a photo op of the two men standing, united in the ashes of burned pews.

At first, it was speculated a spark from faulty wiring had caused the fire until the smell of gasoline rose from the basement. The same basement where Odessa held committee meetings to organize against the resistance movement growing against integration. Blackstone was on duty that night and he discovered several of Penelope's campaign posters underneath the rubble. They were rolled up and used as torches, soaked with gasoline. A few had not fully burned.

The days after the fire were filled with accusations and counter accusations between Penelope's camp and the black community. Agents from the FBI and the Bureau of Alcohol, Tobacco, and Firearms called to speak with her, but she insisted she was too busy, asking them to wait until after the election, which was twenty-eight days away.

They wanted to see her guest list on the day the reverend visited, and to search the house and grounds. Then they began interviewing her land tenants, creating a nuisance. Penelope called her friends. First was Estelle, hoping her husband, the police commissioner could stop the investigation. Instead Estelle suggested a public apology and a large donation to the building fund was the better way.

Then there was Fawn. Not exactly a friend, but she hoped Fawn's lingering love for Jules would help stop the negative reporting and the negative local commentary from being wired nationally. Penelope planned to remind her of the devotion she held for the Velvet Gardens.

Fawn was gracious. "Let me say that the Velvet Gardens is always just a whisper away in everyone's mind." Then she began to tell the same story her poppa had told her about the slave Velvet.

"Please, Fawn. Why do you bring up the same messy story? Can you just talk to your poppa and stop the paper from running the false stories about me?"

"It's not about Velvet. It's about your dad. You know he was good friends with my dad and shared--he never believed his last child died at birth. That's all I was going to say."

"Who said these lies?!"

"Polly, he said. Polly, your devoted servant, told Zak on her dying bed, asking forgiveness. He thought she had been hexed."

"Lies!"

"I know. I know. Just that Rita might be right," Fawn whispered.

"She's not. I'm ashamed of you, insinuating that either I am black or Polly is a liar."

Fawn persisted. "Oh, Penny, it's a rumor. It was started by your father after he heard Polly talking in delirium before passing. Mary Margaret's depressions were about Angel being alive. The rumors were started by your poppa. Don't be angry at me. It isn't in print. I've done all I can to keep Daddy from writing about it for Jules's sake. Understand, Daddy needs to sell papers but will not sink his social circle for a dollar."

Penelope wanted to stop calling for advice. She realized she was just good ink. Any attempt to squash her association with the church fire would only spiral further out of control. Folks were either for her or against her. She had to try Lara Stevens.

"I wouldn't give another cent to those people," Lara said, commenting on Estelle's suggestion. "It was an absolute embarrassment rushing your home like that. I don't care if the church was Polly's sanctuary. She knew her place and they should know theirs."

"Is George going to bring me up on charges, Lara?" asked Penelope.

"I'll do my best. There was some hush talk that the governor is on your side, liking your politics. But George is mad as hell over you withholding that white mink. Maybe if you find it, he may become helpful."

"It's gone, Lara. Disappeared."

"Some of your workers say they saw a woman wearing it walking the grounds at night."

"Has George been talking to my workers? Without my permission!?"

"There I go. Sorry, Penelope. I was not supposed to talk about your case. Honey, I will try my best. George never really talks to me about his business. He is always in the street. I often wake up in an empty bed. Gone. Penny, dear, I have to run. Lots of errands to finish for my girl's graduation. Call me later. By the way, if you haven't done your homework, George tells me your new bartender-slash-overseer is snooping for information linking you to the Miriam murder."

After the telephone call, Penelope was extremely agitated and determined to get the truth out of Earl. Usually she called her workers to the house, but she could not wait. She walked down the back road looking for the scoundrel. Upon seeing Ella, she decided a personal talk with her was more important.

Ella had not spoken to her in weeks. She suspected the woman was holding a grudge because Rita Jane had been arrested and then left for another country, leaving her good home and friends behind.

"Ella!" Penelope called out to the woman hanging clothes on a line outside her small house.

The woman had clothespins in her mouth, so she waved back, then stooped over to pull more sheets from her basket to hang, not wanting to speak.

"Ella, Ella!" Penelope called taking bold strides toward the woman engulfed in flapping sheets with only her yellow kerchief around her pressed hair visible. Then Ella emerged and made the sign of the cross over her heart. Penelope stopped, stunned.

"Miss Penelope. I'm not feeling right about now," Ella said. Lifting her empty basket, she entered her three-room house, leaving Penelope to be blanketed by the white sheets billowing in the wind.

Earl happened upon the encounter but remained silent, watching Penelope fight back the sheets from her face. It was a struggle for her to save face from Ella's snub.

"Miss Penelope," he gently called. The woman stood frozen, trying not to show any response to Ella. She turned to walk back to the big house. He quietly walked beside her, waiting for her to speak. Uncomfortable, he began to talk.

"Miss Penelope. I've heard a lot since working here. It's kinda scary. Workers hear babies crying and screaming women."

Penelope said nothing.

"Ella told workers an evil spirit took over the Velvet house. That she hears footsteps walking up and down the stairs whenever she's in there. Then she said something about the mink coat with blood on it. Said you have it and just making a fuss over its loss to keep the police confused. I did hear Talbot may have given it away. Someone in France."

This confirmed Penelope's belief Talbot was the thief. She wanted to hang him, but Alice would take her skin. She checked her dislike of him because Alice was all she had left to hold onto.

Penelope thought, *Maybe, it's better that the damn coat is gone.* Then finally spoke, "And I've heard plenty of talk about the slave girl named Velvet that Grandpoppa killed a good man for, and now the place is cursed."

"What hurts your workers the most is the fire. They think you had it done."

"Do you?"

"No, but I can find out."

She wondered if he had those kinds of connections. "Don't. It's better to leave it be. It will get around that I was planting information, just because you work for me. What hurts is that crossing, Earl. I am not evil."

"There's also talk of a lady in a white mink coat down the drive at night."

"Have you seen the woman?"

"To be frank, there were times when I thought Miriam was down the road coming to the house. But I know she's dead. And it's just my imagination working through all the gossip."

"Well, I guess Miriam can be added to Polly, and Velvet, and all the other spirits," Penelope said, sighing. "What do you know about George and Miriam?"

"He used to visit Gene's many years ago."

"Did he know Miriam Walker?"

"Yes ma'am. They were intimate. They met often at the bar, sometimes in the back or the alley."

Penelope was silent. The silence grew as they walked the back road.

"So you know a lot about Miriam Walker and Jules?"

"Some."

"Do you think I killed her?" She stared straight ahead, not wishing to see his response as they neared Rita's garden.

"At first. Before I got to know you. Most people think you did. She told everyone she was coming up here the night she died."

"Who brought her to the house?"

"I'm not sure. I wasn't at work that night. She usually met a black car a block or two away. But Gene said that that night another car picked her up. He made some calls afterwards thinking he had the goods on the guy, hoping it would increase protection against any raids or arrests for the type of businesses he was involved in. You know, the general stuff, gambling, bootlegging, numbers, prostitution, laundering money. After those calls, the Brown Derby had no more trouble. But it also lost business. No one trusted Gene, and they stopped coming. He had to close. I think it was some big shot's son."

"Thank you, Earl." They had arrived at the back steps.

"Earl, if you see that woman again, you shoot her. You hear me?"

He looked at Penelope with disbelief, then realized the woman was serious. "I'll try my best if I see her."

"You'll see her. 'Cause I've seen her a few times myself. And I aim to get her off my conscience."

"Yes, ma'am."

"Earl, you can stay until you find another position. Thank you for your help." Penelope proceeded into the house.

* * *

The days after the fire were explosive for Odessa as well. Her house was filled with workers and well-wishers, all energized to take down the invisible wall. The telephone never stopped ringing and people were constantly stopping by to help.

Grandma Philly called every night, begging Josephine to come home. The girl couldn't leave after promising Odessa she'd stay longer to handle the calls, open mail, or run small errands. There was a force, strong and full, that she'd never experienced before. The workers held hands in prayer meetings; they gathered at the dining room table to share meals and stories of the black resistance to the new Jim Crow laws spreading throughout the South to defund public schools if they mixed the races.

The most disappointing mail beyond the threats and hatred were those that were returned unopened, stamped insufficient postage, wrong addressee, or undeliverable. The letters had been sent in support of Odessa being appointed to sit on the governor's commission regarding the feasibility of desegregation of the schools.

"Cowards," Odessa declared. It was easier to pretend the letters were never received than to formally reject her. As unhappy as she was, she was too invigorated to be down about it for long.

By the end of the week, Esther Mae was at the front door with a mouth full of sorrow. "Good evening, Miss Odessa. Am I welcome to come in?"

"Certainly."

"I know it must seem strange, me being at your door tonight. Knowing how my work with Miss Penelope tarnished the good people's opinion of me. Not wanting to be bothered with me. But all those whispers, calling me a Jemima behind my back, was wrong. I saw a lot up there. I quit, you know."

"Esther you don't have to confess to me."

"Yeah, I do. I am proud and ambitious like any woman. The church did right by me. Helped me to vote. I think I should give something back. I'm good with typing and distributing things. I have a good clientele at the hair salon now."

The two sat at the dining room table. Odessa listened quietly, hiding her dislike of Esther Mae's disloyalty. She felt the young woman was selfish, looking out for any opportunity, even when it held back others, afraid to stand for what they believed. So believe in nothing, and it may all work itself out, only *on others' bare backs.*

Esther's apology seemed sincere, as did her offer to work and give back. Holding her hands out to embrace Odessa, she said, "It was my church, too."

28

Rally Together

The church fire galvanized the city into camps. Angry and heartbroken parishioners called for a federal investigation, while others said it was the work of outsiders stirring up trouble in the city. Others believed it was a sign from above teaching black folks what happens when they step out of place. Odessa agreed with all sides, stirring up pity, sympathy, or guilt to raise money to rebuild the church. It didn't matter what they thought, as long as they had money to give.

It was the first Saturday in June and she was happy to see the large turnout of supporters in Jackson Park for a fund-raising event. Colorful tents and display booths selling baked goods, lemon teas, small crafts, and BBQ ribs filled the square-block park. Church choirs from around the area sang on small stages while squads carrying donation baskets reached out to the strolling families of all ages and races.

Odessa had set up a canopy and table with Josephine to sell handmade potholders and towels they'd made last week. Josephine squatted behind the table to pull out the goods from bags to place on the table. Ella entered the park and darted toward Odessa carrying a large tray of strawberry baskets for sale.

"Greetings, sister." Odessa smiled.

"Hope our prayers are answered," Ella began. "I haven't felt right since the fire. I certainly believe Miss Penelope had something to do with it, but I can't be sure. I've been praying that the evil on her hands doesn't affect me."

"We don't know who did it, Ella. No need spreading rumors," Odessa said, though she wished she could pin the fire on Penelope.

"She must have. Seems every night Miss Penelope is seeing ghosts now. She swears a woman in mink, dripping blood, keeps coming to the door. It has to be her conscience. I need to move, leave that old plantation."

Josephine stopped unpacking to listen carefully, stooping lower to avoid being detected.

"Why, Ella? I heard you're bringing in a profit on your plot. After thirty years of hard work on that land, it's finally paying off. Save your money for your older years. You don't have a pension coming."

"I keep telling myself that. Not sure, but it's Miss Penelope. She has everyone frightened. Guests come just to see ghosts. They walk out back over the fields at night, making the dogs bark. They want the tenants to tell them spooky stories. Got them making up lies about the place for big tips. Sometimes it's more than what you get for growing crops. Making us lazy. I believe Miss Penelope's talking about selling the land right out from under us, though."

"Well, you don't say."

Lowering her voice, Ella continued. "It was that girl, Odessa. I know you like her, but Alice says it all began with that girl. Got Rita Jane all excited."

Odessa took her hand to lead her away, knowing Josephine was listening and had been hiding for a long time under the table.

"Come, Ella, walk with me to the car. I've got some things there."

"Alice started hanging clippings on her office walls about that Miriam woman who drowned in the river years ago. Something strange is going on, Odessa. I need the pastor to pray for me. I feel a spell coming."

"Stop. Just say your prayers. Talk to the pastor." Odessa unloaded another box from her car.

Josephine rose to watch the two women, peeved that Ella thought she was spooky.

"Alice is telling guests about the woman, making Miss Penelope angry. They argued over some type of midnight walk with candles to scare the ghost away from the property. Alice says they can make more money, but Miss Penelope just stays up in the attic waiting for the election next week."

Odessa motioned Josephine to help her with two boxes she was carrying but the girl stood still, not wanting to go near Ella.

"You're not believing me, Odessa. I need to leave there. Alice now wants to show the back rooms where Rita Jane went mad, and Polly's cabinet in the basement. She's gone crazy like Miss Penelope." When Ella noticed the girl at the table, her face squinched, whispering, "Be careful, Odessa." Wanting to get away without further talk. "I see Reverend Poindexter. Let me go. Come visit, Odessa. You're welcome in my home."

"I will do that."

Flapping a potholder as a fan, Josephine said, "I overheard her. I'm not evil, I've done nothing hateful."

"Pay no mind to her talk. She's just worried and sad that life has changed around her."

Suddenly the squeal of girlish voices rose above the crowd. Not far away, Talbot entered the small city park. Girls swarmed him. Girls whose dads were public administrators or doctors or lawyers. Daughters of other church ministers who'd came with their mothers and fathers to support the fund-raising and show ecumenical allegiance to the faith that no fire can destroy, surrounded him.

Josephine brightened at seeing him. He saw her too and waved. She smiled. He moved through the crowd toward her table, winged with a few girls holding onto him.

"How are you?" he asked.

"Fine," she said coyly, busying herself with arranging the towels and potholders in an orderly fashion, not wanting him to notice her delight.

"Hello, Miss Odessa."

"Hello, Talbot. You look a little overworked. Tired." She eyed him sternly, hoping he'd get the notion to quickly leave.

"I'm good. Just working more hours with the cigars business." He turned to Josephine. "My mother heard you were going to attend school here in the fall."

"Virginia Union."

One of the girls with Talbot grew impatient. "Let's go, Tally, you promised to take me in the car."

Two other girls who had tagged along picked through the potholders, causing Odessa to keep one eye on them and the other on Josephine.

"Maybe you can come by the house. I drive around at night as security. There's a rumor about—"

"A ghost!" one of the girls interjected. "Poof! She wears a white mink, too."

Odessa quickly added, "Christians only believe in one ghost, the holy ghost. Stop trying to impress these girls with foolishness, Talbot."

"Honest," one of them said. "My mother says it's the woman who drowned in the James a long time ago."

"I saw her too." Josephine's heart pounded.

The girls laughed. Then whined for him to leave.

He knew it was her mother they were talking about. He'd hoped to spur some interest in her to visit the Gardens again, to talk to him. Talbot saw a look of great urgency in her eyes. She wanted to tell him more, but she was afraid Odessa was watching. The older woman's smile twisted with worry, staring harshly past the young man's face, giving the impression he should leave them alone.

"Well, I better go, Jo."

"Bye."

"By the way, I'm going to be at Piper's Hamburgers on Carey Street at seven. Nice place."

He turned away with the girls hanging on his arm, hoping she would show up later.

* * *

Blackstone was on duty cruising around the park when he saw Talbot talking to the black girl. He immediately stopped at the curb to watch, happy to have something to report to Alice. He didn't like the boy any more than he liked the girl. He was angry about being yanked off the Walker case. If only he had not been so rough. He could have softened her, made her believe he was on her side. Instead, she was trying to sue him. Luckily nobody wanted to hear her complaint.

He watched the couple for dirt to report to Alice, in hopes she would give more concrete evidence about the night Miriam was at the Velvet. So far, Alice just repeated herself, whispering that the woman had taken one of Polly's formulas. Never mentioning who gave the woman the poison or the hanger still lodged in her womb. Alice became careful with her calls to Blackstone at the house.

Estelle told Penelope that it was Blackstone who'd found her campaign notices soaked in gasoline at the church. This sent Penelope into a rant she was being framed by the bastard. *How did they get there, Alice?*

Alice had to hear accusations of being a traitor. Or not having the stuff like her father to fight off sabotage. Alice suffered through the condemnation of being an imperfect ally.

Alice suspected Blackstone had bribed Mr. Barton, the printer out of the first set of posters. Barton called to say they were ready but when a worker arrived to pick up the order, he said he had to redo them because the notices and posters suffered some misprints from some spilled liquid. No one questioned his integrity.

Odessa recognized Blackstone sitting, watching them. She also remembered him at the fire appearing remorseful, giving his condolences to Reverend Poindexter. She did not trust his sincerity, nor that of any man who could hit a woman so savagely. Josephine didn't notice the officer because Lorenzo was now at their table.

She smiled when he kissed her cheek, then Odessa's.

"I saw you earlier but your friend had your attention."

"Tally's a nice person. Heard you paid him off. How much?"

"Everything I had for you." He kissed her hand, causing her to blink several times.

Odessa asked, "Where is Senior? Is he at the park?"

"Not yet. Art invited him to a business lunch. Some bankers, I think."

Art believed some banks were holding back on loans to the church and had asked Senior to lend legal support. They were planning to hold a press conference on Monday. Senior saw an opportunity for media exposure.

"When are you going to come and see me and Mint?" she asked.

"Tonight, if Jo will let me kiss her again."

"Hmm. Free kisses are for frogs remember," Josephine said. "But you're already a Prince Charming. There's no surprise for me." She smiled.

Lorenzo knit his brows. "Is that a riddle?" he asked.

She laughed. "It's your saying, so why are you confused?"

"How about seven?" he asked.

Josephine shrugged. "I'm not sure what I will be doing."

Lorenzo felt disappointed that she was putting him off. "Sure. Call me," he said. He waved bye to Odessa and joined Pasqual with Reverend Poindexter.

Later that evening, Josephine tried very hard to listen to the radio while she wrote postcards to friends. She called her grandmother several times, but at seven the urge to meet Talbot was irresistible. Knowing Odessa was still at a meeting counting the receipts from the fair, she left a note that she going to a movie.

Minton was out playing cards with friends.

On a high stool at the front window of Pipers café, Talbot sat eating a hamburger, watching for Josephine. It was seven thirty. Disappointed, he rose to leave without finishing his meal. Then he saw her standing across the street, smiling. When their eyes met, she waved. More to shake off the feeling of warmth that was beginning to seep into her heart. She was moved that he cared enough to keep meeting with her in the open.

"Happy you came," he said, reaching her on the sidewalk.

"Yeah. I'd like to hear what you know about my mom."

Walking to his car parked at the curb, he told her, "I don't believe in ghosts, but Ella and others can't stop talking about it. Miss Penelope is under a doctor's care. Said she's losing her mind over it. To me, it's just an excuse because she's going to lose the election. She's really far behind. And I really don't care. I never saw the Miriam woman."

"I did. I saw her when I stayed there. I want to go there for one more night," Josephine said.

"Sure. Here's my car."

She stopped, hesitant. "I don't think I should."

"What?"

"It may look wrong. I mean the two of us."

"You can lay low in the backseat?"

"No. I'll take a taxi."

"Cool. Meet me on the back road." He tried to kiss her on the cheek. She turned her head away.

"Afraid," he says.

"People are watching."

He laughed. "Let them watch. I'm used to it." He got into his car. "Here's my number." He handed her a napkin with his telephone number. "In case something happens."

As soon as Talbot reached home, he changed his clothes, putting on a fresh white shirt his mother had starched and pressed for the party George and Lara Stevens were having for their daughter's graduation party the next day, Sunday.

Alice was upset. "Talbot, please don't wear that shirt. It's for the Steven's girls. Where are you going, anyway?"

"Out, Mom."

Alice wanted to fuss more but Talbot hurried past her. His father was dozing on the living room couch, snoring louder than the laughter on the TV. The telephone rang as he left.

"Hello, this is Alice."

"Hello, can I speak to Talbot?" Josephine was calling from a phone booth outside the café. She had sat for a while, then walked to the river, worried and nervous, remembering being arrested. Besides Rita Jane wasn't there to protect her. Finally, she called to cancel.

"Who's calling?"

"Josephine."

She was scared something bad would happen. Odessa had told her not to get friendly with Talbot. "It's not that he has a record or is known to do bad things," she'd said. "Just that he is well-liked and *white* - with emphasis. He will only use you. If you let yourself go that far. There are a few fathers who want to marry off their daughters and set him up in the family business or in positions in the city."

She was becoming tired of the black-white thing. Not that she knew much about it. She'd grown up in a black neighborhood where whites were only seen in the grocery stores, and rarely anywhere else unless one went downtown to shop. Blacks went to a black hospital with black doctors, and they read black papers. The schools in the neighborhoods were nearly all black. No one talked about being careful talking to white people.

"Honey, what can I do for you?" Alice continued.

"Is Talbot there?"

Suspicious, she said, "He's out back, can I tell him anything?"

After a long pause, she said, "No. Yeah. No. Tell him the front circle is better."

Disconcerted and disappointed with Talbot, Alice maintained a calm voice. "I will, dear."

Talbot drove down the back road with the car lights out to prevent any sharecroppers from noticing him. He parked on the side road and waited for Josephine's taxi. After a few minutes, he saw car lights make a U-turn at the intersection of the main road to head back toward the front of the house.

He geared up the car and raced to the front entrance of the long road leading into the grounds of the Velvet house. The taxi was exiting, having already left Josephine at the circle. He waved his arm out the car window to get her attention as he approached. She imagined it was the black car with her mother in the white mink.

After he stopped and exited, her vision of the car with her mother disappeared.

"Glad you came. Waited awhile out back. Thought you cancelled on me."

"Didn't you get my message to meet out front?"

"No. just saw your taxi out front. Hey, let's not waste time." Putting his arm around her gently, "First, can I kiss that cheek of yours? The one that ugly man bruised?"

She looked up at him with the sweetest eyes, as he bent to kiss her lips. Gunfire cracked the air. Suddenly, there was another boom, and another. Talbot saw the front doors at the portico open. There stood Alice with a shotgun. He waved his arms, yelling.

"Mom, stop! STOP!"

The gun blasted again. Josephine screamed as he fell to the ground. Alice started shucking the shells, loading it for another round. Blasting the air again and again. All she saw was the white shirt and the girl. Guests yelled for the police. A few had entered the hallway calling for Penelope. The land tenants were awakened, the dogs barked incessantly. Alice's husband ran to the big house after hearing the sound of his gun and his wife missing.

Josephine kneeled next to Talbot. Blood soiling his white shirt. "Tally? Tally!" She began to cry.

Penelope was frightened, thinking it was some sort of retaliation for the church fire. She ran past guests on the staircase leading to the front hall.

"Please, everyone, go back upstairs. Stay in your rooms. Please. Alice!" she screamed, watching Alice load the gun again.

"Stop, Alice. Stop!"

"I see her! I see her!" Alice cried. "See the white mink down there? I hit her. That girl's come back!"

"Alice, give me the gun!" Penelope begged.

"It's that whore's child. It's that evil child. Penelope. She's come for more blood."

"Alice! Alice, stop!" Penelope grabbed Alice from behind, causing the rifle to shoot upward, knocking out the portico's overhead light. A journalist who'd been invited to spend a few days at the bed-and-breakfast grabbed his camera, after hearing the commotion, and began taking photographs of the bedlam.

He'd been invited to gather information to improve Penelope's image after the church fire and boost her election vote. His photographs of Alice and Penelope struggling with the shotgun eventually made front-page news statewide.

Josephine rose screaming for help as Talbot lay on the ground. Alice and Penelope rushed to the circle, pushing through a crowd of workers who'd gathered.

"Call the police! Call the police! Get an ambulance!" someone yelled.

"No police!" Penelope shouted.

At the sight of blood spreading across Talbot's white shirt, Alice dropped to her knees to wrap herself around her son, sobbing. Ella pushed through the group to take Josephine's hand while everyone was distracted.

"Come, child. Come with me."

The girl was shaking, stunned, wide-eyed, and stiff.

"Is he dead?" someone asked.

Ella pulled her away, knowing that after the confusion cleared, the girl might not see the light of day. They would turn on her. She knew if that boy was dead, the girl would be too. The two huddled together to escape down the field road to Ella's house. There she called Odessa to come quickly.

Talbot's father pulled Alice off and searched for the wound. He lifted his barely conscious son into the car and sped to the hospital. Alice cried for forgiveness, asking

God to save her son, as she rocked back and forth holding her son.

Penelope sank to the ground, feeling defeated on the spot. She looked up to see the journalist scribbling away. She knew this was another two-faced coin. Either it was more scandal to ruin her, or another valid reason to keep the races separate.

29

Letters of Intent

A day did not pass in June after Talbot was shot that a threatening letter failed to arrive at Art's office. While most were anonymous, some were signed, often by numerous persons. There were names he recognized as former clients, people of color demanding or pleading that Josephine leave Richmond. Rumors labeled her as an evil persona casting a cloud over the city, stirring bad feelings amongst good people.

His lawyerly instincts resisted; he felt obligated to shield her. The police were alerted of possible danger but saw the letters as harmless without evidence of an actual crime. The letters created fear of a kind that a good lawyer did not tolerate. Fear that he fought hard against because a lawyer could not entertain imaginary defeat. It worried him that his business would suffer if she stayed. He also worried he was becoming too fearful of everyone. People saw themselves as a substitute target for hate if they associated with him.

Odessa was getting the same letters too. She quietly asked if the terms of Josephine's trust allowed her to attend a college up north. As strong as Odessa's belief in resisting hatred was, she also feared for Josephine. She didn't want to tell how much her life was in danger. It fell on Art.

He arranged to speak to the young woman at the outdoor courts in Byrd Park at the end of the Boulevard. When he arrived a long line of kids were waiting to register for his summer tennis camp. Before he could speak to his assistants, he noticed Josephine was already there talking with some of the children.

Bouncing across one of the courts, she waved and called to him. "Mr. Art!"

Upset, he asked her, "Where's Odessa?" You came alone? Don't you know the danger you're in?"

"I ain't afraid," she said.

"It's not about fear." He was lying. He wanted to believe that too, but he was hating himself that he could not quiet the faceless danger of her death. "Have no doubt there are people who are willing to see you go under. You can't travel alone."

"I'm fine. I took a taxi. There are a lot of people here. No one's going to do anything. Besides, I registered to start school in two months at VU."

"Child, you should go home. I can change the terms of the trust so you can attend one near Philadelphia."

"No, Mr. Art. My mother is here. It was not my fault that Tally got shot. What kind of love is that, Mr. Art? You need to write those people right back and tell them to stop. And I have the right to talk to Talbot."

"If you go see that boy again, I will drop you as a client."

"Then I'll get Senior."

"Nobody will take your case if you are arrested."

"You sound scared, Mr. Art. I've seen the letters. They come to Odessa's house too. Kid drawings of witches riding brooms and things hanging from trees. Silliness. Trying to scare me off."

"Come, walk with me," he said. Holding his racket in one hand, he waved to his assistants who were busy taking names and handing out permission slips. "I'll be back," he called to them as he neared his parked car. Odessa called his home, alarmed that she had left early without telling her. They were to meet Art at his office.

Josephine made plans to see Talbot after speaking with Art and didn't want anyone to stop her, so she left early before Odessa awakened. Now Art was taking her to Odessa without her knowledge. "Come on, get in. Let me take you to my office."

He realized Josephine's scope of the world was limited. So he put the issue in terms of her mother. "You are a target for everything they dislike about blacks, and black women in particular. You have a right to make a choice. But It seems to be following your mother's footsteps."

"Exactly, to find out what happened to her."

"Can't you do it without being killed?"

"What?"

"Meaning fate has set a path that you are now walking on. Think how similar it is to your mother's death. You are involved with a young white man at Velvet house, as was your mother."

"I know they were in love."

"Love can cause foolish things. I don't think you're in love with Talbot, but you have put yourself up against the people who had you arrested, and who now want you banished. I have choices to make too. I can't keep you from doing what you want but I don't have to fight for someone who ignores good advice. You need to decide whether you want to survive or die here like your mother." The girl stopped and looked at him in disbelief.

"You will never find out who killed your mother. It's been over sixteen years. People are gone. Only reason you see it in the newspapers is because of politics. Some people believed you caused Miss Penelope to lose the election."

"Odessa is happy. So are others."

Secretly, Art believed Odessa may have encouraged the girl too much. He hated to think she'd used the girl.

"Yes, she lost, and her large plantation is making more money than before," he continued. "People pay to see ghosts roaming around. Crazy Rita Jane, Angel's grave, and shotgun Alice. If you stay you will be part of it. A suicide hanging up there out of grief for your mother's spirit.

The two neared Art's office. Josephine was quiet. Holding back tears, angered over the push to get rid of her. "I will go. But only for the summer."

"Think about schools near your grandmother. Please."

They entered his office where Odessa was waiting worried. She was chatting with his secretary, then rose to hug Josephine. Art nodded that he had scared her as best he could and hoped the young girl would leave quickly.

To the right of Odessa near the front door was Josephine's luggage. She had packed them last night but did not intend to leave until tomorrow. She was to see Talbot today. His chest wound healed enough for him to be released from the hospital.

He wanted to meet her down at the river one more time. To show folks they were the bold ones. They were going to shape their own future. She was to call after meeting Art, but the telephone on the desk seemed a mile away. Her mind scattered into pieces, realizing Odessa brought her suitcases to force her to leave then and now. Jo saw it as a betrayal to their friendship.

"Sweetie, I brought your bags to save you a trip back to the house." Odessa was pleasant as she could be. "We can go onto the train station from here. Odessa recognized her surprise and disappointment. But it was also painful to listen to her husband scold her last night. He went over the edge.

For several nights someone called at 8 p.m. to repeat Josephine would be found in the river. "Her death will destroy us." He yelled and yelled in their bedroom.

Josephine felt trapped knowing there wasn't a way she could walk out Art's office alone, without breaking her bond with the older woman whom she came to admire. She nodded in agreement. She knew Odessa's home was overburdened with workers. Leaving for a while might be helpful but not because of Art's warnings--until she stepped out his office.

Parked curbside sat Blackstone staring at them with annoyance from ear to ear. Odessa took Josephine's hand and marched past him to load the bags in the trunk of her car, parked in front of the officer. When they drove away, he followed. Josephine watched in the side view mirror.

After three blocks she realized he was not the only car that turned each turn they turned, stopped at every stop light they stopped. There were four other cars tailing him. Four black cars. Which one was the LeNoire's, Josephine wondered. For the first time she was afraid of dying, being killed. It was a caravan ushering her out of town.

"We need to turn back, Miss Odessa. We need to go back to Art's." She was very frightened. Odessa was not chatty this time, just deep in prayer for their safety.

Odessa had seen the cars following, and purposefully took wrong streets and turns. It was a way of life for her. She learned to never to drive straight to a destination but to wander through odd streets to let her tracers know she knew.

"No, we cannot turn back." You must be strong. There will always be those who will intimidate your courage."

Once Odessa parked at the station, the black cars did too. With Odessa holding her hand, Josephine began to feel the strength of a warrior as they again walked past Blackstone who pulled up next to them.

"Just making sure you got to the station on time."

Josephine gripped Odessa's hand tighter. Odessa said nothing.

"A thank you, would be nice, Miss Odessa." Blackstone said. "I got word about an escort party this morning. So, thought it might be nice if I showed them the route." He grinned.

Odessa ignored his comments. She had called Estelle after Minton received that threatening call last night, assuring her that Josephine was leaving in the morning. She was not happy they chose Blackstone to be the standby.

Once inside the train station, they watched the black cars reluctantly pull away one by one after the officer motioned them to pass before him. Josephine wondered who were in the cars. *Were they going to kidnap or kill her? Were they going to hang her, or drown her like her mother?* She thought she saw Alice, and then Ella. Her mind began to jumble up over who and how and why. Odessa grabbed her hand to lead her to the ticket booth. The train would arrive soon.

Josephine worried that she had left Talbot waiting. She wanted Odessa to send him a message.

"Can you speak to Talbot?"

"I already did. He called this morning after you left to see Art." Odessa's face became stern.

Anxiously "What did he said?"

"I told him you were not going to meet him this morning."

"And?"

"He said, he'll see you in Philadelphia." She bowed her head, conflicted, not wanting Josephine to see her prejudice. Although she worked for integration, she believed in loving one's own kind.

Josephine put on a show of happiness, giving Odessa a big hug. The train going north arrived, so she gave one last wave before boarding.

As the train pulled farther and farther away from the City of Richmond, Josephine relived the terror she held back from Odessa. She felt disliked, unwanted, an outsider being chased by a caravan of funeral cars. She knew she didn't want to die young, nor follow her mother's fate. Josephine vowed to reject what others said about her mother though. Miriam was all she had, even if it was a woman who tried to live a life of love. There can never be shame from loving. She was never going to let another person chase her from anyone who loved her.

Epilogue

1955 came to an end, but segregation in the schools of Virginia continued. The *Brown v. the Board of Education* ruling set off a decade of battles between state governments, the federal government, and the citizens of each city and town in the state. Art and Senior filed brief after brief in the district courts to enforce the federal law just before the start of school in September. Black students were still attending the same overcrowded, underfunded, and poorly maintained school buildings.

Odessa continued to organize meetings for parents and students to lobby their officials to reject the Southern Manifesto, the doctrine created to keep public funding from public schools that integrated. She endured opposition from some families who were willing to drop out of the lawsuits filed by Art and Senior, when cities proposed to build new and improved schools for blacks only.

Her strong suit was her door-to-door, in-home talks with parents, encouraging them to hold out for the day their children could enter the same classrooms as white students. There should not be two separate school budgets. During this time white parents built private schools for their children, often funded by tax dollars to avoid integration. She believed that in generations to come students would resist the hatred of their forefathers.

Reverend Poindexter's church was rebuilt.

George was running for the state's attorney general's office.

After her campaign loss, Penelope spent most her time remembering her childhood in Grandpa Franklin's attic room. The holiday season came but she refused to accept Pierre's apologies and long letters encouraging her to visit him in New York. Her desire for him was over.

She mourned selling off the winery and more farmland, releasing all but two land tenants in order to buy out Jules and Rita. More and more people had cars and were traveling outside the city. And more and more hotels and motels had been built around Richmond. Even so, the bread-and-breakfast did not suffer.

What boosted the reputation of the house was the wild story of Rita Jane's Angel. It was impossible to convince guests that there were no ghosts in the house. The requests to rent Mary Margaret's and Polly's rooms irritated her stoic stance to preserve the Southern gentility of the place. Finally, she gave in to Alice. She was puzzled by the woman who detested the sight of any superstitious black person but was ready to sell Mary Margaret and Polly's private wing for an extra price on the idea of a ghost sighting.

Sometimes Penelope believed Miriam appeared. She wept to think that the woman she truly hated paid her bills. She avoided Alice when she got into a fit, explaining that you can't keep down rumors, but if the lies make money keep them going. Penelope increased her commission to keep her employed, to keep her from leaving Velvet Gardens so she would not have to grow old with strangers.

Alice became overwhelmed with the guests crazed over Rita Jane's breakdown and Velvet's escape.

Whenever she heard a crazy story from one of the guests, she tried to incorporate it into the history of the place. Then she embellished the story of Velvet and Franklin's love and wanted her husband to walk out onto the portico with a rifle and shoot down the long dirt road. She even had a small burial plot put in Rita's peace garden for the secretly dead child, Angel. She paid Ella to dress up as Polly. But the woman still refused to go down into the basement.

Talbot joined the army to his mother's disappointment. She wanted him to drive a black car for midnight tours in search of the woman in the white mink.

Jules remained unreachable except by his lawyer and refused to ever return to Virginia out of fear of being implicated in Miriam's death. He lives on Lake Montreaux, never missing the muggy South. On occasions he visited Rita Jane in Paris who owned a Southern-American café called La Virginian on the Left Bank.

Her greatest thrill was when Basie came by with his band for a late dinner. To her surprise he played the piano on the small stage set up for many of the expat jazz musicians who entertained customers for the price of a dinner. It quickly became a favorite for writers, artists, locals, and tourists. Art promised to visit in January and bring her a supply of Southern specialty foods.

In the cold winter weather of Philadelphia, Josephine was pleased with her scrapbook dedicated to her mother, filled with newspaper clippings and all the documents from Lorenzo's and Rhoady's files, keeping it inside the suitcase hidden in her bedroom closet. Often writing Talbot who wrote her regularly.

Lorenzo continued to call, more to speak with Grandma Philly, who had become his significant other parent. His calls were also an excuse to keep tabs on Josephine's activities. They chatted some but Josephine preferred to keep a distance between them. He'd invited her to Senior's annual holiday party as well as Grandma Philly. She hadn't decided yet. Everything was a question without an answer for her. She was disillusioned about whether anyone cared. Whether anyone really wanted to know the truth. Everyone lies. The fact that Grandma Philly kept secrets, important things about her mother from her, made her want to leave for good.

She wanted to be involved in Odessa's grassroots campaigns and refused to accept any fear for her safety. A bus boycott began in Alabama that had Odessa pumped with courage now. It was strange to hear Art and Odessa speak of fear when they'd appeared so courageous before angry people who despised their drive for civil rights.

Josephine planned to return, never giving up on her mother's murder even if it meant going to Europe to find Jules.

Hugh had not been seen or heard from since leaving Jules in New York.

Rhoady sent Josephine small gifts now and then, making her his godchild. He promised to find Miriam's killer. He said he had men out on the street looking for Hugh.

Art called once a month regarding the trust and other legal matters. She always asked whether there were any new leads from people seeking the reward money. So far, they were all false and the reward remained uncollected.

Miriam's death remains unsolved.

The Writers

Ivey has written several plays, most notably *Run'ers*, produced at the New Federal Theater in New York City and recipient of an Audelco Award and other playwriting awards. She was a member of several theater workshops in New York City.

She has a B.A. in Psychology from New York University and a M.A. in Theater from Hunter College. She is also a painter who exhibits regularly.

First novel for Belle Chase

•

Special thanks to editor, NaNa Stoelzle

Special Appreciation

For

Fellini

A Wonderful Muse

And

Toni Cade Bambara

A Novelist Who Shared
A Few Notes on Writing